BLACK MARK

PAUL SPENCER

BLOODHOUND
— BOOKS —

First published in 2024 by Bloodhound Books.

www.bloodhoundbooks.com

Print ISBN: 978-1-916978-87-4

For Molly, Malcolm, and Kim. They know why.

ONE

ALL TOMORROW'S PARTIES

B lack tie wasn't my thing even before I got disbarred, but I couldn't say no to Elliott. So we were on our way to the Portland University Club, on a hot Friday night, for the Spirit of Portland Awards gala dinner. If I kept my head down, they might even let me in.

We walked up Jefferson Street towards the club. A crowd of around two hundred Black Lives Matter protesters had gathered in front of the old redbrick Tudor Revival building, held back by police clad in body armor and riot shields. The protesters were mostly young and white, and held the usual assortment of BLM banners, but I saw a few "Fuck Mayor Alioto" signs in there too.

Someone set off a distress flare and the crowd surged forward. The police charged at them with shields and batons raised. Most of the protesters stopped, but one guy, his face covered by a black bandana, took a flying kick at the nearest cop. The kick missed, and as he spun around, the cop cracked him in the head with his baton. The protester collapsed, blood streaming down his face. The cop grabbed a set of FlexiCuffs from his belt, but before he could use them, two people grabbed the fallen man by his arms and dragged him back through the crowd.

"I knew Alioto was unpopular," I said, "but these guys really don't like him. I hope his team brings him in the back door."

"That asshole has backed the cops since the protests began," Elliott replied. "Maybe he wouldn't be in such shit if he listened to people for a change, instead of sending in the goon squad."

The crowd had settled into an uneasy détente, content to glare at the heavily armed police lined up against them. Elliott and I made our way past the police cordon towards the university club's huge oak door. As we did, one of the protesters pointed at Elliott. "Hey, guys, it's Elliott Russell!" he shouted. "Elliott! Elliott! Come join us!"

Elliott gave him a brief wave and kept walking.

One of the cops raised his eyebrows. "Are you Elliott Russell?" he said.

"Yes I am."

The cop smiled, winked, then raised his hand in a pistol shape and mimed shooting him.

I lunged at him, but Elliott grabbed my arm and dragged me back.

"Leave it, Mick," he said. "I get that shit all the time."

I shrugged him off and glared at the cop. He smiled back at me. I took a deep breath and followed Elliott inside, then stopped inside the door.

"What the fuck was that about?"

"Same old shit. The cops fuck with me every chance they get. Last week I got a speeding ticket fifty yards from my office. Assholes had been waiting outside. They said I was doing sixty-two in a thirty zone, but I hadn't made it out of second gear."

"I don't know how you stay so calm. I don't think I'd keep my cool if a cop pretended to shoot me."

"Trust me, it ain't easy."

I nodded, and we walked through to the lobby. Most of the attendees were already there, standing around in small groups, sipping drinks and chatting. They all wore the same uniform: tuxedos for the men and dark evening gowns for the few women present. But one group stood out from the rest and we walked over to them.

"I feel like a hooker at a debutante's ball," I said to Elliott.

"If you think you're out of place," he replied, gesturing at the other guests, "how do you think I feel?"

I knew what he meant. The group we joined was Elliott's Northeast Neighborhood Coalition colleagues. He and the NNC team were the only African Americans in the room. Even the servers were white.

A couple of the NNC crew did a double take when they saw a white guy walk up.

"Guys, this is Mick Ward," Elliott said. "My lawyer from back in the day."

The man to my left Billy Hinds shook my hand. "Good to see you again, Mick."

"Good to see you too." Billy was an older man, with an uncanny resemblance to Morgan Freeman. He was Elliott's second in command at the NNC and I'd known him almost as long as I'd known Elliott. I nodded to the rest of the crew. The two guys to Billy's left, Ray and G-Dog, had helped me out on a construction teardown gig recently. Some of the others looked familiar, but I couldn't remember their names.

I tapped Elliott on the shoulder and pointed at the bar. "You want anything?"

"No, I'm good."

"I'll come with you," Billy said. "I could use a drink."

At the bar I ordered a neat Scotch. Billy had a bourbon on

the rocks. There were a few high-top tables off to the side, so we stood at one with our drinks.

"How's Elliott doing?" I asked.

"Working too hard, as usual." Billy took a swig of his bourbon and looked at me carefully. "You doing okay?"

"I'm fine. Come on, it's Elliott's big night. Let's enjoy it."

"That's why I asked," he said. "Elliott will need you between now and the election in November."

"Don't worry, I'm not going anywhere. Now let's grab another drink and rejoin the crew."

We grabbed our refills and started back toward the NNC group. A tall, silver-haired man in ceremonial police uniform held out his arm to block my path, spilling half his drink in the process.

"Well I'll be damned," he said, his florid face somewhere between a smile and a sneer. "If it isn't the patron saint of lost causes. Didn't expect to see you back amongst the high and mighty."

"Chief Walker," I replied. "I'm surprised you're not out front helping your goons beat the shit out of the mayor's fan club."

Walker scowled at me as I pushed his arm aside.

"Why did he call you that?" Billy asked as we rejoined our group.

"Back when I was a defense lawyer, I had a reputation for taking on shitty cases other lawyers wouldn't touch. He thinks it's funny because the patron saint of lost causes is a cop icon."

"Lost causes like me?" Elliott said with a smile.

"Ha. You were easy compared to some of the losers I represented."

A bell chimed and we went through to the Tudor-style dining room. Dark wood panels lined the lower half of the walls, matching the exposed beams in the ceiling. A giant fireplace sat unlit at one end of the room, with a low stage set up in front of it. The main floor was filled with round tables draped in long white tablecloths, around which gathered Portland's finest politicians, lawyers and civic leaders.

The Northeast Neighborhood Coalition table was at the back of the room. I saw plenty of my ex-colleagues as we made our way there, but none of them met my eye.

I sat down between Elliott and Billy.

Elliott leaned over to me. "I just want to get this over with," he said.

"Come on, the exposure is good for your campaign. And this city needs you on the council."

"It better be," he replied. "Some folks don't think I should be here."

"Damn right," G-Dog said from across the table. He pointed at the door. "We should be out there, with our people."

"They stopped being our people when they trashed downtown. White kids smashing windows for fun ain't what we're about."

G-Dog shook his head.

Waiters dressed like English butlers took drink orders, then served the meal. I washed the bland salmon and wilted salad down with another Scotch. Maybe not the gourmand's beverage pairing of choice, but I know what I like.

As the waiters returned with dessert and coffee, the MC stepped up to the podium to begin the evening's program. I zoned out through most of it, drinking my coffee and applauding politely when everyone else did.

Elliott nudged me. "Mick, I think this is it."

"And now," the MC announced, "presenting tonight's main award for Outstanding Community Leader, the Mayor of Portland, Thomas Alioto."

A round of lukewarm applause ushered a fat man with thick

gray hair and a politician's smile to the stage. He shook the MC's hand and waved to the crowd, then stepped up to the microphone. Like Elliott, Mayor Alioto was in the throes of an election campaign. Unlike Elliott, he'd had far more exposure than he could have ever wanted. For weeks, Portland had been gripped by nightly Black Lives Matter protests after Portland Police shot and killed Andre Gladen, an unarmed African American man seeking help after a mental health episode. The unrest had turned ugly. Scenes of cops teargassing protesters and kids in black ski masks kicking in Apple Store windows made nightly news across the country. Alioto had been crucified for his inability to quell the unrest.

Alioto kept his speech short and generic, talking about the importance of a diverse community and strong local leadership, the sort of remarks that play well to a crowd that's in favor of diversity as long as they don't have to get too close to it.

"And now," he said, when he was done pandering, "it gives me great pleasure to present this year's award for Outstanding Community Leader to a man who embodies all that is great in this city of ours. As an administrator at Jefferson High, he established after-school programs that increased graduation rates by sixty percent in Portland's Humboldt neighborhood. He's worked tirelessly to ensure that those in our minority community have access to affordable housing. Under his leadership, the Northeast Neighborhood Coalition has dramatically reduced food insecurity for thousands of local children. Ladies and gentlemen, Elliott Russell!"

Elliott stood and made his way to the stage, waving in response to the applause. As he approached Chief Walker's party, Walker pushed his chair out to block his path. Elliott scowled, then went around the other side of the table.

Cameras flashed as he stepped up to the podium. The

mayor handed him a plaque, and the two shook hands. Neither of them smiled.

"Thank you," Elliott said. "I'm honored to receive this award and I accept it on behalf of my colleagues in the Northeast Neighborhood Coalition. A leader is only as good as his team."

Elliott paused and looked around, expectantly. The crowd managed a brief smattering of applause. He took a deep breath and continued.

"I know a lot of people aren't happy about me getting this award. I know a lot of you blame me for what's happening on our streets each night."

Now the crowd was nodding and muttering.

"But there's a reason we're marching in the streets. There's a reason we're frustrated. We are a city divided, and if we're going to come back together it's going to take work from us all. Mayor Alioto, Chief Walker, I'm looking at you. I'm *asking* you. Work with me. Together, we can unite our communities. We can be a city where Black children aren't afraid of cops. A city where everyone believes their voice will be heard. That's the Portland I want to live in. That's the city I want to represent. A city we can all be proud of. Join me. Help me. Let's make it happen."

Our table burst into loud applause as Elliott stepped down from the stage, while the rest of the crowd offered a more restrained response.

Elliott headed for Chief Walker's table on his return. Walker had pulled his chair back in, but he said something to Elliott as he passed.

Elliott stopped. "What did you say?"

Walker muttered something and turned away.

"No!" Elliott snapped, and cuffed Walker on the shoulder. "If you're going to call me a thug, have the balls to do it to my face."

Walker stood up, towering over Elliott. "Don't you touch me, boy."

"Don't you call me boy!"

I was out of my seat and by Elliott's side before Walker could respond, with Billy Hinds hot on my heels. I grabbed Elliott's arm and pulled him away from Walker, while Billy stepped into the space between them.

"Come on, buddy, let's go," I said. "That old prick isn't worth it."

Elliott glared past Billy at Walker, breathing hard through his nose.

"Yeah, you're right," he said. He beckoned to the NNC table. "Come on, guys, we're out of here."

Elliott marched out of the room. The crowd had fallen silent, and his footsteps echoed across the marble floor. He tossed his award on Mayor Alioto's table as he passed. The crowd looked on with shocked expressions as the NNC team stood up and walked out behind him.

Chief Walker watched them go. "Classy bunch of friends you've got there, Mick."

I laughed at him. "Elliott Russell has more class in his little finger than you'll ever have, you washed-up old soak."

Billy and I caught up with Elliott and the rest of the crew outside the front door. Elliott was still seething.

"I wish you hadn't grabbed me, Mick. I was gonna punch that asshole Walker out."

If I'd known what was coming down the road, I'd have let him.

TWO
DIGGING TO CHINA

It was a hundred and five in the shade. While the smart people stayed inside with the AC cranked up, I was out in the sun digging a fucking hole. Being broke sucks.

I shoveled a load of dirt, wiped the sweat from my brow with the back of my glove and took another swing at the rock hard earth. The impact jarred my wrists. The shovel's blade barely penetrated six inches, but that was enough. I scooped out the remaining dirt and eyeballed my work. It looked right to me.

Elliott sat on the steps by his back door, flicking paint flakes off the railing and drinking a beer. He wore a gray T-shirt and the kind of baggy khaki cargo shorts you'd usually see on a middle-aged white dude. He was a tall man, easily six foot five, but barely two hundred pounds. Sitting on the steps like that he looked like a stick figure folded in half.

"Man, there's nothing I like better than watching a white man work for a living," he said.

"Screw you, you lazy prick," I said. "Grab a post and help me out."

Elliott drained his beer slowly, then loped towards me, rolling his shoulders in time with his stride. Unfortunately for him, his skinny limbs made him look like a badly operated puppet.

"You're not in a gang anymore. Cut the crap and get over here."

He sighed and dropped the theatrics. "Ten years ago, I'd have popped a cap in your ass for coming back on me."

"Ten years ago you were in jail and I got your ass out. Bring me a post."

Elliott went over to the pile of fence posts and grabbed one by its end. He strained to get it upright, then wrapped it in a bear hug and carried it towards where I stood. He had to stop every couple of steps and rest it on the ground.

"Damn, that's heavy," he said, breathing hard. "A little help here?"

"All that indoor work's made you weak," I said.

I grabbed the post and swung it into the hole. They were heavy, but I'm a big guy – almost as tall as Elliott, and much heavier. Until recently, I'd spent two years doing manual labor in a streetcar factory, and I had the muscles to show for it. Elliott held the post in place, while I maneuvered it into position. When I was done, the top lined up perfectly with the guide string.

"Not bad," he said. "It almost looks like you know what you're doing."

"Master craftsmanship, buddy," I replied. "Now, how about you grab us a couple of those beers? I could use a break."

I sat on the dirt pile I'd just created while Elliott went inside for the beers. It was late on Saturday afternoon. Digging holes for the fence posts was backbreaking work. Weeks of hot days had baked the clay soil rock hard. Normally, summer in Portland was a brief pause in the Pacific Northwest's eternal rain. But even though it was only June, this year was on track to be the city's hottest on record. I'd been working most of the day and I was soaked in sweat.

Elliott had moved into the house a couple of weeks ago, a rundown old Craftsman-style place he'd bought in Portland's Humboldt neighborhood. The previous owners lost it to foreclosure and they'd trashed the place before they left. Amongst other things, they kicked the back fence down, leaving the house exposed to the alley and a vacant lot behind it. The vacant lot was a popular hangout for local teens, so Elliott needed a new fence fast.

I'd been getting by on handyman gigs lately, so I offered to build a fence for him for free. Elliott insisted on paying me, so I gave him a price that just about covered the materials.

We had been close since I took his case ten years ago. Usually, I didn't stay in touch with clients from my defense lawyer days, but I could tell Elliott was different, from the moment I met him. When he finished his jail term, I gave him a job and helped him find his feet. It didn't take him long. And years later, he stood by me when my wife left me, my son died and I hit the self-destruct button on my legal career. He let me stay at his place when I had no money and nowhere to go. And he talked me down one night when I was seriously considering swallowing the business end of my gun.

He came back with the beers and handed me one.

"Last night was fun," I said, as I took off my gloves and downed a long swallow. The icy liquid was deliciously refreshing.

"Yeah, sorry about that. I shouldn't have let Walker get to me."

"Don't sweat it. He was an ass and you were right to call him on it."

"Probably didn't help my campaign, though."

"Don't be so sure. The people in your district will love a guy who told the Chief of Police to go fuck himself."

"I hope so."

"Trust me, buddy. Walker's as popular as a fart in an elevator."

When I first met Elliott, he was just another gangbanger, headed for jail and lucky that a bullet didn't get him first. Now he might just win a seat on the City Council. If more of my clients had turned out like him, I might still be a lawyer.

I dropped that thought like a hot rock. Almost three years had passed since I was disbarred, and it still ate me up every day. Sometimes I wished I was back in the courtroom, but most times I wished I'd never been a defense lawyer at all. I'd spend hours daydreaming about being an auto mechanic, putting in a good hard day's work, and going home to a couple of beers and a quiet life.

Elliott must have seen the look on my face. "What's wrong, Mick?"

"Nothing. Just thinking about old stuff."

Elliott raised his eyebrows at me, but he didn't say anything. We sat there for a while. Pretty soon the silence got too much for me, so I waved my beer bottle at his house. "I like this place."

"Thanks. It's good to hear you say that, even if it's a dump."

"Yeah, but it's *your* dump."

Elliott laughed. "Don't get me wrong, I'm happy to be here. Especially after what I went through to get the place."

"Did the banks give you a hard time?"

"Everyone gave me a hard time. Realtors didn't want me as a client, sellers didn't want me on their property. But yeah, the banks were the worst. I thought my criminal record would make it hard to get a loan, but most of them shut me down before they even knew my name. You'd think they'd never seen a Black man before."

"This is Portland. They probably haven't."

Elliott shook his head ruefully. "True that. Everyone talks about attracting a diverse population, but no one's in a hurry to do it."

"Get on the council," I said. "Make it happen."

"I plan to." Elliott took a pull on his beer, then gestured at the house with his bottle. "There's plenty more that needs fixing if you've got time. If you'll let me pay you, that is."

Elliott was right. The house needed new siding and a coat of paint, and the back deck looked ready to collapse. Inside was just as bad, with holes in the drywall and cigarette burns on the carpet, which stank like a wet dog too.

"I've got nothing but time right now."

Elliott looked at me over the neck of his beer. "Are you doing okay, Mick?"

"I'm getting by," I lied. "Hey, what are you doing tonight? There's a Timbers game on later. I'm going to watch it at Holman's. I'll probably call Tony too. You want to join us?"

"I'd love to, but there's an NNC board meeting tonight. Duty calls and all that shit."

"What's on the agenda?"

"We're working on an ordinance to limit the number of new multi-occupancy dwellings in a neighborhood."

"Aren't you in favor of development if it's bringing money into the area?"

"Smart development, yeah. But what's happening now is just Black folks getting kicked out of their homes so developers can tear them down and build condos for hipsters." Elliott sighed. "We've got to stop it."

"Sounds like fun. I'm sorry I'll miss it." I drained my beer and handed Elliott the empty. "Anyway, enough of that crap. I'm going to finish up here so I can get to the game."

"I'll leave you to it," he said, and he took the bottles inside.

I picked up my shovel and moved to where I'd marked the position for the last hole. The ground had been dug over recently. I slammed my shovel down into the dirt and it gave more easily than I'd expected. I emptied the soil off and dug in again. The ground was definitely softer here. After a hard day of digging, it was a relief. Maybe I could get done in time to shower before I went to the pub.

The rest of the hole practically dug itself. Then, when I was almost done, my shovel hit something and stopped. I tried again, but it still wouldn't penetrate any further. It kept hitting something soft but unyielding. Was it a root? There weren't any trees nearby, so that was unlikely. I tried to scrape the dirt away, but I couldn't clear enough to see what was blocking me. I got down on my knees and cleared the earth away by hand. There was definitely something down there, something smooth and pliant. I moved more dirt and took a closer look. My blood ran cold.

It was a human hand.

THREE
THERE GOES THE NEIGHBORHOOD

I cleared away more dirt, revealing fingers curled as though holding a ball. The rest of the body remained buried. The skin was cool to the touch, and dark, most likely African American. Then the smell hit me, garbage left in the sun too long. I stood up and wiped my hands on my jeans hurriedly.

"Elliott!" I yelled.

He opened the back door. "What's up?" he said. He did a double take when he saw where I stood. "Why're you digging there?"

"Why do you think? I'm fixing your fence."

"That's the space for the driveway. Where else am I gonna park my car?"

"Never mind that. You better come over here."

Elliott frowned as he walked over to me. I pointed at the hole. He looked down and froze.

"Oh shit," he said, his eyes wide. "Is that what I think it is?"

"Yeah."

"What the hell is it doing here?"

"You tell me. It's your yard."

Elliott stared at me, eyes wide. "What? You think I know anything about it?"

I didn't know what to think. Did Elliott know about the body? But his reaction was genuine, his shock too real. And I couldn't believe my friend was a murderer.

"Okay, let's think about this," I said, doing my best to remain calm. "There's a body buried in your backyard. Someone put it there. Why?"

"Only one answer I can think of. To set me up." Elliott shook his head. "Shit, what are we gonna do?"

"Good question." I considered the hand, those yearning, grasping fingers. I kept expecting the body to move, to struggle free of the shallow grave. "I honestly have no fucking idea."

"I can't go to the cops," Elliott said. "I'm a Black man with a felony record. You know what'll happen if they find a body at my house."

Elliott had a point. A dozen years as a defense attorney had taught me many things, chief amongst them being that cops don't look past the obvious answer. Show them a dead Black man in an ex-gangbanger's backyard, and they'd have Elliott tagged as the killer by sundown. But what else could we do?

"Oh man, that stinks," Elliott said, pinching his nose. "Can't we just cover it up?"

"What, fill in the hole?" I gestured at the vacant lot behind Elliott's property. "The body's barely two feet down. It's going to rot quickly in this heat. The smell's going to draw every dog in town. How long do you think it'll stay buried?"

"Fuck!" Elliott snapped. He ran a hand over his head and glared at me. "So, what do I do?"

I rubbed my eyes, thinking furiously and coming up blank.

"Your only other option is to run," I said.

"What?" Elliott looked at me like I was crazy.

"Why not? Get the hell out of here and don't come back."

"No," he said. "I won't do it. I've worked too damn hard to rebuild my life. I ain't running away just because some punk dumped a body at my house. Anyway, what if whoever did this comes after me?"

"If you run far enough, it won't matter."

"I'd still be looking over my shoulder every day. For the killer or the cops."

I looked down at the hole. The body appeared loosely buried in dirt and dry leaves, as though it had been dumped in a hurry. Despite the smell, the hand wasn't visibly decomposing, so it hadn't been there long. Maybe no more than a day or two. I looked over my shoulder. There was still no one else around.

"I'm going to regret this," I muttered under my breath, as I cleared more dirt away.

"What are you doing?"

"Before we make any decisions, let's see if we can find out who your mystery guest is. Help me move this, see if we can find some ID or something."

Elliott hesitated, then scooped out a handful of earth. We dug together, clearing away an arm clad in a pale blue business shirt, then the shoulder and the neck. Elliott jerked his hand back, his eyes wide.

"What's wrong?" I asked.

He looked at his hand, as though it was on fire. "I just touched his fucking skin!"

"He's not going to bite you."

Elliott stood back as I shifted soil away from the face. I had most of it exposed when he spoke again.

"Stop."

"What now?"

"We don't need any ID," Elliot replied, his voice flat. "I know who he is."

FOUR

THE NAMING OF THE DEAD

"You know him?"

"Yeah, I do." Elliott nodded his head. "It's Malik Betts."

I looked down at the dead man's face. His eyes were wide open, he had short dark hair and a neat round bullet hole in the middle of his forehead.

"Never heard of him."

"He's the guy I was on my way to shoot when I got busted."

I became Elliott's lawyer when he was arrested on possession charges. Drugs and a firearm. A patrol officer saw him flashing a Glock 19, and they found the drugs in his pocket when they searched him at the station house. Strangely, the officer who made the arrest had searched him at the scene, but he didn't find any drugs. Somehow, twenty grams of crack cocaine magically appeared on the ride to the station. I'd seen that shit too often and it pissed me off. I fought Elliott's case hard and got the drug charge tossed. He did six months for the Glock. But that beat the hell out of a five-year stretch for crack he never had.

"Why were you going to shoot him?"

Elliott stared straight ahead. "Because he killed my little brother."

I didn't say anything. It was an old lawyer trick to keep a witness talking. People hate silence. Give them a long one, and sooner or later they'll fill it. Elliott didn't let me down.

"It was stupid gang stuff," he said. "I knew Malik since high school. We both went to Jefferson. Never had much to do with each other until he became a Blood and I joined the Oakhurst Street Crips. The only reason we ended up in different gangs is because we lived on different streets."

"And he killed your brother?" I asked.

"Yeah, he shot him."

"How do you know?"

"Because the bullets were meant for me."

"Okay," I said, eyebrows raised, "tell me more."

"I was walking Lincoln home from school. Betts and three of his boys cruised up on us in a pimped-out Impala. Betts leaned out the window and called my name. I saw the gun as soon as I turned around, so I grabbed Lincoln and tried to pull him onto the ground. Betts fired maybe five shots. I just hit the deck and closed my eyes. When I opened them again, Betts and his boys were gone and Lincoln was lying next to me, not moving. Not even breathing. There was blood everywhere. I couldn't tell if it was mine or his. One of the bullets went through my arm, but two of them caught Lincoln in the chest."

Elliott stopped and took a deep breath. Tears welled up in his eyes, and he wiped them away with the back of his hand.

"Was Lincoln a gang member too?"

"Lincoln wasn't in no motherfuckin' gang!" Elliott snapped back. "He was eight years old!"

The tears came again and this time Elliott couldn't hold them back. He put his face in his hands and wept, great heaving sobs shaking his body. When the tears eventually subsided, he wiped his face on his sleeve.

"I'm sorry," he said. "I ain't done that in a while."

I nodded and waited for him to compose himself. Elliott took a deep breath and rubbed his face.

"Why did Betts want to kill you?" I said.

"Gang shit. Betts was slinging dope on our turf. I made him stop."

I waited for him to say more, but this time he didn't.

"And of course, you didn't go to the police," I said.

"Damn right. I was gonna take care of that punk myself."

"Is that why Betts wasn't convicted? No witnesses willing to testify?"

"Exactly. Cops arrested him, but they had to drop the charges."

"So what happened after that?"

"Betts left town. No one saw him around for a few years. You know the rest. I did my six months, got out and took a job with some dumbass defense lawyer." He managed to smile at me. "That's not the end of it, though."

"What happened?"

"Betts came back to town a few years ago, started selling real estate. Tried to make himself out as some sort of inspiration to the Black community. Gangbanger made good, or so he liked to say. Really, what he did was sell old folks' homes to urban hipsters for below market value. Used his redemption story to con people into believing his bullshit.

"Anyway, the Coalition managed to shut down a planned condo development up in Kenton. It was going to be massive. Dozens of older African American families would have had their homes bulldozed. I led the campaign and Betts was pissed because he already had deals in place to sell the condos. He came to a Coalition meeting a couple of months back. We got into it pretty good."

"You fought?"

"Yeah. Crowd separated us quickly, but it was enough to make the news. Gave some lazy-ass reporters a chance to drag up the old gang thing too."

I tried to figure out what the hell was going on. If someone wanted to frame Elliott for murder, they'd found the perfect way to do it. What with Betts killing Elliott's brother, the two of them brawling in public, and now Betts's body in Elliott's backyard, it looked like an open and shut case. There was only one problem. Elliott didn't do it.

Something else occurred to me.

"Did you have the locks changed when you moved in?"

Elliott looked confused. "Of course. Why?"

I went over to Elliott's back door and peered at the lock. There were fresh scratches around the key slot.

"Come over here," I said.

Elliott joined me by the door. "What?"

"We need to search your house. Whoever put Betts there knows they need something more to link you to the crime." I pointed at the lock. "See these scratches? Someone picked this lock recently. I'm guessing they planted something inside."

"Shit." Elliott pulled the door open. "You take the kitchen. I'll start in my bedroom."

I followed him inside and went to the kitchen. Like the rest of the house, it was badly in need of an update, with scuffed linoleum flooring, paint peeling off the cabinet doors, and appliances that looked like they came from the Brady Bunch set. But I wasn't here to decorate. I started my search in the cabinets. Elliott didn't have much stuff, so it was easy to make sure nothing was hidden behind his cooking supplies. The fridge and freezer were empty too, save for some beer and a couple of frozen pizzas.

I bent over and pulled open the oven door, then straightened up when I heard Elliott's shout.

"Motherfucker!"

I hurried through to the bedroom. Elliott stood by the open bottom drawer of his nightstand, a pile of socks by his feet.

"What is it?"

He pointed at the drawer. There, at the back, was a 9mm Ruger SR9 and a box of ammo.

"I take it that isn't yours?" I said.

"Fuck no! I haven't touched a gun since you got me out of jail." Elliott's shoulders shook. He looked scared and alone. "Now what?" he said. "I'm lost here, Mick. Help me out."

Someone was framing my friend for murder, and if they had been stood in front of me right then, I'd have ripped their fucking throat out. But right now we had to clean up this mess.

"First things first," I said. "We get rid of the gun."

FIVE
LET'S GO FOR A DRIVE

I grabbed a plastic shopping bag and a pair of tongs from the kitchen, then went back to Elliott's bedroom and used the tongs to put the gun and ammo in the bag.

"Is there anything else we should get rid of?" I said.

"Like what?"

"I don't know. Drugs. Whatever." I scratched my head. "Look, just grab anything obvious."

"I ain't got nothing like that," Elliott said. He pointed at the shopping bag. "What are we going to do? Throw it in the river?"

I opened the bag and looked at the gun. There were a couple of greasy smudges on the stainless steel slide, and the matte black grip was dirty too.

"No, let's keep it. It might come in handy later."

"Are you crazy? Where are we going to keep it?"

"Don't worry," I said, "I know a place. But first there's something else we have to do."

I went back outside, grabbed the shovel, and stood over the hole containing Malik Betts's body. I took a deep breath and heaved dirt over his empty, staring eyes, my stomach churning. I covered the rest of his face quickly. Concealing Betts's body felt deeply wrong, but we couldn't risk someone else coming down the lane and seeing it. I kept moving dirt until the hole was full, then tossed the shovel aside.

"Okay, let's go."

My car was parked out front of Elliott's place. At first glance, it didn't look like much; just another mid-eighties BMW Sedan, with faded green paint and Bondo patches on the rear rocker panels. The window trim leaked and given how much it rained in Portland, the car's interior smelled like wet carpet, even in summer. It had 210,000 miles on it and I'd owned it since I was in law school. It ran well, though. I'd taken care of the major mechanicals before I lost my career, and the little beemer never let me down, despite its shitbox appearance.

We got in and I headed south towards Interstate 5. Saturday afternoon traffic was light, as we eased onto the freeway.

We drove in silence for a while, Elliott gazing out the window at the lights flashing by. I took the Morrison Street exit off the freeway. Downtown loomed across the river, its skyscrapers cradled by the West Hills beyond. Further south, the green-tinted glass condo towers of the South Waterfront district shone like a man-made forest. Somewhere in a penthouse atop one of those towers, my ex-wife lived with the man she left me for.

Neither of us spoke as we bumped along the badly potholed streets among the empty warehouses and used furniture stores crammed against the east side of the Willamette River. I parked in a spot by the disused rail tracks under the Morrison Bridge. A hot, dusty wind whipped at my clothes as I climbed out of the car. Traffic rumbled past on the bridge overhead. I looked around and I couldn't see anyone.

"Okay, let's go. It's over here." I pointed at a dimly lit doorway in the western end of the warehouse building across the street.

I punched my combination into the keypad on the door and swung it open. There were no lights on inside, and when I flicked the switch by the door, nothing happened. My unit was at the end of the hall, so I fired up the flashlight on my phone and led us down there. I hadn't been here in about a year, but everything looked the same. I unlocked the padlock on my unit's door and opened it, then pulled the light string. A single bare bulb hanging from the ceiling lit up, swirls of dust motes dancing in its harsh glow.

My unit was ten feet by six, the walls lined with ceiling-high stacks of bankers boxes, and it smelled of damp cardboard. The space in the middle was cluttered with junk. A couple of lamps, a desk, an end table, and a box of shoes. Just about everything I'd kept after the divorce.

I went over to the desk, pulled the bottom drawer out, and set it on top. The drawer had a false bottom. I slid it out, put the bag with the gun and ammo inside, then reinserted it and put the drawer back in the desk.

"Should be safe there."

Elliott looked at me, eyebrows raised.

I grinned at him. "What? You think you're the first client who had something to hide?"

We locked up my storage unit and went back outside.

"Now what do we do?" Elliott said.

"There's only one thing we can do," I replied. "We go back to your place and call the cops."

"Are you out of your fucking mind?"

"Get in the car. I'll explain."

I got in without waiting for Elliott's response. He waited outside, arms folded, his chest heaving like bellows. I put the key in the ignition but didn't start it up. Eventually, Elliott opened his door and sat down. He slammed the door shut and stared straight ahead.

I started the car and drove off.

"Why don't we just get rid of the body?" Elliott said.

"We can't. Think about it. Whoever is framing you was smart enough to plant that gun too. They know you might move the body, so they'll have a plan."

"Like what?"

"I'm guessing they kept a shirt with his blood on it, or something like that. When the body isn't found in a couple of days, they plant it at your house or in your car and drop an anonymous tip to the cops. Then your rival is missing and his blood's at your house. The cops will be convinced you killed him." I shook my head. "No, we have to call the cops. If you call them first, you're one step ahead of whoever is setting you up. The gun is gone and you look like you've got nothing to hide."

"Easy for you to say! You're not the one with the whole city's police force on his ass!"

"Yeah, I've got an idea about how to deal with that. But first I need to make a call."

I pulled out my phone and thumbed through my contacts while keeping one eye on the road as we pulled onto the Interstate and cruised past the Moda Center. I was restoring the E30 to its original condition, and that meant no hands-free option. I found the contact I wanted, put the phone on speaker, and hit the call button. Casey answered on the third ring.

"Law Offices of Casey Raife. Who's calling?"

Casey was the defense attorney who represented me when I was in big trouble three years back. She'd recently gone into private practice after years running the Major Crimes Team at Multnomah County Public Defender's Office. Casey's fearless approach and no-nonsense style made her a match for any attorney I've known. Besides, now she was in private practice she could probably use the business.

"Casey, it's Mick Ward. I need your help."

"Jesus, Mick, what have you done this time?"

"It's not for me. A good friend is being framed for a murder he didn't commit."

"What? Tell me more."

"Do you know Elliott Russell?" I glanced at Elliott. He was still staring out through the windshield, but his face had softened.

"The activist guy who's running for City Council?"

"Yeah, that's him."

"We haven't met, but I know who he is. He raised a ruckus at a City Council meeting I was at recently."

"Yeah, that sounds like Elliott."

"You say someone is framing him for murder. But how sure are you that he didn't do it?"

Elliott glared at me.

"I'm certain," I said, quickly.

"Okay," Casey said, "what's the story?"

I gave her the details. She asked a couple of questions, but mostly just listened.

"Wow," Casey said when I finished. She paused. "I'm in Sunriver for a defense attorneys' conference. I need to wrap up a few things here before I head back, so I won't be in Portland until close to midnight. I don't suppose you can hold off on calling the police until tomorrow?"

"No. Someone might find the body before then. Hell, whoever's framing him could be calling in an anonymous tip as we speak."

"Yeah, you're right." Casey sighed. "You know the drill, right, Mick? Elliott doesn't say a goddamn word to the cops. Not one."

"Absolutely."

"Good. By the way, that was smart thinking, getting rid of the gun. Now make sure he keeps his mouth shut."

"Don't worry, I still remember some things about being a lawyer."

"Glad to hear it. And be careful what *you* say, too. I'm going to go wrap up here and hit the road. Call me first thing tomorrow."

She hung up.

"Who the hell was that?" Elliott said.

"Your lawyer." I looked at Elliott and he frowned back at me.

"So you're just going to hand me off to some lawyer I've never met before and walk away? You're the one who dug up the goddamn body!"

"And I'm the one who just got you a lawyer." I took a deep breath. "Look, I know it sucks, but you're in for a tough ride. You need Casey's help. She's as good as they come."

"What about you?"

"What about me? I got disbarred, remember?"

"But there must be something you can do," Elliott said, his voice softer now.

"I wish there was. But you need a lawyer and I stopped being one when I punched a prosecutor in open court. I'll make sure the cops don't get out of line today, but the sooner you get Casey working for you, the better off you're going to be."

Elliott shook his head and went back to staring out the window. I hated the look of disappointment on his face and I hated not being able to do anything about it. But he needed the best legal representation he could get, and that wasn't me anymore.

We drove the rest of the way back to Elliott's place in silence. The sun was setting as we got out of my car and walked through to his backyard.

I grabbed my work gloves and the shovel, and walked over to where Betts's body was buried.

28

"What are you doing?" Elliott said.

"Making it look like we just found a body."

I dug until I figured I was close to the body, then knelt down and removed dirt by hand until I'd exposed Betts's hand and part of his forearm.

"Okay, that's far enough," I said.

I dropped the shovel and stretched, groaning at the popping sounds coming from my spine. It was almost nine o'clock and the sun had fully set, the sky taking on a deep blue hue. At least it wasn't so hot now.

I took out my phone and looked at Elliott. "You ready for this?"

"No," he said, "but you're gonna do it anyway."

I dialed Portland Police Bureau.

"I need to speak to Detective Eddie Buchanan. It's urgent."

I waited while the call was connected.

"This is Buchanan. Who's calling?"

"Detective Buchanan, it's Mick Ward."

"Oh great, that's all I fucking need," Buchanan said. "I've spent the whole goddamn day trying to run down two meth heads who robbed a Korean deli, I'm buried in paperwork, and I'm late for my wife's birthday dinner. Now some washed-up ex-attorney I haven't seen for years is calling me. This better be real important, Ward."

I looked at Malik Betts's hand, his dead fingers reaching for something they would never find.

"Yeah, it is," I said.

SIX

NOWHERE TO RUN

W e went inside to wait for the police to arrive. The kitchen was just off the back deck, so we stopped there. Elliott sat at the kitchen table and I leaned on the sink.

"What's the deal with this Buchanan guy?" Elliott said. "Why did you call him?"

"Buchanan's a decent guy, for a cop. And he's the only Black detective in the Portland Police, so you won't get any racist shit from him." I didn't tell him Buchanan was also the one who told me that the cops conspired with the DA to set me up and get me disbarred, so I knew he played it straight.

"Okay." Elliott rummaged through a pile of papers on the Formica table and pulled one out, then he unfolded it and slapped it down with his palm.

"See that?" he said, stabbing a finger at the page. "Blueprints for the yard work. The driveway goes where the body is. You shouldn't have been digging there."

"If I hadn't, in a day or so the police would be finding a dead body in your yard and the murder weapon in your nightstand. So maybe it's a good thing you never showed me those plans."

Elliott put his head in his hands. He sat there for a while, then looked up at me, close to tears. "I'm sorry I got mad at you before, Mick. I know you're trying to help. But I gotta tell you, I'm pretty damn scared here."

"I know you are. Hang in there, buddy."

"What happens now?"

"Buchanan will be here soon, with his partner and a crime scene team. Buchanan will want to interview you. You remember what Casey said, right? About not talking?"

"Yeah, I knew that already," he said. "I haven't forgotten everything you taught me."

"Good. That's crucial. Don't say a word—let me do the talking, and that won't be much. The crime scene team will seal off the scene and search it, dig the body up, take soil samples and whatever other evidence they can find."

"What about my house? Will they search my house?"

"I expect so," I said. "They'll claim they don't need a warrant. I think they do, and I'll try to stop them, but we're probably going to have to let the lawyers fight over that later."

"I can't believe this shit is happening. Twenty-four hours ago I was getting a big award. Now I'll be lucky if I don't end up in jail tonight."

"They won't arrest you," I said. "Not yet. They need something more than the body to have probable cause."

I tried to think of something more, something comforting, to say, but I struck out. An awkward silence followed, eventually broken by the sound of cars pulling up outside.

The front curtains were open and blue lights flashed against the walls. We left the kitchen and went out onto the front porch.

"Remember, don't say a word," I said, gesturing for Elliott to stay behind me.

Three vehicles had pulled up outside Elliott's house: an unmarked blue Ford Crown Victoria, a Portland Police patrol car and a black Crime Scene Unit van. The crime scene team got out of the van and put on yellow protective suits and boot covers. Meanwhile, two guys in plain clothes, one Black and one white, got out of the unmarked vehicle and approached us, followed by two uniformed officers from the patrol car.

The two guys walking towards us wore sports coats and white shirts, their ties loose and top buttons undone. I knew them both all too well. Detective Eddie Buchanan was the taller of the two, with a shaved head, a sagging belly and deep wrinkles in his tired face. Like I'd told Elliott, he was the only Black detective in the Portland Police and earning his badge had been a tough road. Buchanan always rode his cases hard. He pushed at every detail, like he knew he had to be twice as good as the white guys. But he played by the rules and he did right by me when he could have kept his mouth shut. The guy next to him was another story.

Short and stocky, with mouth curled in a permanent sneer and a thick scar on his lower lip, Detective James Malone looked every bit what he was—an old-school prick. Back when he was in uniform, before cops wore body cameras, he was notorious for beating the shit out of suspects and booking them for resisting arrest. He looked like a bar-room brawler after one too many bouts. He had a reputation as a racist too, so Buchanan had to love working with him.

"Mick Ward," Buchanan said as they approached me. "Still causing trouble after all these years."

"Good to see you Detective," I replied. I nodded at Malone. "I see they let you keep the puppy."

Malone moved towards me, but Buchanan put an arm out to stop him. "Settle down," he snapped. "Okay, Ward, what's the deal with this body?"

"Detectives, this is Elliott Russell, the homeowner. Mr. Russell has an attorney, Casey Raife. I believe you know her.

Ms. Raife is on her way back to Portland from a conference in Sunriver, and Mr. Russell will not be speaking to you until he has had a chance to meet with her. Before we go any further, I need you to acknowledge that you understand."

"Elliott Russell the BLM guy, right?" Malone said. "I'm gonna enjoy locking your ass up."

I ignored him and looked at Buchanan. "I'm waiting."

"Fine, whatever," Buchanan said. "Now, can you tell us what's going on here?"

"This way, guys," I said, and led them around the side of the house.

I stopped the group by the hole containing Betts's body. Buchanan leaned forward and peered in.

"Getting dark here. Flores, give me your flashlight."

He held out a hand, without looking, and one of the uniform cops pulled a flashlight from his belt and handed it over. Buchanan shone it into the hole, illuminating Betts's lifeless hand.

"Everything you see is as we found it," I said. "Like I told you on the phone, I'm helping Mr. Russell build a fence. I was digging a hole for one of the posts when I found this. I called you as soon as we realized what it was."

"Kind of dark to be building a fence, isn't it?" Buchanan said.

"You know me, Detective. I'm a hard worker."

Buchanan straightened up and shone the flashlight up and down the alley behind Elliott's place. "Okay, Flores, let's get this area sealed off and let the forensic guys go to work. Mick, let's go inside and you can give us a full statement."

"I'll make a statement," I said, "but we can do it out here. You're not going inside Mr. Russell's house without a warrant."

"Jesus, Mick, you're not a lawyer anymore. Did they take your brains when they pulled your ticket?" Buchanan gestured at the hole. "Unless this guy buried himself, this whole area is a murder scene."

"It's well established that it takes more than a homicide to create an exception to the Fourth Amendment warrant requirement. Without exigent circumstances you've got no right to search, Detective," I said. "So we're doing this outside."

"Either of you guys could be the killer. Which means we need to search the house for evidence before you have a chance to get rid of it."

Elliott shot me a glance, which I ignored. "Seriously?" I said. "You have no probable cause to suspect either of us, which means any search will be unconstitutional. What's the over/under on how long it will take Casey to get any evidence you find tossed out of court? Five minutes?"

"Not my problem," Buchanan said. He turned to Flores and the other uniformed officer. "Go search the house, guys."

"The guy who lives here started all that BLM protest bullshit downtown," Malone called out to the departing officers. "Don't be afraid to make a mess."

Flores grinned back at him. "Yes, sir!"

Elliott looked at me again. I made a 'calm down' gesture with a hand behind my back. "Have it your way, Detective. I've told you everything you need to know. Mr. Russell and I will wait on the deck until you're finished."

There was a new outdoor table and chairs on Elliott's back deck. I'd helped him pick it up from Home Depot last weekend. We sat down. He leaned forward and whispered to me urgently.

"What do we do now? They're going to find those blueprints!"

"Not a big deal," I whispered back. "They don't prove anything and I meant what I said about Casey getting evidence tossed. Buchanan is making a mistake searching your place and I think he knows it. Relax. We just need to wait this out."

The forensic team, now fully kitted out in overalls and blue footwear covers, approached and surrounded the area with crime scene tape. One of them took several photos of the hole, the camera flash illuminating Elliott's yard like a strobe light. Once the photos were done, two other members of the team knelt down and carefully removed dirt, pausing occasionally for the photographer to take more snaps.

A while later Flores came out of Elliott's house.

"What have you got?" Buchanan said.

"Not much, sir," Flores replied. "There's a laptop computer and some papers with plans for the fence, but that's about it. No weapon, no contraband."

"No weapon?" Malone said. "You sure?"

"Yes, sir. We looked everywhere."

Malone was about to say something else when one of the forensic team approached.

"Detectives, I think you need to see this," he said.

He led Buchanan and Malone over to the body. I got up and followed them, gesturing for Elliott to stay put.

Enough dirt had been moved to expose Betts's head and the technician shone his flashlight on the gunshot wound between his eyes.

"We'll need to wait for the autopsy for confirmation," he said, "but it looks like the cause of death is obvious. Gunshot wound to the head, at close range—significant presence of residue around the wound indicates that the shot was fired from no more than a foot away. From the size of the wound, I suspect we're looking at 9mm ammunition. No rope marks on his arms or signs of other restraints. Also, no skin under the fingernails, or visible contusions, so it looks like he didn't struggle."

The technician moved his light to the back of Betts's head, illuminating a gaping hole surrounded by black dried blood.

"Exit wound is consistent with standard ammunition, rather

than hollow point. There's very little blood in the soil we removed and we are yet to find any sign of brain, skull, or hair matter either, which indicates that the killing took place elsewhere and the body was transported here for burial." He waved a hand at the hole. "We still need to exhume the body, and we may find more as we do so, but I wanted you to see this."

"Thanks, Cartwright," Buchanan said. He turned to me. "You recognize this guy?"

"Never seen him before in my life."

"Mr. Russell," Buchanan called, "can you come over here, please?"

"Stay there, Elliott," I said, quickly. I looked at Buchanan. "I told you, he's not saying a word to you guys until after he's spoken to his lawyer."

"Have it your way." Buchanan gestured at Betts's body. "You know, we've seen a few gang killings like this in the last year or so. Shot in the face so the victim can see it coming. Mr. Russell used to be a gang member, didn't he? You sure he's not still active?"

"Do you honestly think I'd tell you if he was?"

"Yeah, you're right. I should stop wasting my breath." Buchanan turned away, then stopped and pointed at Elliott. "Oh, and Mick? You know he can't stay here tonight, right? We have to seal the crime scene."

I nodded, kicking myself for not thinking of this before. Regardless of whether Elliott was a suspect, the police had the right to keep him out of the crime scene to prevent accidental destruction of evidence.

"Okay, I'll tell him. He can go inside and grab some stuff now you're done searching, right?"

"Yeah, but I want an officer to accompany him."

I nodded again and went over to break the bad news to Elliott.

"Yeah, I figured as much," he said when I told him.

"You can stay at my place."

He laughed. "No thanks. I've seen your couch. I'll call Billy. He's got a spare room."

"Fair enough. Let's go get some stuff."

I signaled to Buchanan and he had Officer Flores escort us into the house. Inside, the kitchen looked like it had been hit by a tornado. Drawers and cupboards were open, their contents scattered over every flat surface. The living room was worse, with the sofa and chairs overturned and their cushions piled in a corner. I'd seen cops pull this kind of petty bullshit more times than I could count, and it still fried me every time. From the thunderous look on Elliott's face, he was even more pissed than me.

Flores caught Elliott's angry expression and smiled at him. "Looks kinda like downtown, huh?"

Elliott ignored him and went to the bedroom. Flores followed, so I hung back and waited in the kitchen. Elliott emerged a minute later, with an overnight bag.

"Let's go," he said.

Buchanan was waiting for us on the deck. "Mr. Russell, you're free to go. We will want to speak to you after you've had the chance to confer with your attorney, so don't go too far."

"You know better than that," I snapped, still steamed about the mess the cops had made of Elliott's place. "Mr. Russell won't be saying a word to you, especially once Casey has reinforced that message. And he can go where he damn well pleases. Come on, Elliott."

We walked around to the front, where our cars were parked. Elliott threw his overnight bag in the back seat, then closed the door and leaned against his vehicle.

"Fucking assholes," he said. "You see what I mean, about the shit they pull?"

"Yeah."

Elliott paused and took a deep breath. "I'm still lost here, Mick. What happens now?"

I thought about finding the body, getting rid of the gun, and dealing with the cops. I was exhausted and I couldn't imagine how Elliott felt. When we started this morning, his biggest problem was how the press would respond to his clash with Chief Walker at the awards dinner. Now he had to wrap his head around someone framing him for murder.

"Go to Billy's place," I said. "Try to get some sleep. We'll talk to Casey tomorrow and make a plan from there."

"Okay, I'll try," he said. "Thanks, Mick. For everything you did today. I'd have been screwed without you."

He grabbed me in a bear hug before I could respond, then got in his car and drove away. I watched his taillights receding, trying desperately to shake the feeling that things were about to get a whole lot worse.

SEVEN
MAN OVERBOARD

I woke to the shrill chirp of my phone ringing. It took a few seconds for the fog in my head to clear. I looked at the bedside clock. 7:17am. *Shit.* I'd planned on sleeping at least a couple more hours.

I grabbed my phone, looked at the caller ID, and groaned. This was all I needed. For a moment I considered not answering, but I knew she'd just keep calling back until I did. Better to get it over with.

"Yeah?" I grunted.

"Where's my alimony, Mick?"

"Good morning, Sarah."

"Don't be a smartass. The check's late. Again."

"You call me this early, on a Sunday, to give me grief about money you don't even need?"

"Don't put this on me. You were supposed to pay me a week ago."

"Jesus Christ. You're living with a guy who just made partner at Miller Nash. You should be paying *me* alimony. Why don't you just marry him? Then you could stop bleeding me dry."

"Maybe if you stopped drinking away what little money you make, we wouldn't be having this conversation."

I didn't answer.

"Just send the check, will you?" Sarah said, eventually. "I can hold off cashing it for a few days if you need me to."

I hung up before she could and dropped the phone on the bedside table. My head was pounding. After I left Elliott's place last night, I'd gone to Holman's, my local bar, to wash away the day's chaos with a couple of stiff drinks. That led to an ill-advised pilgrimage to my son's grave, which in turn led to a few nightcaps in front of late-night TV, so it was never going to be an easy morning. Sarah bitching only made things worse.

I closed my eyes and laid back down, but I couldn't get back to sleep. No matter how hard I tried, I couldn't stop thinking about Elliott—who might hate him so much they'd kill someone and dump the body in his yard. No matter which way I tried to spin it, I drew a blank. Eventually, I gave up and dragged myself out of bed. I found a clean pair of boxers and a T-shirt amongst the mess on my floor, then wandered over to the kitchen and made toast and coffee.

I drank the first cup standing by the pot, then poured a second and used it to wash down a couple of aspirin. I took the toast and coffee over to the couch and sat down.

Christ, what a great start to Sunday. It annoyed the hell out of me that they didn't just get married. But then, I sent him a thank you card every year on the anniversary of Sarah leaving me for him, so he had a reason to be pissed at me.

I was going to keep sending them, though.

I had time to kill before our meeting with Casey, and I sure as hell didn't want to sit around moping about Sarah, so I put on my workout gear and went for a run. The day was already warming up and I was soaked in sweat after a few blocks. I cut through Laurelhurst Park to Stark Street, then headed east along Stark for a while, past the nursery and the rows of Craftsman bungalows. I turned right at 60th and took a lap around the base of the dormant volcano that was the centerpiece of Mount Tabor Park. When I'd completed it, I stopped and gazed up at the peak. Back when I was a teenager, my father and I used to run to the top to train for cross-country events. I was a decent athlete in those days, and he ran Masters events well into his sixties. Now he was gone, and I'd be lucky to make it halfway up that hill. But still, it felt good to sweat out some toxins. I stretched out, then slowly jogged home.

After a quick shower, I drove downtown and parked in the underground lot at Pioneer Square, then emerged onto the sidewalk by the Apple Store. The windows were still boarded up and the boards were covered in anti-police graffiti. Protesters had smashed windows and looted stores along much of downtown Portland's retail corridor when the Black Lives Matter demonstrations had turned violent. The protests still happened each night, and although they were more subdued and largely nonviolent, Apple and many other retailers had kept the boards in place rather than risk another round of shattered glass and stolen merchandise.

Casey's office was in an ornate 1920s redbrick building, a couple of blocks south of Skidmore Fountain, at the north end of downtown. It had been converted into office space for small businesses and Casey's practice was on the second floor, with a view of the river from the window. The office itself was big enough for a large wooden desk, a separate conference table with four chairs, and bookshelves on two walls. A small room off to one side held a photocopier and a supply cabinet. As with just about every other lawyer's office I'd ever seen, all the flat surfaces were covered in piles of paperwork.

"Hey, Casey, good to see you again."

"You too," she said.

Casey wore a blue two-piece suit, her straight brown hair cut to shoulder length. She was in her mid-thirties, tall and athletic. She held out her hand and I shook it. She had a solid grip, but not so firm you'd think she was trying to prove anything.

Casey moved a couple of stacks of paper off the conference table and gestured towards it. "Have a seat."

I sat down and Casey joined me.

"How's life in private practice?" I said.

"It's okay. The money's better, but I liked my clients more when I was a public defender. Most of my cases these days are white-collar crimes. Rich defendants are a whole new breed of assholes. A murder case is a refreshing change." Casey took a deep breath. "Anyway, what have you been up to?"

"Not much. I lost my job when United Streetcar went under a year or so ago. I've been doing some odd jobs here and there. Mostly small construction jobs, some night security gigs at Dante's or Revolution Hall. Building a fence for Elliott, until yesterday."

"Speaking of Elliott, you know *you* should talk to a lawyer too, right? If he gets convicted, and the cops find out about you and the gun, the first thing they're going to do is charge you with aiding and abetting."

"Yeah, I know. First sign of trouble, that gun's going in the river."

"If you were my client, I'd advise you to ditch it right now."

Casey had a point. Under Oregon law, the penalty for aiding and abetting is the same as for the underlying crime. So, I could be facing the same sentence as a murderer. I'd have to keep a close eye on how things played out.

"I'll think about it. If things go bad, I could always hit up your old friends at the Public Defender's office."

"You could do much worse."

42

"True that."

Casey looked at me thoughtfully. "What happened to you, Mick?"

"What do you mean?"

"You know exactly what I mean," she said. "You were a damn good defense lawyer. And the crazy cases you took—man, even I wouldn't go near some of your clients. You were the patron saint of lost causes. And then one day you blew it all up. Why?"

"Simple. The justice system is a swamp full of shit and I got sick of swimming in it."

Casey threw her hands up. "Oh, come on, that's bullshit and you know it. If you weren't happy, you could have just quit your job like a normal person. Instead, you slugged a prosecutor in front of a judge. There has to be more to the story."

There was a lot more to the story, but I didn't want to tell it. Fortunately for me, Elliott chose that moment to walk in.

We both stood up and Casey stepped forward to greet Elliott.

"Welcome, Mr. Russell," she said as she shook his hand. "It's a pleasure to meet you."

"Good to meet you too," Elliott replied, "though I wish it was under different circumstances. Thank you for seeing me on a Sunday."

"Of course, no problem. Please sit down."

Elliott sat down and nodded to me. "Mick."

"Good to see you, buddy," I said. "You get any sleep?"

"Not much."

"Yeah, me neither."

Casey grabbed a legal pad and a pen. "Right, Mr. Russell. Let's start by having you walk me through what happened yesterday. I know the basics from the phone conversation with Mick, but I want to hear it from you."

Elliott talked Casey through the day's events, starting from when we first found the body. He spoke in short, sharp sentences, scowling and stabbing the air with fierce hand gestures to illustrate key points. A long night of brooding had stoked the fires of anger at whoever had done this to him. I could almost feel his rage from across the table.

When he got to the part about the cops searching the house, Casey held up a hand to stop him, then frowned at me.

"You let them search the house?" she said.

"I couldn't stop them," I replied. "I told Buchanan he didn't have exigent circumstances, but he went ahead anyway. Besides, I figured it could come in handy. This way, you've got a chance of tossing anything they find, on Fourth Amendment grounds."

"Speaking of which, what did they find?"

"Plans for the yard work and Elliott's laptop. The plans aren't great for us. They show a concrete driveway going in where Betts was buried. You know they'll spin that as a plan to hide the body."

"Then I'll have to make sure those plans never make it to court," Casey replied. "Anything to be concerned about on the laptop?"

"No," Elliott said. "It's mostly work stuff and my campaign files."

"How about your social media?"

"That's clean too. Has to be, otherwise my campaign would be over in a heartbeat."

"Good." Casey looked at her notes. "You say the police didn't identify Betts at the scene?"

"Not before we left," I said. "But they will soon enough."

"Yes, they will. Elliott, Mick said you have a history with Betts. Tell me about it."

"Okay." Elliott took a deep breath and rubbed his face. He told Casey about Betts shooting his brother and about having been arrested on his way to take revenge. Tears welled in his eyes, but this time he managed to hold them back. Without missing a beat, he told Casey about his recent fight with Betts at the Coalition meeting.

"And that made the media?" she said.

"Yeah, front page of the Metro section in *The Oregonian*," he replied. "Probably the TV news too."

"So, the police will find out about it soon enough." Casey pursed her lips and made some more notes. "Now for the obvious question. Who's setting you up?"

"Shit, I don't know. I haven't seen Betts since the fight at the Coalition meeting. Maybe he screwed over some business partner or something."

"Then why frame you?" Casey said. "Why not just dump Betts out in the woods?"

"That's obvious. Whoever killed Betts wants me out of the picture too. Or they figure if I take the fall, they get away with it."

"Do you think it's a gang thing?"

"I doubt it," Elliott replied. "That was all a long time ago."

"Are you sure? If there's one thing I know, it's that gang members hold grudges."

"Maybe," Elliott said, but he didn't look convinced. "What about the cops?"

Casey shook her head. "I'm no fan of the boys in blue and we all know about Andre Gladen and George Floyd, and all the others, but this isn't their style. If they wanted you locked up, they'd just pull you over and plant drugs on you."

"No, hear me out. Ever since I organized the BLM protests, they've been on my case. Coming to my office with bogus noise complaints. Stopping me as I'm leaving work. Mick saw a cop mime shooting me Friday night and I almost got in a fight with Chief Walker."

"All true," I said, curious to get Casey's take.

"I don't doubt it," she replied. "But there's a big difference between fucking with you, and killing Betts and dumping his body in your yard. What about your work with NNC—could that have a connection?"

"Unlikely. We do community programs and housing policy advocacy. Nobody gets killed over that."

"Well, think about it some more. We're going to need something to go on."

"I will. Anyway, now you've heard all this, what's your take? Am I in trouble here?"

Casey put her pen down. "It's complicated. Do you want the good news or the bad news?"

"The good news. I could use some."

"Without the gun, the police don't have any evidence connecting you to the killing. Unless they come up with something else, it's going to be very hard to convict you of murder."

"All right, what's the bad news?"

"The bad news is it won't take the cops long to find out about those clashes with Betts. It's enough probable cause for them to arrest you."

"What?" Elliott snapped. "I'm going to be arrested?"

"Yes."

"But you said they don't have enough to convict me?"

"They don't. But probable cause for arrest is a much lower bar. Betts killing your brother and you fighting with him is enough."

Elliott put his head in his hands. "Shit. What happens now?"

"Buchanan knows I'm representing you," Casey said. "Once

they decide they have probable cause, he'll get a warrant, then contact me and make arrangements for you to surrender yourself. You'll be taken into custody, then arraigned, typically the next day."

"What about bail?"

"It depends on what they charge you with. If they go with aggravated murder, it's unlikely. With a lesser charge, we might be able to swing something."

"So how long until they lock me up?"

"I'd guess a few days. A week at the outside."

"And I'm supposed to just carry on with my life until then?"

"Pretty much, yeah." Casey sighed. "I know this is a lot to take in. But like it or not, your life changed forever when someone buried Malik Betts in your backyard. There's no going back to how things used to be."

Elliott glared at her. "I fucking knew this day would come," he muttered. "All right, I'm guessing you don't work for free. How much is this case going to cost me?"

"That depends. I won't know for sure, until we know how deep it's going to go. But you can assume somewhere between one hundred and two hundred thousand dollars as a ballpark figure."

"And I gotta come up with that money right now?"

"No, but to get started I'll need a retainer of ten thousand dollars."

"Damn, that's more than I was expecting," Elliott said.

"Do you need a payment plan?"

"No, I'll find a way to cover it. I've got some savings, and NNC has litigation insurance. It covers criminal defense. We should be able to tap into that. Not sure it'll cover two hundred K, but it's enough to get started. If we keep the tab on the lower end of your estimate, I might even keep my house. What does my ten grand get me, counselor?"

"Please, call me Casey. You'll get the best defense I can give you. First, we go through your movements for the past week or so. That way, once we get the time of death, we can work on establishing an alibi. I'll hire an investigator to look for witnesses —and other potential suspects. I'll work on legal research and preparation for arraignment, specifically focused on trying to get you bail. But the real work starts once we get the initial round of discovery from the prosecution. Then we know what they're basing their case on and we can figure out how to attack it."

"All right," Elliott said, "when do we start?"

"Can you be here tomorrow, at nine? I need to get some things off my plate so I can focus on your case. That'll take me the rest of the day today."

Elliott stood up. "Yeah, nine is good. Mick, you want to meet me here again?"

"I won't be here, buddy," I said.

I looked at Casey and she gave me a brief nod. "Mick isn't part of the defense team," she said. "The meeting tomorrow will be just the two of us."

"But there must be something he can do to help?"

"Casey's right," I said. "You need a lawyer, and she's the best. I need to step back and let her get on with it."

"Okay, I guess," he replied. "I'll see you tomorrow, Casey."

Elliott walked out, his shoulders hunched, as though a ton of bricks was pushing them down.

I meant what I said about him being in good hands with Casey. And besides, the last thing Elliott needed was a failed lawyer like me. But that didn't stop me feeling like the world's biggest asshole.

EIGHT
A LITTLE HELP FROM MY FRIENDS

Monday morning, I called my old friend Tony da Costa and asked him to meet me for breakfast at City State Diner. City State was a short walk from my apartment. They served a mean Bloody Mary, and the interior paid homage to classic diner style, with everything from chrome-edged black Formica tables to hipsters in trucker hats perched at the bar. Tony was already there when I arrived, seated at a table in the back.

"Hey, Mick," he said as I sat down. "How are you doing?"

"Good to see you, Tony."

Tony was a private investigator I'd hired regularly back when I was practicing, and we stayed friends after I was disbarred. He was about five ten, thin as a rake, and he moved like a whippet. He claimed he'd been a boxer as a kid in Mexico. He didn't look big enough, to me, but he sure was quick and his nose looked like it had been broken more than once.

A waitress appeared before we could get past our greetings. I hated slow service, so that was another reason I liked City State. I went for a Bloody Mary and eggs Benedict. Tony ordered coffee and the smoked salmon hash, with a side of fresh fruit. The waitress took our orders and left with a cheery smile.

"Thanks for coming," I said.

"Always happy to eat a good breakfast," he said. "What's going on?"

"I need your help."

"Is this related to our case?" he asked. Tony had persuaded one of his lawyer clients to hire me to do document review on a construction defect case at a new strip mall on the west side. We had a meeting with the lawyer tomorrow morning, and I hadn't started yet.

"No, that's not it. Something else came up over the weekend." I looked around the crowded diner. "You want to take a walk?"

Tony raised his eyebrows. "Sure, let's go."

He left, gliding between the tables like a dancer. I told our waitress we'd be back soon and followed Tony outside. He was leaning against the wall by the door, hands in his pockets.

"Come on," I said, and headed around the corner onto Couch Street. Tony walked alongside me. Apart from the occasional cyclist, there was no one around.

"What's going on?" Tony said.

"It's about Elliott. He's in trouble."

Tony stopped. "What?"

"Keep walking," I said, "it's a long story."

We set off again. As we walked, I told him the whole thing: finding Betts's body, the planted gun, the history between Betts and Elliott, and our meeting with Casey. Tony knew Elliott well and he had to be just as shocked as me by what had transpired.

"Man, there's only one way we can help him," he said when I'd finished. "Get his ass across the border pronto."

"He won't go."

Tony shrugged. "Force his hand. Go back to his place to

finish the fence. Find the gun, call the cops. While you're waiting for them to show up, call Elliott and tell him he's got no choice now. Tell him my cousin has a taco bar in Sayulita. He's always looking for reliable staff."

I laughed. "You're a sick bastard."

"Am I right, or what? You're missing something obvious here."

"What?"

"Elliott did it."

"Don't be ridiculous!"

"Jesus, listen to yourself. This guy admitted to you he was going to shoot Betts the night he got arrested!"

"Yeah, but that was ten years ago."

"If you killed my little brother, I'd spend the rest of my life hunting you down."

"No way. Look at how far he's come. He wouldn't throw all that away."

"You better hope you're right. Because if he's guilty, by helping him you became an accessory after the fact."

"Yeah, I know." So now both Tony and Casey were on my case about accessory liability. I knew I should get rid of the gun; that way there would be nothing to tie me to the crime. And I knew helping Elliott was risky. He could be convicted of murder, regardless of whether he did it. And if he was, I could be convicted of being an accessory, which meant spending a long time locked up in a dark place.

Our drinks were waiting for us when we got back to the table and our food came as we sat down. I took a long pull on my Bloody Mary. Nice and spicy, and a healthy belt of vodka to give it an extra kick. Perfect.

We made small talk while we ate. I got the sense Tony didn't know what to say about Elliott's situation. I was happy to let it ride. Hearing Tony say I should stay away from the case made me feel better about leaving Elliott in Casey's hands. Still, I couldn't shake the feeling that I should be doing more.

Tony ordered more coffee when we finished eating. I thought about another Bloody Mary, but I had a big day ahead, so I decided against it.

"Anyway, let's talk about this construction case," I said.

"Right, that." Tony put his coffee down and scratched his head. "You found anything in the documents yet?"

"Not yet, but I'm going to hit it hard today. Anything in particular I should be looking for?"

"Anything that could light a fire under the defendants."

"Yeah, I can do that. They've hit us with a ton of documents, but if it's there, I'll find it." It was the oldest trick in the book when big businesses got sued by the little guys. Bury the plaintiffs in paper. The plaintiff's attorneys worked on contingency, which meant they didn't get a penny unless they won the case. Meanwhile, the defense attorneys got paid by the hour, and the defendant's insurance was footing the bill, so they were perfectly happy to spend their days stuffing bankers boxes full of paper. They thought they were being clever when they gave you a thousand pages in response to a single document request. But sometimes they got sloppy and let critical information through in their rush to build a bigger pile of paper. And a trained eye could find those nuggets.

"Thanks, man. We're meeting at Kristen's office at nine tomorrow."

"Sounds good," I said. Kristen Campione was the plaintiffs' attorney in the case. "See you then."

I stood up and drained my Bloody Mary. We shook hands and I went home.

Back at my place, I pulled out the boxes of documents Tony had given me and dumped them on the floor by my couch, then grabbed a Coke from the fridge and pressed it against the back of my neck. It must have been ninety degrees out, and it wasn't much cooler inside. I popped the Coke and opened a couple of windows. There wasn't much of a breeze, so I turned on my battered old fan.

I opened boxes until I found the case file Tony had prepared for me. I read through the complaint and answer, along with the summary memo. It was a standard construction dispute. Several small business owners who'd bought premises in a new strip mall were suing the developer. Plaintiffs claimed defective construction, false advertising, and fraud. According to them, the storefronts in the strip mall were advertised as high-end business facilities and priced accordingly. But the actual places were shoddily built, with cheap superficial decorations hiding major construction defects. Defendant's answer basically said that the buildings passed city inspections—and besides, you bought it already, so tough luck.

I started in on the discovery responses. The defendants had sent a couple of boxes full of everything from emails to supply contracts to a hand-drawn wiring layout sketch on the back of an envelope. Half of one box was filled with copies of invoices for construction materials: concrete, drywall, carpet, windows and doors, and everything else. The documents weren't presented in chronological order, which was another standard defense tactic. I sighed and grabbed a pencil and legal pad.

I made a quick first pass through the documents to map out the events and key players. First, I turned my pad on its side and drew a timeline. I marked one end with the date construction began, and the other end with the date plaintiffs filed suit. Then, as I went through the documents, I made notes along the timeline. Working in pencil allowed me to erase and move things around as I found new information. Maybe I could have done it faster on my computer, but I felt more connected when I worked by hand. I moved steadily through the documents, my timeline becoming more like a spider's web with every page.

After a couple of hours, I needed a break, so I stood up and stretched, then called Elliott.

"Hey, buddy, I wanted to see how you're doing."

"Just sitting here waiting for the hammer to fall."

"Yeah, that's tough," I said. "How was the meeting with Casey this morning?"

"She told me not to talk to anyone about it so I don't break the attorney–client privilege. That means you too, right?"

"Come on. You know I'd never say anything."

"Still, you're on the outside now," he said, curtly. "I don't think I'll take that chance."

His tone annoyed me. "What do you want from me? I found you the best lawyer I could."

"And then you cut out."

"If I cut out, would I be calling you now?" I took a deep breath. "Look, I can't help you on the legal side of things. But if there's anything else I can do, just say it. You know I'll be there."

Elliott was silent for a while. I was about to hang up when he spoke again. "I know. I'm sorry. This shit is hard, you know?"

"Hang in there. Call me if you need anything."

I hung up, feeling better now that we'd cleared the air. Then I looked at the stacks of discovery documents I still had to review and sighed. It was going to be a long night.

NINE
MEET THE NEW BOSS

M y alarm shouted me awake at eight the next morning. I rubbed my eyes and sat up, fighting my way back to the land of the living. I'd been working on the document review until 3 a.m.

I stumbled into the bathroom for a quick shower, then dried off, dressed and downed a mug of cold coffee left over from the pot that had kept me going last night. My meeting with Tony and Kristen was at nine, so I had to get moving. I threw my laptop and notes into a plastic shopping bag and drove downtown.

Kristen Campione's office was on the 24th floor of the 1000 Broadway Building downtown. The building's copper mirrored façade and staggered sides made it more interesting than most office towers, although the dome on top made it look like a giant stick of deodorant. Kristen's office suite was decorated in lawyer chic: dark wood door with brass handle and nameplate, shelves of law books lining the walls, and furniture that wouldn't look out of place in a remake of *Gone with the Wind*. Kristen's receptionist showed me into the main conference room, where Tony was already waiting.

"Hey, Mick," he said. "You look like shit."

I sat down and put my notes in front of me. "You're not exactly Miss Universe, yourself."

Tony was about to say something else when the receptionist appeared with coffee. I took a sip, then sat back and sighed.

"Long night, huh?" Tony said.

Before I could answer, Kristen Campione walked in. She was short, dark-haired, pushing fifty, and so full of pent-up energy she was like a firecracker about to go off.

"Tony, Mick," she said, nodding at us. She pulled out a chair, slapped a stack of documents down on the table, and sat. "Let's get started, shall we?"

Without waiting for an answer, she fanned her documents out, put on reading glasses and pursed her lips. "We have the summary judgment response due in a week and the hearing on it in two. If we lose, we're dead. What have we got?"

Kristen pushed her reading glasses up on top of her head and looked at us expectantly.

Tony looked at me. "Mick?"

I made a mental note to kick his ass later. "Okay, I took a pass at the documents you gave me. Good news and bad news. The bad news is that there are no smoking guns. No email saying 'let's cheat the customers', or anything like that. The good news is that the documents do raise some questions."

I spread my notes out in front of me, trying to decipher my late-night scrawl. Kristen raised her eyebrows, but not in a bad way. She was old-school enough to like seeing someone work longhand.

"If you look at this timeline," I said, sliding a sheet over for her to look at, "you'll see that the inspection dates and construction sign offs don't quite align. There's normally a minimum of a week between sign off and inspection, but on these buildings it's much less. The same day, in one case. It could be just a scheduling thing, but to me it smacks of collusion. It's worth digging deeper."

Kristen spun the sheet around to read it, then frowned and handed it back.

"Okay, good. We'll file supplemental discovery on that. Before we do, Tony, go talk to those inspectors. See if you can get anything out of them before they lawyer up. Mick, what else?"

"There are some blueprints in the documents they handed over. It wouldn't hurt to have a construction expert look at them, to see if they're up to code. And if they are, maybe have the expert check out the mall itself and see whether the build matches the blueprints. Could be they cut some corners."

Kristen nodded. "We've had an expert look at the buildings already, but I agree it would be worth having them review the blueprints too."

"That's all I've got right now," I said. "I want to take another pass at the documents, but I doubt there will be much more. The answers aren't buried in that pile of paper."

"They never are," she said, "but you've made a good start. Okay, next on the agenda. Background on our plaintiffs. Tony, any skeletons we need to worry about in their closets?"

I didn't listen to Tony's answer. My mind kept racing back to Elliott's situation and the trouble I could be in too. Wading through paperwork last night, had got me thinking. Maybe I could spend some time digging into Betts's business dealings, to see if anything unusual came up. Maybe help Elliott out and help myself at the same time.

The meeting wrapped up without me needing to be involved again. Tony was late for another appointment, so he left in a hurry. I got up to leave.

Kristen gathered up her stack of documents. "Having fun, Mick?"

"What do you mean?"

"Being back in the saddle. It's been a while since you've done legal work."

"It has."

"Well? Are you enjoying it?"

What a question. I loved it for giving me the old thrill of the hunt. I hated it for reminding me of what I'd thrown away. I wanted to go back to the way things used to be. And I didn't like being reminded of how it made me feel.

I shrugged. "Pays the bills."

Kristen raised her eyebrows. "Right. Good catch on the inspection dates," she said. "Let me know if you find anything else."

"Will do," I said, surprised by how much Kristen's compliment meant to me.

"Oh, and Mick? I meant it when I said good work. I've got a couple of other cases coming up where I could use some help. Are you interested?"

"Sure. Call me if you need me." I managed to keep my voice calm, but civil cases were indoor work with no heavy lifting and paid three times what I was getting for the various gigs I'd been subsisting on lately. Hell yeah, I was interested.

I pictured being able to pay my rent on time. It was a strange but pleasant feeling. I'd never made much money, even when I was a defense lawyer. Most of my clients weren't exactly rich. That had always been a bone of contention between Sarah and me. She wanted me to switch to some other area of law, like real estate or mergers and acquisitions, where my clients could afford to pay their bills. But I wasn't interested in helping wealthy people move piles of money around. When we divorced, Sarah cited irreconcilable differences; the biggest difference being between what I earned and what she wanted to spend.

It was hot out again, so I didn't feel like going home. Since I was downtown, I hit up an old haunt. The Lotus Tavern was a Portland institution about a five-minute walk away. I hadn't been there since I'd been disbarred, and I felt like catching up. As the closest bar to both the county and federal courts, the Lotus did strong traffic in drinking lawyers. It was one of the few bars west of the river that could make a Top Ten Portland Dive Bars list, and to be honest, I missed the place.

It looked the same: Faded Oregon Trail mural above the mirrored bar, walls stained yellow by decades of smoke, the smell of stale fryer grease hanging heavy in the air. It felt like home. I didn't recognize the bartender, but that wasn't a surprise. Lawyers are hard to deal with when they're alone and sober. When they're drinking in large groups, they're a nightmare. Staff turnover was high at the Lotus.

Most lawyers weren't done with work yet, so the place wasn't too busy. I parked myself at the bar and ordered a beer. It felt good just being there. I caught a look at my reflection in the mirror behind the counter. My short brown hair was losing the battle against invading gray and my stubble was even worse. I had just turned forty, but the face staring back looked ten years further down the road.

I shrugged at myself and sipped my pint, remembering the times I'd been in the same place. Celebrating victories, drinking away defeats. And the day my career ended. After Judge King called security, to have me removed from the courtroom, I'd come here and bought drinks for everybody in the bar. At first, everyone loved me, but the crowd thinned out as word filtered through about what I'd done. I used to think I lost a lot of friends that day, but later I realized I'd learned who my friends were.

I pulled out my laptop and spent the next couple of hours

trawling through online real estate records, pausing only to grab a stale ham sandwich for lunch. I took notes as I went, trying to build a picture of Malik Betts the real estate agent. His business Phoenix Realty had been operating for six years. He worked mostly seller side, and of late his numbers had increased dramatically. So much so, that he was on last year's list of Portland's top fifty agents based on volume. He didn't make the list based on dollars, but that was probably down to him mostly working in poorer neighborhoods like where he and Elliott grew up. In the last couple of years, he'd done mostly condo sales. He worked alone, but he was a member of all the usual trade groups. On the face of it, he was a moderately successful independent real estate agent.

I took down the names of a few recent clients, then checked my watch. It was after five. I stood up and stretched, my shoulders and back stiff from hours spent sitting in the same chair. My neck cracked as I rolled my head from side to side. Christ, I was getting old. I gathered up my notes and laptop. My phone rang as I was about to leave.

"Hello?"

"Mick, it's Elliott. The news is out."

"What do you mean?"

"I've been getting calls non-stop from reporters for the past hour. The first one asked me if I had any comment about the body of Malik Betts being found at my house. I hung up on him and ignored the rest."

"Shit, that was quick. Did you call Casey?"

"Yeah. She said to play it cool. Easier said than done."

"No doubt. Anything I can do to help?"

"Yeah, there is. There's a City Council meeting in an hour. The NNC's proposed ordinance to limit new multi-unit developments is on the agenda, so I need to be there. I could use some help making sure the press keep their distance."

"Are you sure you need to go?"

"Yeah, I thought about it, and I need to do it. We've had too many people working on the ordinance for too long to let it slip just because of me. Besides, Casey told me to carry on with my life."

"Then count me in," I said. Working security at nightclubs had taught me plenty about dealing with unruly crowds, and this one should be mostly sober. I could do it in my sleep.

"Thanks," Elliott said, his voice softer now. "Can you pick me up at the Albina Community Center? I'm up there running an after-school computer education group."

"No problem. I'm on my way."

TEN
DOING THE LORD'S WORK

When I got to my car, I pulled out my phone and checked the KOIN news website. Sure enough, the lead headline was "Body Found in Council Candidate's Yard." I read the story. It named Betts as the victim, mentioned Elliott by name, and stated that the police had refused to comment on whether he was a suspect, which was tantamount to saying they were sure he did it.

I'd hoped the police would take longer to identify Betts and his connections to Elliott. But now they had and the press was all over it. At least Elliott hadn't been arrested yet.

I drove up to the Albina Community Center. The NNC had set up a computer lab in a small room off to the side of the main hall. There were two rows of five desks, each occupied by an African American child working away at a computer. The kids looked to be about ten years old. Elliott leaned over one girl's shoulder, pointing at the screen and offering her tips. Other than his voice, the only sound was the clacking of keys.

Elliott saw me. He finished talking to the girl, patted her on the shoulder, and came over.

"Thanks for coming," he said.

"No worries. You holding up okay?"

His pocket buzzed before he could answer. Elliott took his phone out, looked at the screen, then killed the call.

"Yeah, I'm fine," he said. "You heard anything?"

"Not yet."

"I suppose I'll be arrested soon?"

"I don't know. Maybe they leaked the story to the press to try to shake something loose."

Elliott didn't look convinced. He checked his watch. "It's almost six, and the meeting is at 6:45. We should hit the road."

He turned back to the room. "Okay, gang, it's time to wrap up. Sign off and shut down, please."

Audible groans echoed around the room, but the kids did as they were told. They packed up their stuff and left, high-fiving Elliott on their way out. He watched them go, then went around the room to make sure the computers were shut down.

"I'm gonna miss this," he said.

"You'll be back here soon enough."

Elliott didn't speak as we drove downtown. When we got there, I took a pass by City Hall to see what was happening. From a distance I saw two TV broadcast vans parked outside, their antennae and satellite dishes raised. As we got closer, it became apparent there was a large crowd gathered outside the rotunda entrance. When Elliott saw how many reporters were there, he shook his head.

"That's worse than I thought," he said. "You think you can get me through that crowd?"

"Easy."

We parked and walked back toward the four-story sandstone building.

"Okay, here's how we play it," I said. "I'm going in hard. Stay close to my back and hide your eyes with your hand so they can't get a good face shot. Let's go."

The crowd recognized Elliott as soon as we got close. A couple of reporters peeled off toward us, holding microphones and shouting, "Mister Russell! Mister Russell!"

I spread my shoulders to make myself as wide as possible and made a beeline for the front door. The first two reporters stepped back quickly to avoid being run over. As we approached the main crowd, another reporter tried to block my path. I planted my hand on his chest and shoved him back. He stumbled and fell, knocking over a cameraman as he went down. Everyone else got out of our way.

There were two security guards by the oak doors. They swung the doors open, to let Elliott and me through, then held the press pack back.

"Thanks, Mick," Elliott said. "Can you stay for the meeting? Those guys will still be here when we're done."

"Of course."

We made our way to the council chambers. The meeting hadn't begun, but Mayor Alioto and the four other council members were already in their seats at the front of the room, facing the public gallery. They were all flicking through papers and muttering to aides. Billy Hinds had a seat in the front row of the gallery, with a space next to him. Elliott went and joined him. The rest of the gallery was almost full, but I found a seat near the back.

I spent most of the meeting playing around on my phone and trying not to nod off. The NNC's proposed ordinance was the last item on the agenda. When it was called, Elliott and Billy made their way to the speakers' table in front of the council members.

Mayor Alioto picked up a sheet of paper. "Our final item today is initial reading and comment on a proposed amendment to Title 33, Chapter 270 of the City Code, Planned Unit Developments," he said. "The amendment, brought forward by the Northeast Neighborhood Coalition, would limit the number of new multi-dwelling structures that can be erected within a given residential zone to one every two years. To begin, Mr. Russell, would you please explain why the NNC believes this amendment is necessary?"

Elliott stood, and a murmur went through the crowd. The news about Betts must have spread.

"Thank you, Mr. Mayor," Elliott said. "We believe this amendment is necessary, because in recent years, too many members of our community have had their homes taken in the name of profit. The city uses eminent domain to evict families who have been in their homes for generations, so developers can build cookie-cutter condo blocks and get rich by selling the units to people new to the city. In the past five years, twenty-three of these developments have been approved in North Portland and Northeast Portland alone. Over two hundred families have lost their homes and soaring housing costs mean they've been forced to leave the neighborhoods they lived in their entire lives. It is tearing our communities apart and it has to stop."

Elliott sat down. Several people in the gallery tried to speak at once. Mayor Alioto held up his hands.

"Please," he shouted, "we will take questions from the council first, then the public." He looked at the people on either side of him. "Commissioner Salmon?"

"Thank you, Mayor," said the man at the far right of the council seats. His nameplate identified him as Commissioner Rick Salmon. "Mr. Russell, I'm sure you are aware that Portland is facing a housing crisis. Your proposed amendment would make solving this crisis more difficult, by limiting high-density accommodation development. How do you propose to remedy that?"

"Commissioner, I don't know how to solve a housing crisis," Elliott said. "I do know that evicting people from their homes and pricing them out of their own neighborhoods isn't the answer."

The woman at the other end of the council bench pulled her microphone toward her. "Mr. Russell," she said, "the city already has a comprehensive review process designed to prevent the kind of abuses you allege. Is there a need for your amendment?"

"I'm glad you brought that up, Commissioner Eugenie," Elliott replied. "You say these developments are approved through an open process. But let me give you an example of how that process works. When the recent Sunshine Portland development on Northeast Rosa Parks was announced, the city requested comments from residents of the area. Forty-six different African American families submitted comments opposing it. The development was approved anyway, and not one of those families even received a response. Do you know why? Because Black folks have no voice in Portland. They are evicted from their homes and forced to leave neighborhoods their families have lived in for generations because they can't afford to stay. That's why we need the amendment."

Eugenie sat back, frowning. Mayor Alioto looked along the bench, but neither of the other commissioners responded.

"All right," he said. "We'll take public comments now." He looked around the room, then pointed at someone. "Mr. Charles Sinclair, we'll hear from you first."

A tall, sixtyish man with gray hair and a matching suit stood up. "Thank you, Mayor," he said. "Mr. Russell, I understand your concern. But surely you agree that Portland is facing a housing crisis? We have a homeless problem, that's getting worse by the day, and the only way to solve it is to build more affordable housing."

"Mr. Sinclair, you claim to be an advocate of affordable

housing," Elliott said. "You're President and CEO of CDS Construction, aren't you?"

"I am," Sinclair said, straightening his shoulders.

"And your company has built fifteen of those developments I mentioned, correct?"

"I believe so, yes."

"Can you tell us what percentage of the units in those developments are allocated to affordable housing?"

Sinclair frowned. "Not off the top of my head, but I assure you our company is committed to providing–"

"Bullshit," Elliott said.

"I beg your pardon!"

"You heard me," Elliott replied. He jabbed a finger at Sinclair. "I'll tell you the number. Less than two percent of the units are allocated to affordable housing. The rest of them are sold at prices that working-class Black folks can't afford. How is that solving any problem?"

"Don't you dare lecture me!" Sinclair snapped.

Elliott stood up. "And don't you dare act like you give a damn about my community. How many of your buyers are people of color?"

"Are you calling me racist? How dare you! We do not discriminate. Anyone is free to purchase–"

"Yeah, right. Just like anyone is free to have their home stolen by the city so rich folk like you can build more little boxes and make more money. I guess it's just coincidence that it only happens to Black folk."

"I've heard enough!" Sinclair yelled, his face red. "I'm sick of you interfering where you're not wanted. This is the last time!"

Mayor Alioto stood up. "Please! Everyone, let's keep it civil. Mr. Russell, I have to ask you to apologize for the accusations you leveled at Mr. Sinclair."

"Oh, you do, do you?" Elliott said. "Well, Mr. Mayor, I regret to inform you that you can shove your apology up your ass."

Elliott walked out of the chamber, leaving disbelieving stares in his wake. I hurried out too and caught up with him in the corridor outside.

"That was fun," I said.

"Motherfucker is lucky I didn't kick his ass."

"Look at you, picking fights with Chief Walker and now this Sinclair dude. You're almost as bad as me."

"I'm sick of it, Mick," he said. "Sick of these assholes getting rich by screwing people over. They're destroying our community and no one is doing anything about it!"

Elliott was so wound up, I could almost feel the heat coming off him.

"I know, buddy," I said.

"You're going to tell me I should take it easy, aren't you?"

"Fuck no. I'm right there with you. I hate what those assholes and their cookie-cutter condos are doing to Portland. They're stealing this city's soul. Any time you want me to deck somebody for you, just say the word. It's not like I haven't done it before."

Elliott laughed. "Thanks, man. I appreciate it."

"I meant it," I said. "Now, let's get you through that mob outside. Who knows? Maybe I can punch one of them instead."

ELEVEN
WELCOME TO THE JUNGLE

Elliott had left his car at the NNC office, so I dropped him off there and went home. I'd barely made it in the door when my phone rang.

"Hey, Mick, it's Casey. Is Elliott with you? I've been trying to call him, but he's not answering."

"No, I dropped him off about twenty minutes ago. What's up?"

"Buchanan called me," she said. "A warrant has been issued for Elliott's arrest. I'm trying to reach him so we can arrange for him to turn himself in."

"Damn. That was quick. What's the charge?"

Casey paused. "Ag murder."

Aggravated murder, or 'ag murder' in lawyer speak, was the most severe murder charge under Oregon law. It carried the possibility of a death sentence. Oregon hadn't executed anyone since 1997 and a governor's moratorium on any further executions had been in place since 2011, but there were still more than thirty people on death row and the moratorium could be lifted at any time.

Casey's news hit me like a smack in the face. "On what grounds?"

"They're saying the physical evidence shows an execution-style killing, which strongly indicates a broader criminal enterprise, or murder for hire."

"That's complete bullshit." I paused for a moment. "No, it isn't. Betts's murder probably was an execution. But Elliott didn't do it."

"Let's hope you're right. Do you know how I can reach Elliott?"

"Not if he's not answering his phone. Let me call him. He's been ducking calls from reporters and he might not have recognized your number."

"Okay, call me back," Casey said, and hung up.

I called Elliott. It rang three times and went to voicemail. I hung up and tried again, but the same thing happened.

I texted Casey.

No reply. I'll try Billy.

I called Billy Hinds and he answered right away.

"Hey, Billy, it's Mick. Is Elliott with you?"

"No, I haven't seen him since the meeting."

"Is he still staying with you?"

"Yeah. I was expecting him home by now."

Billy's house was no more than a five-minute drive from where I'd dropped him off at the NNC office. Elliott should have been there a while ago.

"That's strange," I said. "Do you know where else he might have gone?"

"Can't think of anywhere off the top of my head," Billy replied. "Maybe he had car trouble?"

"I suppose. If you hear from him, can you tell him to call Casey right away? It's important."

"Sure, no problem."

"Thanks, Billy."

I hung up and tried Elliott's number again, but he still didn't answer. I left a message telling him to call Casey ASAP, then called her myself.

"No luck," I said. "I can't reach him and Billy hasn't heard from him either."

"Damn. Okay, I'll keep trying. Can you do the same?"

"Sure."

I hung up and thought about what to do. I spent the next half hour reaching out to everyone I could think of who knew Elliott. I called Ray and G-Dog, but neither of them knew where I could find him, nor did anyone else I tried. I tried Elliott every few minutes too, but the calls kept going to voicemail. When I finished my list, I called Billy and Casey again. Billy still hadn't seen Elliott and Casey hadn't heard from him either. I was sick of sitting around, so I grabbed my keys and drove up to the NNC office

It was just after 11 p.m. when I arrived. The parking lot was empty and no lights were on in the building. I looked around, and immediately I saw flashing red and blue lights a couple of blocks to the south. Two police cars were parked facing each other across the street, blocking both lanes.

I ran towards them. About a dozen people were gathered by the cars. Two more police cars were parked across the street fifty yards to the south, blocking off traffic from the other direction as well. Crime scene tape had been strung between trees, temporary barricades closed off a section of the street, and six uniformed officers milled around inside it. There was a vehicle parked by the side of the road in the closed-off area. Elliott's car. Two white-suited forensic technicians pored over it, and two more were examining the surrounding street and sidewalk.

I went over to one of the officers by the tape. "What's happening here?"

"Sir, you need to stay back, please," he said.

"I'm not trying to get through. I just need to know what's happening here. That's my friend's car."

"I can't tell you anything, sir. Please, step back."

I looked around, then ran over to the crowd of people.

"Does anyone know what's happening?"

"I heard shooting," one person said.

"An ambulance just left," another replied.

My heart sank. I called Tony.

"Hey, Mick, what's up?"

"You still have contacts inside PPB?"

"Yeah, why?"

I told him about the scene.

"Holy shit," he said. "Let me make some calls and get back to you."

"Okay."

I hung up and paced around the police cordon, looking for clues as to what might have happened, but I couldn't make out much in the dark. I took out my phone and looked at Portland news sites. Nothing on *The Oregonian*. Nothing on KOIN. My phone rang as I hit the KGW website. Caller ID said it was Tony.

"You're not going to like this, Mick," he said

"What is it?"

"I don't know it's Elliott for sure, but I'm told there was an all-units call to an officer-involved shooting in North Portland a half hour back."

"Shit. Is he okay?"

"My contact heard three bullets to the torso," Tony replied. "Victim was transported to Legacy Emanuel. That's all I know."

"Okay. Thanks, Tony. I've got to go."

I ran back to my car, calling Casey as I went.

"What is it, Mick?"

"Elliott's been shot. They're taking him to Legacy. I'm heading there now."

"Okay, I'll meet you there."

I drove to the hospital, fighting the urge to break every speed limit and run every stop sign.

Legacy Emanuel Medical Center was a sprawling hospital complex that sat on twelve blocks a couple of miles north of downtown. There had been a hospital on the site for over a hundred years, with the current complex being built mostly in the seventies and eighties. The architecture was typical of that era: no-frills concrete and glass structures, done in straight lines and painted beige. Although from the outside it looked unremarkable, it housed one of the State's finest trauma centers. Elliott would be in good hands.

I parked outside the emergency room and ran inside. The waiting area was mostly empty. A couple of uniformed cops lounged by the vending machine, drinking coffee. I ignored them and headed for the admissions desk. Casey was already there, talking to the duty nurse.

"I'm sorry, I can't let you see him," the nurse said.

"Who's your boss?" demanded Casey.

"The duty surgeon. Doctor Ross."

"Call him."

The nurse looked at Casey, her mouth wide.

"I'm waiting," Casey added.

The nurse picked up her phone and made a call. She spoke softly so we couldn't hear, but her body language made it clear that the person on the end of the line wasn't happy. She exhaled heavily as she hung up.

"He'll be here in a moment."

"Thank you," Casey said, but the nurse ignored her.

A few minutes later a doctor in bloodstained green scrubs appeared, a stethoscope draped around his neck. He was tall and tanned, dark-haired with streaks of gray at the temples. He was breathing heavily and he looked like his team had just lost the Super Bowl.

"What's this all about?" he said.

"Doctor, my name is Casey Raife. I'm Elliott Russell's attorney. I'd like to see my client, please."

"I can't allow that," Doctor Ross said, hands on hips. "We're preparing him for emergency surgery."

"My client has been arrested for a capital crime. I need to see him."

"I don't think you understand, Ms. Raife. Mr. Russell is gravely injured and he needs surgery right now." He gestured at the dark red mess down his front. "If you'll excuse me, I have to go scrub up."

Over the doctor's shoulder, I saw a gurney being wheeled out into the hall, surrounded by nurses and orderlies. One nurse held an intravenous drip bag aloft, and another was pressing something down onto the person on the gurney. I caught a flash of dark skin.

I ran past the doctor, with Casey close behind me.

"Hey, you can't go there!" Dr. Ross shouted.

I ignored him and kept running. As I expected, it was Elliott on the gurney.

"Elliott!" I shouted.

He turned his head slowly, then blinked, his eyelids heavy and fluttering.

"Mick?" he said, his voice barely above a whisper. "Is that you?"

"I'm here, buddy. How are you doing?"

One of the orderlies stepped away from the gurney and held his arms out. "Sir, you have to leave now."

Elliott lifted his arm and pointed down the hall. "Are the cops here?"

"No, just me." I gestured over my shoulder. "Casey too."

"Oh. Good." He dropped his arm and closed his eyes, his head lolling to the side. "Don't let him shoot me again."

"What are you talking about?"

"I told him, Mick," he said. "The cop. I put my hands up. I told him not to shoot me."

TWELVE
ROUND ONE

The orderlies hurried down the hall with the gurney, leaving Casey and me staring at each other in shock.

"What did he just say?" she said.

I ignored her and ran back to the waiting room. The two cops were still drinking coffee by the vending machine. I marched over to them.

"Which one of you assholes shot him?"

"Excuse me?" the cop nearest me said.

"You heard me. Which one of you gutless punks shot a man with his hands up?"

The other cop tossed his empty coffee cup in the trash, hooked his thumbs in his equipment belt, and stepped in front of me. "Sir, nobody here shot anyone. You need to step back."

I was about to say something else when Casey grabbed my arm. "Mick, let me handle this."

She put herself between me and the officers. "I'm sorry about that. He's upset because his friend has been shot. I'm Casey Raife, the shooting victim's attorney. We heard the police were involved. Can you tell us what happened, please?"

The cop looked Casey up and down. "I'm afraid I don't

know a whole lot, ma'am. We answered a call about a shooting at a traffic stop. Apparently, the suspect pulled a weapon and was shot by the arresting officer. When we arrived at the scene, we were told to accompany the ambulance to the ER and await further instructions."

I stepped forward, but Casey put her hand on my chest. "Thank you, officer," she said, then turned to me. "Come on. Outside."

I glared at the cop, then followed Casey into the parking lot.

"What the hell are you doing?" she said.

"You heard that bullshit," I replied. "Elliott didn't pull a gun on anyone. He doesn't even *have* a gun!"

"And what good does taking a swing at a cop do him?" she said. I went to protest, but she cut me off. "Don't even try to deny it. I saw the look in your eye. You were about to throw a punch when I stepped in."

I put my hands in my pockets and exhaled noisily. "Fuck! What do you expect? You heard Elliott. Some asshole cop shot him when he had his hands up!"

"I know. I'm as pissed about it as you are. But Elliott is alive, and the best thing we can do for him right now is to get out of the way and let the doctors do their work. Go home. Come to my office in the morning. We'll see how Elliott is doing then."

I wanted to stay, to wait and find out how Elliott's surgery went. But Casey was right. There was nothing I could do, and those cops inside would be like a red rag to a bull, especially if the surgery went badly.

Casey's face softened. "I know you're upset. I know how much Elliott means to you. But you hired me for a reason. I'll do everything I can for him. You need to let me do my job."

"Okay," I said.

"Thanks. Go get some rest."

Casey smiled at me, then walked over to her car and left. I

looked back at the ER. Those cops would still be inside. But whoever shot Elliott, it wasn't them. There was nothing I could do here tonight. Reluctantly, I got in my car and headed home.

I called Tony on the way and told him what I'd learned. He hadn't heard any more from his contacts in the Portland Police Bureau, but he promised to get an update as soon as he could.

When I got back to my apartment, I opened a beer and paced around my living room. What the hell happened tonight? There was no way Elliott pulled a gun. Even if he did have a weapon, which I highly doubted, he was far too smart to draw it around a cop. No one knew the dangers a Black man faced in a police confrontation better than Elliott. He'd organized the BLM protests in the wake of Andre Gladen's shooting and he'd been stopped countless times himself as a result. Sure, he had a temper, but he wasn't stupid. Whatever went down tonight, it wasn't because Elliott started anything.

I swigged from my beer, trying to figure things out. Did the cops provoke Elliott? Did they manufacture some other excuse to shoot him? Nothing made sense. Meanwhile, my buddy was in surgery, fighting for his life. He had to pull through. And if he didn't, I would move heaven and earth to make sure whoever shot him got what they deserved.

I drained my beer and opened another. I tried sitting on the couch, but that didn't help, so I stood up and paced around the room some more. The frustration, the waiting, the not knowing was unbearable. I was full of rage, made worse by the fact I was powerless to help Elliott.

Unable to think of anything else to do, I fired up my laptop and searched local news websites. Sure enough, KOIN had a breaking news story: "Murder Suspect Shot During Arrest."

The story didn't tell me anything new; it just stated that Elliott Russell, a suspect in the murder of Malik Betts, was shot during his arrest earlier this evening. Neighbors reported hearing gunfire, but there were no witness accounts and police had no comment. I checked the other local sites. They all carried versions of the same story, but none of them gave any extra information.

I sighed, closed my laptop and drained my beer. Casey was right. There was nothing to do but try to get some rest.

I went to bed, then proceeded to spend the next few hours staring at the ceiling. I could barely close my eyes; sleep was out of the question. I tossed and turned for hours. Finally, around dawn, I dragged myself out of bed and went for a run. I pushed it further than usual, mostly to kill time and burn out the fire, losing myself in the pounding of my feet and the rhythm of my breath.

It worked as well as I could expect. When I finally made it home and got in the shower, I no longer felt like I was ready to explode. I got dressed, forced down a quick breakfast, then called Casey. We agreed to meet at the Starbucks near her office.

Casey was already there when I walked in. She had dark rings under her eyes and she clutched a large coffee as though it was the last life preserver on the Titanic.

"Get yourself one of these," she said. "You look like I feel."

I got my coffee and we found a table that looked reasonably private.

"You heard any more?" I said.

"No. I called the hospital, but they won't give out information to anyone who isn't family."

"Not surprising. You think we'll get more if we go over there?"

"There's one way to find out."

We took a taxi across the river to Legacy and went to the emergency room again. If anything, the waiting room was even more empty, which wasn't too surprising given that it was early Wednesday morning. Not exactly prime accident and illness time. The cops were gone too, which was a relief. We went to the duty nurse.

"Excuse me," I said, "we're here to see Elliott Russell. He was brought in last night with gunshot wounds."

"Are you family?" the nurse replied.

"No, but I'm his best friend and she's his lawyer. We need to see him."

"I'm not sure I can tell you anything."

"Look, can you call Dr. Ross? He was treating Elliott last night. Can we speak to him?"

"Hold on a moment."

She turned away from us and made a call, speaking softly so we couldn't overhear. After a moment she nodded and hung up.

"Wait over there," she said, pointing at the empty chairs. "Dr. Ross will be here shortly."

I thought I was tired, but when Dr. Ross arrived, he looked like a walking corpse.

"I remember you from last night," he said. "You're Mr. Russell's attorney, right?"

"I am," she replied. "How is he?"

"Well, the good news is that he's alive, and it's likely he'll pull through. Beyond that, it's too early to tell. He lost an awful lot of blood, so there's a risk of acquired brain injury. He's in an induced coma and we won't know much more for a week or two."

"Can we see him?" I said.

"I just told you he's in a coma."

"I know, but Elliott is like a brother to me. I'd really like to see him."

Doctor Ross looked at me. I raised my eyebrows and shrugged.

"Very well," he said, his shoulders visibly sagging. "He's in room 104, down the corridor on the left. Please remember he's gravely injured."

Elliott's room was easy to spot. It was the one with a uniformed police officer standing outside. Casey ignored him and made for the door. He put an arm out to stop her.

"You can't go in there, ma'am."

"I'm his attorney," she said, and pushed his arm aside. I followed her in.

Inside, the room looked like a scene from every TV hospital drama ever made, only this time it was my best friend in the bed, hooked up to all the tubes and machines. There was an oxygen mask over Elliott's face, but he wasn't intubated. There was some sort of frame under the blankets to lift them clear of his body from the waist down. His eyes were closed, and his breathing was soft and regular.

There was a chair by the bed. I looked at Casey and she gestured to it.

"You should sit there," she said.

I sat down. My friend's chest rose and fell in time with the soft beeps of one of the monitors. Casey took Elliott's chart from the end of the bed and flicked through it. She frowned and handed it to me.

I'd seen plenty of medical records before, mostly when I was representing someone accused of a violent crime. The prosecution would gleefully present the victim's records, detailing their injuries in sickening detail. It was their way of letting you know how badly your guy was fucked if you put him in front of a jury.

It didn't take me long to find what I was looking for. Elliott had been shot twice in the abdomen and once in the right thigh. He'd undergone emergency surgery on the wounds just before midnight and received four pints of blood via transfusion. His spleen had been removed. One of the bullets could not be taken out because it had lodged against his spine. I skipped to the admission notes and what I read made my blood run cold.

Conscious when admitted. No sensation in lower extremities.

I closed the file and took a deep breath.

The door to Elliott's room swung open and Detective Buchanan marched in, with Malone right behind him.

"What the hell's going on here?" he demanded.

"I could ask you the same thing, Detective," Casey replied, her voice expressionless. "Please leave."

"You haven't answered my question, Ms. Raife."

"Nor am I going to. I'll say it again since you're obviously hard of hearing. Get out."

Buchanan looked like his head was going to explode. The beeping from Elliott's monitor seemed louder in the silence.

"Let's take it outside," I said, with as much control as I could muster.

Buchanan started to say something, then thought better of it. He left the room, ushering Malone out in front of him. Casey followed them.

I squeezed Elliot's hand. "I'm gonna get the fucker who did this, buddy," I said, and joined the others in the hall.

"Now, Detective, what can I do for you?" Casey said.

"You can start by explaining what the hell is going on," Buchanan replied. "I'm on my way over to see how my murder suspect is doing when I get a call from Wittkowski here–" He jabbed a finger at the sheepish-looking uniformed officer, "– saying some attorney ignored his command to stay out of that room."

"You're the one who's got some damn explaining to do," I said. "He had his fucking hands up!"

"Mick," Casey said, and put a hand on my arm. She turned to Buchanan. "Detective, we should go somewhere else to discuss this."

"Fine," he said. "There's a cafeteria back past reception. Wittkowski, don't let anyone in that room who isn't a doctor or a nurse. I don't care if it's the goddamn Pope, if anyone tries to get in, shoot them."

Buchanan stomped off toward reception, with Malone in tow.

I stared at their backs, fighting the urge to kick their miserable asses. Casey squeezed my arm again.

"Let me do the talking, Mick," she said. "Don't make things worse for Elliott."

I took a deep breath and nodded.

We walked down to the cafeteria, which was a drab room painted in industrial pale green and smelling of boiled vegetables. Buchanan and Malone were sitting at a table by the coffee vending machine. All the other tables were empty, bar one, where an elderly woman had her arm around a young man, patting his shoulder as he sobbed quietly into his hands.

"You want a drink?" I said to Casey.

"Sure," she said. "Coffee, no sugar, thanks."

I made a show of figuring out how to work the machine, taking as long as I could to order two coffees. Casey stayed with me, her face expressionless. Eventually, I handed her a drink and we joined the detectives at their table. The look on Buchanan's face made it clear I hadn't improved his mood, which did improve mine.

"Now, Detective," Casey said, taking the lead, "can you explain why you barged into my meeting with my client? I want to make sure I get the details right for the judge."

"Spare me the crap, Counselor," Buchanan replied. "You're the one who needs to explain what you were doing visiting a murder suspect in custody without permission."

"He's not in custody. This is a hospital, not a prison."

"He was arrested last night, and he'll be in prison as soon as he can be moved," Malone interjected. Buchanan shot him a look.

No one spoke. I fought the urge to hurl my steaming coffee in Malone's face. Casey sipped hers calmly.

"All right, I get it," Buchanan said. "You're his attorney, Ms. Raife. You'll get your chance to visit with him. But I want all visits arranged through my office. No surprises."

Casey snorted. "You know damned well I don't need your permission to meet with my client. And when he regains consciousness, no one from the police or the prosecutor's office is to question him without me present. If you so much as ask him how he's feeling, I'll have you in front of a judge before you can blink."

"Fine. Whatever." Buchanan jerked a thumb at me. "Going to tell me what this guy is doing here?"

"Why do you care?" Casey said.

Buchanan smiled. "Your client had some very interesting things to say about Mick when the ambulance brought him in last night."

"I assume Mr. Russell was sedated at that time?"

"You'd have to ask the doctor, but my guess is yes, given how talkative he was," Buchanan said.

"Did you read him his Miranda rights?"

"What?"

"I thought not," Casey said. "So, you're planning on using

information you extracted from a suspect without reading him his rights, while he was too heavily medicated to understand or waive those rights even if you had. My job just got easier."

She stood up.

"One more thing. Tell the DA's office to compile everything related to my client's arrest. It's going to the top of my discovery list. Dashcam video, arrest reports, recordings of calls to HQ. Everything." Then she turned to me. "Let's go."

I went to stand, but Buchanan put a hand up. "Not so fast. You can leave if you like Ms. Raife, but Mick is staying. We're not done with him."

Casey raised her eyebrows.

"It's okay," I said. "If I don't talk to them now, they'll want me to come to the station later, and this place smells better."

"You know I can't stay, right?"

"Yeah. I'll be fine. I'll see you back at your office."

Casey nodded and left. She had to leave to ensure she didn't create a conflict of interest. As Elliott's attorney her duty was to him, and if she learned anything that would help his defense she'd be obliged to use it, even if it screwed me over. Besides, I'd sat through hundreds of police interviews with my clients. My biggest challenge would be keeping my temper.

I folded my arms and glared at the detectives. "All right. What do you want?"

"Why was Russell asking for you last night when we brought him in?" Buchanan said.

"I don't know," I replied. "Maybe because some asshole cop shot him when he had his hands up."

"Does the name Malik Betts mean anything to you?"

I made a show of thinking about it. "No. Should it?"

"You represented Elliott Russell on weapons and drugs possession charges in 2009, didn't you?"

"You know I did."

"Did he ever tell you why he had a gun that day?"

"Have you ever heard of attorney–client privilege?"

"You're not a lawyer anymore," Malone snapped.

"Jesus, you haven't gotten any smarter, have you?" I looked at Buchanan. "You want to explain the survival of privilege to Captain Shit For Brains over here?"

"Don't be a smartass, Mick," he said. "Why didn't you tell us you knew the victim's identity?"

"Because I had no idea who the victim was."

"Putting aside the fact I know you're bullshitting me, why didn't you tell me that Elliott Russell knew who the victim was?"

"We called you after we dug up a human hand. I doubt Elliott could've recognized the victim from that. I sure as hell couldn't. And if you recall, Elliott stayed on the deck while you uncovered the rest of the body."

"Because you told him to," Buchanan said. "Was that because you knew he'd recognize the victim?"

"No, it's because smart people don't talk to the police when they're likely to be charged with a crime they didn't commit. Now look at me, being all stupid and talking to you guys like you're my friends. I think I'll take my own advice and inform you that I won't be saying anything more until I've spoken to a lawyer."

Buchanan sighed and ran a hand over his shaved head. "Mick, I'm going to give you another chance because we go back a long way. I'm trying to do you a favor here. Russell is going down for this. He killed Betts. You know it and I know it. Don't get caught in the crossfire."

"Are you arresting me?"

"Not yet."

"Then I've said all I have to say. Have a nice day, detectives."

"You're not leaving yet." Buchanan slid a pad and pen across to me. "I want a written statement."

"One of your colleagues shot my friend. He may not survive, and if he does, there's a good chance he'll be a paraplegic. And you want to frame him for a murder he didn't commit. You can shove your written statement up your ass."

I stood up. Malone stood up too, but Buchanan waved an arm at him.

"No, let him go. We know where to find him." He looked at me. "Last chance. You going to help us out?"

I left without answering.

THIRTEEN
WELCOME TO THE MACHINE

I marched into Casey's office and stood in front of her desk.
"I want in."

"What?" she said, frowning at me.

"You heard me. I want in. I want to be on Elliott's defense team."

"You're not a lawyer anymore, Mick."

"It doesn't matter. Someone is framing Elliott for murder and now the cops have shot him. I'm going to find who's responsible and make them pay."

"Have you forgotten how the legal system works?" Casey said. "This isn't some vigilante operation."

"I know. Look, you said it yourself. A murder case is a ton of work. There's legal research, motion drafting, witness interviews and everything else. I can do all those things."

"Have a seat. There are a few things we need to talk about."

I sat down. "What kinds of things?"

"You, to be blunt." Casey leaned forward. "I know you want to help Elliott, but if I'm going to even consider having you on the team, I need to know I can trust you. This case is going to be very high profile. Lots of media attention. Lots of pressure. You don't have a great record under pressure."

I sighed. "I knew this would come up sooner or later."

"I mean it. You used to be a damn good defense lawyer. What the hell happened?"

"Too many cases with bad results, I guess."

"You helped a lot of people, Mick."

"Maybe I helped some people. But I was drowning in all the people I couldn't help. More than once, I lost cases when my client was innocent. Seeing them go to jail tore me up. After a while it became like a tidal wave, like trying to bail out a sinking ship with a thimble."

"We all have our dark days in this profession. I still don't understand why you did what you did."

"Okay, I'll explain, but first tell me what you think you know."

"I know what everyone in the legal community knows. You lost a case and you slugged the prosecutor."

"All true. But do you know why I slugged him?"

"Does it matter?" Casey said, her eyes wide.

"It does. It's a long story, but you need to hear it. First, let's go back to a year before it happened. District Attorney Evans was running for reelection. He based his campaign around being tough on criminals, especially pedophiles. Do you remember what they used to call me?"

"Yeah, the patron saint of lost causes. So what?"

"Well, one of my lost causes was a high school custodian accused of peeping on the girls' changing room in the gym. They found a webcam hidden behind a row of lockers. The custodian had a prior conviction for solicitation of prostitution and Evans went after him hard. In a campaign speech, Evans said he was going to lock my guy up and throw away the key.

The only problem was, at trial I proved that the headmaster was the one who planted the camera. My guy went free. I made Evans look like an idiot.

"He managed to get reelected anyway, and he made it his mission to come after me. Right after the election, I had an armed robbery case. I knew my guy was innocent, but I couldn't prove it. Then a witness called me out of nowhere and said he could give my guy an alibi. It sounded too good to be true. I should have known better, but I had nothing else, so I ran with him.

"Of course, it was a setup. He changed his story on the stand and said my guy did it. Turns out he was a confidential informant who owed the cops a favor. They used him to fuck me over, and they didn't give a damn that an innocent man got a five-year mandatory minimum sentence. The witness was in the gallery when the verdict came down, and the prosecutor actually winked at him. I saw it and I lost my shit. So, the prosecutor got a black eye, and I got disbarred."

"Okay, that's messed up," Casey said, "but surely there were better ways to deal with it than punching the guy."

"I've thought of hundreds in the last three years," I replied. "But my life was fucked up for other reasons too."

"What reasons?"

"Short version is that my son died of leukemia and my wife ran off with my best friend. So yeah, I was in a dark place and my judgment wasn't great. But that was a long time ago. I'm over it now." That last bit was a lie, but Casey didn't need to know that.

"Given that you almost slugged a cop last night, I'm not so sure."

"I was pissed, but I didn't hit anybody. And I'm all out of wives and sons, so no danger there." I leaned back. "Did I pass the test?"

Casey tilted her head to one side. "After everything you've been through, are you sure you want this?"

Defense law is brutal. Sometimes you have to fight for truly evil people: rapists, killers, the worst of the worst. And then there are my 'lost causes': the wrongly accused, the little guys getting crushed under life's inexorable wheel. In the end, the weight of it all blew me apart. After I got disbarred, I swore I'd never get involved in another case, and a week ago I wouldn't have done it for a million bucks. But this was for Elliott, and I couldn't walk away.

"Damn right I do."

"I can't pay you much."

"I'm not doing it for the money."

"All right," Casey said, "we'll give it a try."

"Good. Maybe now we can talk about more important things, like Elliott's case."

"There's not much to talk about right now. There won't even be an arraignment until Elliott is well enough to participate." Casey gestured at a stack of folders on her desk. "It's a good thing, in a way. Gives me time to clear some of these other cases so I can focus on Elliott's defense."

"I assume you're thinking SOD defense here?" SOD was a lawyer acronym for 'some other dude,' as in 'some other dude did it.'

"Yeah. At least until we get discovery, which won't be until after the arraignment."

"From what the doctor said, that could be weeks away," I said. "I'm not going to sit on my ass and do nothing while we wait. Besides, there's an important question we need to answer."

"What question?"

"Remember what you told Elliott? The cops didn't have probable cause to arrest him because there was no evidence linking him to the actual killing. Well, they've got something now. What is it?"

"I have no idea," Casey said.

"Me neither," I replied. "But I'm going to find out."

FOURTEEN

ALL IN THE FAMILY

The sun blasted my eyes, as I turned off the Ross Island Bridge, south onto Highway 43. I winced, pulled the visor down and pushed my sunglasses up tight against my face. It was a hot, sunny Tuesday morning, a week after Elliott's shooting, and I was on my way to Lake Oswego to talk to Malik Betts's father.

I'd spent the past week researching Betts's business dealings without learning anything interesting, so I figured it was time to go knock on doors and ask some questions. Betts's family was a good place to start. There wasn't much information available publicly, so I called Tony for help, and he sent me an email with some names and addresses.

I drove along the river, the sun glaring off the Willamette's muddy brown surface. The road swooped down and right, into downtown Lake Oswego, with its high-end boutiques and art galleries. Lake Oswego was one of Portland's richest and most exclusive areas. For much of its history, you needed more than just money to buy a place here. A small group of real estate agents handled all the town's property transactions, and they'd only sell to the right kind of people. Given that Lake Oswego used to be known as Lake No Negro, Betts senior must have had some serious juice to get in.

Dr. Marcus Betts lived with his wife in a Hamptons-style Dutch Colonial on Uplands Ridge, between the Lake Oswego Country Club and the lake itself. I parked in front and walked up the curving driveway to double front doors, painted pristine white and set between square columns. I hit the brass doorbell button.

A tall, thin African American man answered the door. He wore khaki slacks and a green cardigan over a white business shirt. There were patches of gray in his neatly trimmed hair. His face was drawn tight, as though his skin was being pulled back by a clip. His eyes were bloodshot and he looked somewhat dazed.

"Who are you?" he demanded.

"Doctor Betts?" I replied. He nodded. "My name is Mick Ward. I'm here about your son."

Betts frowned at me. "What are you talking about?"

"Can I come in please? We need to talk."

"I don't even know who you are."

"Please, it's important." I stepped forward, keen to take my opportunity while Betts was off guard. Sure enough, he stepped back and let me in.

The door opened onto an immaculately furnished sitting room: a floral print sofa and chairs surrounded by polished wood tables, and a large wall unit containing photographs and commemorative plates. Most of the photos were of Dr. Betts with prominent Portland society figures: the mayor, Clyde Drexler, Paul Allen and a bunch of other guys in suits that I didn't recognize. The opposite wall was dominated by a large crucifix. A woman I guessed was Dr. Betts's wife stood by one of the armchairs, trembling and dabbing her eyes with a tissue.

"What's going on here?" Dr. Betts asked.

"Doctor Betts, I'm very sorry about your son," I began. "I know it's no consolation to you, but I understand what you're going through."

I watched his face for some sign of emotion, but none came. I pressed on.

"I assume the police told you that they know who killed your son?"

"They did. That Russell guy, the one who's running for City Council." Doctor Betts spat out the words like they were rotten food.

"They're wrong. Elliott Russell didn't kill Malik."

"I think the police know what they're doing."

"I wish that were true, but this is a setup. I'm going to find out who's behind it, and I need your help to do it. Can I ask you some questions about your relationship with Malik?"

"Not until you tell me what's going on here."

"Please, bear with me. Were you and Malik close?"

"You've got a lot of nerve, coming in here and asking me that," he said. Behind him, his wife's shoulders shook.

"I know this is a terrible time for you," I said. "Don't let the police make it worse by going after the wrong man."

Now, Dr. Betts glared at me and pointed at the door. "Get out of my house."

The look on his face told me not to push it.

"Okay, I'm leaving. Sorry to have disturbed you. Here's my number if you change your mind." I put a card on the table by the door and left.

Outside, I checked my phone for messages. There was something from Tony about the construction defects case, which I figured could wait until later. I was about to get in my car when I heard a voice behind me.

"Mr. Ward, wait."

I turned around. Betts closed his front door and walked over to me.

"I'm sorry I was abrupt back there," he said, "but there are things I don't want Cora to know about. You see, when Malik came back to town, he told me he wanted to be a real estate agent. I helped him get set up, get licensed, and I introduced him to a few people. At first, it seemed to be working. He made some sales, did all right. But then one day he showed up here in a Bentley. I'm not stupid. You don't make Bentley money selling a couple of condos a month."

"No, sir, you don't. Do you know where the money was coming from?"

"Not with any certainty. I just assumed he was up to his old tricks." He sighed. "Did you mean what you said about this being a setup?"

"Yes, sir. I'm convinced of it."

He nodded at me, his eyes wide and full of pain. "Then, you find out who's behind it."

He walked back inside, his shoulders stooped as though carrying a great weight. I got in my car and headed north on Highway 43. About a mile or two north of Lake Oswego, I pulled into a parking lot overlooking the river, to give myself time to think. Betts Senior saying that Malik had been 'up to his old tricks' had to mean he thought he was dealing drugs again. But even then, street dealing doesn't buy you a Bentley. So, Malik must have been a major player. I'd suspected a gang motive for his murder from the start, and Dr. Betts had seemingly confirmed it. But I needed to be sure, and that meant talking to some gangbangers.

FIFTEEN
JUST ANOTHER SUNDAY IN THE NEIGHBORHOOD

B ack when I was still a lawyer, Elliott had referred me to a
couple of his fellow Oakhurst Street Crips after my work
on his possession case. Unfortunately, that meant I didn't know
any Bloods—once you represent a member of one gang, no rival
gang member will hire you. I didn't even know which chapter
Betts had been in. But I figured I could call Billy Hinds and get
him to ask around. The NNC did a lot of work with ex-gang
members on both sides, and some of them were less ex than
others. Meanwhile, I looked up the 'Crip' section in my mental
Rolodex and came up with a couple of names who might be able
to help.

I figured my best bet was DeAngelo Kennedy. DeAngelo
was a smart guy who could have succeeded in any field, and his
chosen field was selling drugs. Over the years, I represented him
on a string of dealing and possession charges, mostly with good
results. Each time, I did all I could to get DeAngelo back on the
straight path. But from the day I met him it was obvious that
darkness rode him like a racehorse. Eventually, the futility got to
me and I stopped trying. Shortly after I'd won him an acquittal
in our last case together, someone beat a young crack addict to

death in an alley near DeAngelo's house. The killer was never caught, but word on the street was DeAngelo did it because the guy owed him fifty bucks.

I didn't like the idea of getting in touch with him again. I used to rationalize defending guys like DeAngelo as the price I had to pay to fight for all the good people our justice system loves to fuck with. Sometimes I even believed it. But it's hard to convince yourself you're doing the Lord's work when you set a guy free and he kills somebody.

But if anyone could get me information to help Elliott, it was DeAngelo. It took me a few days to track him down, but by Sunday I'd established he was still in town, running a crew up in North Portland, in the Vernon neighborhood.

I drove up MLK for a while. In most cities, if you find yourself on Martin Luther King Jr. Boulevard, you're in the wrong part of town. That used to be true in Portland, but now MLK was all artisanal coffee shops and Whole Foods. I took a right on Ainsworth. A couple more turns got me to some back streets the hipsters hadn't discovered yet. It didn't take me long to find the corner I was looking for.

Two African American guys sat on a wall, checking their cell phones and casting surly glares at the rest of the world. They both wore gold chains and big watches encrusted with fake diamonds. Jackpot. I parked my car and walked over.

"I think you're in the wrong neighborhood," the taller one said. He pushed himself up from the wall and stood in front of me, hands on hips.

"I know where I am," I said. "I'm looking for DeAngelo Kennedy. He still live around here?"

"What's it to you?"

"I told you, genius. I'm looking for him."

"I don't like your attitude."

"I don't care. Is he here or not?"

"You better get your ass out of here, white boy," he said. Over his shoulder, I saw his partner stand up and move to my right.

"Look, guys," I said. "I want to talk to DeAngelo. Just get him for me, okay?"

"You ain't getting shit."

His eyes moved right and I caught the signal just in time. His partner swung a punch at me. I ducked under it and slammed my fist into his stomach. As he doubled over, I grabbed the back of his head and rammed my knee into his face. He buckled, and I let him drop. Meanwhile, the tall guy aimed a kick at me. I caught it in the ribs, rolling with it to ease the impact, but it still knocked the wind out of me. I went down, pulling his leg with me. He came down on top of me and caught me with an elbow to the eye. We wrestled, but I had a size and weight advantage. I pushed him away and got to my knees. As he tried to stand, I hammered a punch into the side of his head. He stumbled and managed to regain his balance, but it gave me time to get up. When he charged again, I grabbed him in a bear hug. I squeezed his chest with all my might as he banged his fists ineffectually against my back. I could sense the fight leaving him, but then something cold, round and hard pressed into the back of my neck. I knew that feeling—the barrel of a gun.

"Let him go," said a voice behind me.

I did as I was told, putting my hands in the air. My assailant made to come at me again.

"Stop," the voice commanded. "Just get his gun."

My assailant glared at me, then patted me down.

"I don't have one," I told him.

"Check him for a knife."

"I don't have a knife either."

"Man, you are one crazy motherfucker, raising hell on our turf when you ain't got no weapon."

I felt the pressure on my neck ease. I lowered my arms and turned around slowly.

"Hey, DeAngelo," I said, "it's been a while."

DeAngelo Kennedy was a giant of a man. I'm six-three and two forty, with most of my weight in my upper body. DeAngelo made me look like a little boy. He must have been four inches taller than me and sixty pounds heavier. He looked soft, but there was a mountain of muscle under the surface. He was wearing expensive jeans and a flowing shirt big enough to be a kaftan. He had a large diamond stud in each ear, and his were genuine. Unlike his boys, he wasn't wearing a watch or neck chain.

He shook his head, tucked his gun in his waistband and ran a hand through his Afro.

"Shit, Mick Ward," he said. "What you doin' up here?"

"Looking for you." I dusted off my jeans and nodded at the first guy who came at me. He was on his knees, hands over his face, with blood dripping out between his fingers. "Sorry about your boy."

DeAngelo rested his hand on the handle of his gun. "Yeah, don't be making a habit of that." He looked me in the eye. "Why you lookin' for me?"

"I need information," I said.

"What do you think I am, a motherfuckin' library?"

"Cut the crap, DeAngelo. I just want to ask you a couple of questions. You know Malik Betts?"

"He a Blood. Piece of shit." DeAngelo spat in the dirt.

"You seen him around lately?"

DeAngelo smiled. "I heard the news. Ain't nobody seen him around lately."

So DeAngelo knew Betts was dead. What did that mean? Did he kill Betts? Did he know who did? I tried my silence trick, trying to draw out a reaction, but he just kept looking at me.

"I heard he was still in the game," I said eventually.

"Oh, he was in the game all right. Big time. Motherfucker was making bank. I was thinkin' it might be time to put his ass in the ground, but someone beat me to it."

"I'm guessing you heard his body was found in Elliott Russell's yard?" I said. "You know anything about a beef between him and Betts?"

DeAngelo scowled at me. "Now you tryin' my patience, saying that name."

"Look, you know Elliott, and you know there's no way he could have killed Betts. He could use your help."

"Why would I want to help that bitch? Ever since he got out of jail, Mr. Goody Two Shoes been tryin' to put me out of business. Don't bother me none if some cop put a cap in his ass."

"Seriously? You're just going to stand by and let him go down?"

DeAngelo's mouth tightened into a sneer. "I'm gonna say this nice because you did a good job for me." He took out his gun and tapped the barrel against his temple. "Elliott Russell was a Crip. Then he turned on the Crips. Elliott Russell is not welcome around here. You understand me?"

"You know what?" I said. "Ten years ago, when Elliott was arrested, the cops offered him a get out of jail free card if he ratted on you guys. He didn't say a word."

DeAngelo looked at me thoughtfully, then stuffed his gun back in his pants. "All right, I'll tell you one thing. Betts wasn't dealing in the hood here. Word is he was in the meth game. I heard he cornered the market on selling ice to a bunch of crackers out in Clackistan."

Clackistan was Clackamas, a rundown suburban community southeast of Portland that thoroughly deserved its nickname. Look up 'white trash' in the dictionary and you'll see a picture of Clackistan.

"Interesting. Thanks, DeAngelo."

De Angelo nodded once. "We good now. You should leave."

I didn't need to be told twice. I got in my car and pulled away.

I drove back to MLK and pulled into a Popeye's Chicken. I parked away from the other cars in a space at the back and switched the engine off. Today was hot again, so I opened the car window to let some air in. I looked at my face in the rearview mirror. My right eye was red and swollen where I'd caught that elbow, and I felt a throbbing pain behind it. It would be a spectacular shiner tomorrow. And I still felt the panic that gripped me when DeAngelo put his gun to my head. Maybe getting back into the defense world wasn't such a great idea after all.

I tried to think about what to do next. DeAngelo hadn't given me much, but maybe it was more than he thought. He clearly hated Elliott, and as a prominent Crip he had plenty of motive to kill someone high up in the Bloods food chain. He claimed someone else did it, but could DeAngelo have killed Betts? It was possible, but to me it didn't make sense. If Betts was dealing meth out east, he was no threat to DeAngelo's turf. And killing a high-ranking rival invited the kind of retribution that DeAngelo could do without. Plus, why go to the trouble and risk of burying the body in Elliott's yard? I wanted to ask more questions, but I'd already overstayed my welcome in this part of town.

I called Tony instead and told him I needed to talk. He was home, so I drove over to his place, with a quick stop on the way to pick up some beer to help us beat the heat.

Tony lived in a small pink 1920s bungalow in Southeast

Portland, just off Division. The previous owner had renovated and flipped it, and Tony kept it in great shape. When I pulled up outside, he was weeding his herb garden. He waved at me.

"Mick, good to see you. Let's go inside."

I followed Tony into his kitchen. He washed his hands, dried them on a tea towel, neatly folded it, and hung it on the oven door. As usual, the countertops were spotless.

I opened two beers and handed him one, then we sat at his kitchen table.

"Something smells delicious," I said, waving my beer bottle at the oven.

"I'm slow-roasting a leg of lamb. My nephews are coming over for dinner. You want to join us?"

I'd met Tony's nephews. They were both big, heavily tattooed and fond of chunky gold jewelry. Their forced machismo made me uncomfortable and I knew from experience it embarrassed the hell out of Tony. The lamb smelled great, but I had no desire to hang out with those guys.

"I'll pass. I need to work on a few things for Elliott."

Tony wiped his brow. "How are you doing? You don't look so good. And what happened to your eye?"

I touched the swelling around my eye and winced. "Yeah, it's a bit sore."

"What's going on?"

I told Tony about my morning with the Oakhurst Street Crips.

"Holy shit," he said. "What's the deal with this guy who pulled a gun on you?"

"DeAngelo Kennedy. Crip dealer from way back. He's bad news, but I had to see if he knew anything about Elliott and Betts."

"And you believe him when he says his guys didn't do it?"

"I do. They had nothing to gain by whacking Betts, and a lot to lose if it had started a war with the Bloods."

"So maybe it's a Bloods thing?" Tony said. "Some internal rivalry?"

"Could be. That's my next angle to pursue."

Tony pointed his beer at my eye. "Be more careful next time, huh?"

"Yeah, for sure." I drained my beer and stood up. "Anyway, I'll let you get back to your roast."

Tony stood up too. "Wait a minute. I've got something for you." He fished an envelope out of his pocket and handed it to me. "Kristen gave me this. Payment for your work so far on the construction defects case."

I stuffed it in my jeans. "Thanks, man. I needed that."

"You doing okay, Mick?"

"Yeah, fine." I'd be lucky if the check covered half of what I owed people, but I wasn't going to tell him that. "Damn, that lamb smells good. See you soon, buddy."

SIXTEEN
LIFE'S A PICNIC

The Fourth of July dawned hot and dry, another baking day in what was already a long, brutal summer. I got up late, then went for a run to clear my head. I wanted to take my usual route around Mount Tabor, but the sun had other ideas. I was soaked in sweat and gasping for air by the time I reached Belmont and 60th. Heat stroke didn't appeal to me, so I turned around and headed home.

I took a cold shower, thinking about my busy day ahead. The main event was the annual Northeast Neighborhood Coalition picnic, and Casey had invited me to her sister's holiday barbecue too. I'd told Billy Hinds that I'd get to the NNC picnic early to help him set up, so after I'd showered I drove up to Unthank Park, a small municipal park in North Portland, crammed in between MLK Boulevard and Interstate 5, right in the heart of NNC territory. I arrived around noon to find Billy struggling to erect a shade tent on his own. I hurried over to help him, and we soon had it set up and secured.

"Thanks, Mick," he said. "We're going to need this today."

"No doubt."

With the shelter in place, we decorated it with red, white,

and blue ribbons and balloons. Then we set up trellis tables and folding chairs, and unloaded coolers of food and drinks from the back of Billy's van. Hauling full coolers was tough work on a day like today. We were both ready for a break by the time we were done.

Billy sat in one of the folding chairs. "Man, I wish we had beer in one of those."

"You and me both." I opened a cooler, pulled out two bottles of water and tossed one to him. He caught it, then looked at me and frowned.

"What's up with your eye?"

I touched the swelling and winced. It had been four days since my run-in with DeAngelo's boys. Most of the discoloration had gone, but it was still tender.

"Had a friendly disagreement with someone," I said, then changed the subject quickly. "How's the NNC doing without Elliott around?"

"It's tough, man. We're still trying to get the City to restrict multi-unit developments, but none of us have Elliott's juice. The man just knows how to work people, how to get them onside. It's a tough sell without his contacts and influence. And now this Betts shit has gone down, well, a whole bunch of people won't even take our calls..." Billy's voice trailed off.

"Yeah, I get it. By the way, did you manage to get any information about Betts and the Bloods?"

"Oh yeah, I meant to tell you. You were right that it ain't about crack. Apparently, Betts was running with the 8 Deuce Mob Bloods, the same crew he was with back in the day. Some guys confirmed the Deuce Mob had expanded into selling meth to trailer trash out in Gresham and Clackamas. Only problem is, now Betts is gone, the meth supply has dried up and the Deuce Mob ain't happy about it."

"Betts was supplying meth? Where was he getting it?"

"I got no idea."

I drank some water. What Billy said made sense. After all, DeAngelo Kennedy had told me that Betts was moving up the food chain. Supply and distribution was a big step up for a street dealer, and a smart one if you could make it. Still, I wanted to know where the drugs were coming from. Maybe Betts had crossed his suppliers, and that's how he wound up dead.

"Maybe supplying is how Betts made big money," I said. "I heard he was cruising round in a Bentley."

Billy raised his eyebrows. "More than just the Bentley, you know. He had a luxury suite at the Moda Center for Blazers games, and he was hanging out at all kinds of fancy restaurants. Man, I wish he'd taken them brains and used them for good. Just think what he could have done for our community."

Billy looked off into the distance, lost in thought. But I was right back on alert. I'd spent enough time with big law firm people to know how much a suite at the Moda Center cost, mostly because they loved to tell you at every opportunity. Add that to the Bentley and the fancy restaurants, and there *had* to be something going on with Betts and his business. No way a mediocre independent real estate agent could afford that kind of flash. And supplying tweakers in Clackistan wasn't going to make you rich any time soon, either. I'd have to talk to Casey and Tony about it, see what we could find.

Before I could ask Billy any more about it, a school bus pulled up and a group of kids piled out. Billy groaned and pushed himself to his feet.

"I'm getting too old for this shit," he said. "How about you go help Ray and G-Dog keep those holy terrors busy while I finish setting up?"

I did what Billy asked. Between the three of us, we managed to corral the kids long enough to get a game of flag football going. That lasted about fifteen minutes before degenerating into a no holds barred scramble. We let them wrestle for a while, then called it when G-Dog rumbled across the line for the winning touchdown with two kids attached to each leg.

I dragged one of the coolers over and tossed sodas and water to the kids. Ray helped me while G-Dog threw the football with a couple of the older boys. When everyone had a drink, we closed the cooler and sat on the lid.

"Thanks for coming out, Mick," Ray said.

"Happy to help. I just wish Elliott could be here with us."

"Yeah, me too, man." Ray paused, then looked at me. "What happened? You know, when the cops shot Elliott. How did it go down?"

"We don't know yet. We're trying to get that information, but the cops don't want to give it to us."

"You think you'll get it?"

"They have to hand it over eventually."

Ray took a swig of his water and stared off into the distance. "Man, if they shot him when he wasn't doin' nothin' wrong, this town's gonna explode."

"I hate to say it, but you might never know. Given the protest situation, the judge will probably seal the evidence. Which means that only the lawyers get to see it."

Ray nodded, but he didn't look convinced.

Back at the shelter, Billy had two grills fired up. He was cooking burgers and dogs, while some more volunteers had shown up and were putting chips and snacks out on the tables. The kids mostly congregated over there now, going at the food like a swarm of locusts. Ray and I grabbed our drinks cooler and went over to join them.

I stayed for another couple of hours, mostly tossing footballs and baseballs with the kids to avoid having to talk to the adults. Elliott's situation was the elephant in the room. Everyone wanted to hear that he was going to be fine, that he wouldn't be going to jail, and I couldn't tell them that. I felt like I was letting the side down, even though there was nothing more I could do.

Around four, I made my excuses and left. I thought about going home to freshen up before Casey's sister's barbecue, but her house was only a mile away in the Alameda Arts neighborhood, so I just drove over there.

I texted Casey when I arrived. The house was a 1920s bungalow, with a low-pitched roof and a broad covered porch at the front. It had recently been repainted in a deep red and tan combination, and the front lawn had been replaced with a raised bed vegetable garden. Casey stepped down from the porch to greet me. She wore jeans and a US Women's National Team soccer jersey, which made me feel better about not going home to freshen up.

"Thanks for coming," she said. "How's your eye?"

I'd called Casey last night and told her about my encounter with DeAngelo. "Not as bad as it looks."

"Come through and I'll introduce you to my sister."

The house was furnished like a feature article in a lifestyle magazine. Casey led me through to the backyard, where about a dozen people stood holding plates and wine glasses, talking in small groups. Casey waved to one of the groups and a woman in a short floral dress came over to us. She looked me up and down.

"So this is the guy you told me about," she said. She pointed at my eye. "He's a fighter. I approve."

Casey scowled. "Mick, this is my sister Louisa. Louisa, this is my colleague Mick."

Louisa held out her hand. "Nice to meet you."

"And you," I replied, shaking her hand. Louisa looked like Casey might if she spent half her income on her appearance. In addition to the floral dress, her hair was coiffed and subtly tinted, her face was made up like a model's, and her sandals looked like they cost more than my entire wardrobe.

"Have you eaten?" she said.

I'd been too busy avoiding the adults to go near the food at the NNC picnic. "No, not yet."

"Oh, then come with me. We've got grilled cedar-planked salmon."

"Sounds good." I wished I'd grabbed a burger back at the park.

Louisa led me to a table stacked with food. There was a large salmon fillet on a charred plank in the center, with various other dishes grouped tightly around it. Louisa handed me a plate and told me to help myself, then refilled her glass and went back to the group she'd been with. I surveyed the table and was relieved to see a tray of sausages, so I grabbed a couple of those and a bread roll. I rummaged around under the wine bottles in the drinks tub and found a can of Fat Head IPA. Normally I don't like hoppy IPAs, but any port in a storm.

Casey came over. "Sorry about that," she said. "I did tell Louisa you're a colleague. That vamp act is just her trying to wind me up."

"No problem." I took another mouthful of sausage and washed it down with beer. "How's the barbecue?"

"As exciting as watching paint dry." Casey waved her glass at the crowd. "Architects, mostly, with a couple of interior decorators thrown in. Not the most interesting people in the world."

"Wow, I'm glad you invited me then."

She laughed. "How was the NNC picnic?"

"Interesting." I gave Casey a summary of the information Billy had shared.

"Supplying meth, huh? Not what I would have expected."

"Me neither. The good news is I might know someone who can tell us more. Old biker client I had a few years back. He and his guys weren't strangers to the meth scene. I'll go see him, see what he has to say."

"Okay. Let me know what you find out."

I gave a mock salute. "Yes, boss."

Casey looked over my shoulder and smirked. I turned around. Louisa was approaching us, along with a well-tanned man in a linen sports coat and narrow rectangular glasses.

"Michael, you have to meet Enrique. He did my sunroom."

Casey grinned again. "Enjoy," she said, and walked away.

SEVENTEEN
FRIENDS IN LOW PLACES

Monday afternoon, I drove down to Felony Flats, the locals' name for the rundown Southeast Portland neighborhood known for its high crime rate. It was also home to three different motorcycle clubs classified as outlaw gangs by the Oregon Department of Justice. Sonny Gradzinski, the man I was going to see, founded the Speed Brothers, the largest and most notorious of those gangs, back in the late seventies.

I drove down Foster and turned onto 62nd Avenue. Most of the houses were in a state of disrepair, and Gradzinski's house fit the neighborhood perfectly. The paint had been light blue at some point, but it had long since faded to gray. One of the front windows had been broken and boarded up. The narrow porch had an old couch on one end, its fabric ruined by years of rain and mold. A large black Pitbull dozed on the porch. The dog stood up when I approached, growling and straining at the chain leash holding it back.

Sonny Gradzinski pushed the screen door open and came outside.

"Shut up, Mutley," he said. The dog sat down and looked up at him, wagging its tail nervously.

Gradzinski stood on the porch, hands on hips. He had thinning gray hair pulled back in a ponytail and a white handlebar mustache. A leather biker vest, black T-shirt and faded blue jeans hung loosely on his wiry frame.

"Mick Ward. Can't say I was expecting you."

"You're looking good, Sonny."

Gradzinski snorted. "Yeah, right. I'm looking old."

"You mind if I come in? I need to talk to you."

"Sure."

I followed him into the house, giving the dog a wide berth. Inside, the house was much like the exterior. The green hall carpet was worn through to the thread in several places and there was a fist-sized hole in the plaster near the door. The floor creaked underfoot. I had to turn sideways to squeeze past the two immaculate Harley Davidson Shovelhead motorcycles parked in the hall.

"I see your priorities haven't changed," I said, as we entered the kitchen.

"Never will," Gradzinski replied. "You want a beer?"

"Always."

Gradzinski grabbed two beers from the fridge and handed me one. He sat at the kitchen table and gestured for me to do the same.

"I hear you're not a lawyer anymore," he said.

"Yeah, I hear the same thing. A lot." I took a drink of my beer. "Long story. I'm still in the game, though."

"That what you came here about?"

"Yeah. You heard about Elliott Russell being charged with murder? The guy the cops shot?"

"Yeah, the Black Lives Matter dude. I heard about it. What's it to do with you?"

"He's innocent, and I'm helping his lawyer out."

"Glad to hear it," Sonny said. "Anyone who's against the

cops is a friend of mine."

"I figured you'd say that," I replied. I picked at the label on my beer. "You remember you said you owed me a favor?"

"Anything, anytime. That's what I said," Gradzinski replied. "I meant it."

Gradzinski's son Sonny Junior had been my client in one of the two murder cases I'd handled previously. It happened when a fight with a rival gang went wrong. Four guys jumped Junior and a friend in a local dive bar. They were in trouble until Junior landed a big right hook. The guy went down, hit his head on the bar rail, and he didn't get up again. His three friends fled.

DAs don't like biker gangs and they went straight to an aggravated murder charge. Junior had been facing life in prison at best, and the DA was making noises about the death penalty. Junior was willing to plead to manslaughter, but the DA wouldn't go any lower than second-degree murder.

That carried a twenty-five-year mandatory minimum sentence, so I called his bluff and threatened to take the case to trial. I knew the State didn't have a witness—the people in that bar weren't the type to talk to the cops. Without anyone to put Junior at the scene, chances of a conviction were slim. The DA knew it, too. Eventually, he cracked and offered a voluntary manslaughter plea. I thought about taking the case to trial and going for acquittal, but putting a giant hairy tattooed biker dude in front of a jury is a big risk. I didn't want to gamble with Junior's life, so I countered with involuntary manslaughter and the DA accepted it. With time served and good behavior, Junior was out six months later.

After the plea deal was finalized in front of the judge, the DA took off like a greyhound. I took my time gathering my things and Sonny was waiting for me when I got outside. He hugged me, fought back tears, and promised me that any time I needed a favor, I could come to him.

I considered Gradzinski as I gathered my thoughts. The old biker's arms were still muscular and well-defined, but his skin had taken on the crinkled paper look of age. His eyes were still bright, though, and his menacing gaze made me just as uncomfortable now as it had ten years ago.

"I don't like doing this, Sonny, but I need your help."

"I told you. Name it."

"I need information. About the meth business in town."

Sonny's eyes narrowed. "Don't ask me to rat anyone out, Mick."

"No, of course not. But can you tell me what's been happening on the scene lately? I heard that the Bloods have moved into the market. Not what I would have expected."

"They're welcome to it," Sonny said.

"But where's the supply coming from? Didn't most of the big labs up here get shut down?"

"They did. It's coming from Mexico."

"What?"

"Yeah, you heard me," Sonny said. "A couple of years back, some guys from Sinaloa came to town looking to do business. Said they had a big supply and needed help with distribution. Not just local, either. They were looking to supply the entire Pacific Northwest. They came to us, and I heard they contacted the Gypsy Jokers and the Mongols too. I told them to pound sand and so did the other clubs. No way I'm getting involved in some cartel bullshit. Those guys are crazy."

"I guess the Bloods did a deal with them."

"Yeah. Must have been a good deal too. Right now there's more meth on the street than you can shake a stick at. It's like Christmas for every tweaker east of I-205."

"So the money's flowing too, then."

"Yeah, whoever took the Mexicans up on their distribution offer is making bank. No skin off my back, though. I'm too old to be dealing meth anymore." Sonny finished his beer and pointed the bottle at me. "What's this got to do with your buddy's case?"

"It's a long story. Short version is that someone's trying to frame him for that murder, and the dead guy is connected to the meth trade."

"You need any help?"

"Not right now."

"If that changes, you call me." Sonny stood up. "What you asked me now, that was nothing. I still owe you for what you did for Junior."

He held out his hand, so I stood up and shook it. "Will do. Thanks, Sonny."

I drove home, thinking about what Gradzinski had told me. Betts must have been the Mexicans' partner. Like everyone else, I'd heard stories about how ruthless the cartels could be. But even so, it wasn't likely they'd killed Betts, given what Billy had told me about the supply drying up when he died. If the Mexicans were going to execute Betts, they would've had replacement distribution arrangements in place. Besides, even if they did kill Betts, there was no reason for them to frame Elliott.

Still, now we knew where some of Betts's money had come from. Maybe we could follow that money and see where it led.

EIGHTEEN
HUNTED

The doctors brought Elliott out of his coma just over a week later. I wanted to go see him right away, but the doctor wouldn't let him have visitors until they were sure he was stable. I kept pushing and they finally agreed to let us visit a couple of days later.

Casey was waiting at reception when I arrived at the hospital, leaning against a wall, scrolling through her phone. She wore a Seahawks T-shirt and tight jeans that fit her athletic physique well. I struggled to drag my gaze up to her face.

"Casual Thursday?" I said.

"Very funny," she replied. "I got a copy of the indictment this morning. They confirmed the aggravated murder charge."

Casey's news instantly knocked the humor out of me. "No surprise there, I guess."

"Yeah, I know." Casey pushed herself off the wall. "Shall we go see Elliott?"

There was a different uniformed officer by Elliott's door. He let us in without objection when Casey told him who we were. Elliott was still hooked up to all kinds of monitors and drips, and an oxygen mask covered his face. He looked frail, his eyes sunken and dull, and his cheeks hollow.

"Hey, Mick," he said, his voice hoarse. "Good to see you."

"Good to see you too, buddy. How are you feeling?"

"Like shit." Elliott lifted his right hand, which held a small plastic device connected to one of the IV drips. "They gave me this morphine pump, but I'm trying not to use it. I want to keep my head clear."

Casey pulled another chair over and sat down. "What have the medical staff told you?"

"Not much. Apparently I was in a coma for about a month."

"That's right. Have the police been to see you?"

"No, you're my first visitors. What's happening in my case?"

"I guess you know you've been arrested," I said. "They charged you with aggravated murder."

Elliott sighed. "I figured they'd do that."

"Do you mind if I look at your chart?" Casey said.

Elliott nodded his head slightly. Casey grabbed the chart from the end of the bed and flicked through it. She frowned at a page and handed it to me.

There were notes from earlier that morning indicating Elliott still didn't have any feeling below the waist.

He must have seen the look on my face. "The doctor told me what's going on."

"What did he say?"

"One of the bullets is lodged against my spine. He thinks they might be able to remove it, but he's not sure it will help. It depends on how much damage it's already done to my spinal cord."

"When are they going to do it?"

"Probably late next week. They have to wait until the swelling goes down some." Elliott coughed, then flicked his eyes to the table beside the bed. "Would you hand me that water?"

There was a plastic cup with a drinking straw poking through a hole in the lid. I held it up to Elliott's mouth and he took a couple of sips.

"Thanks." He looked at Casey. "What happens next?"

"The next step is arraignment," she said. "But it won't take place until you're well enough to appear in court."

"That could be a while," Elliott said with a rueful half smile. "Do I have to be there?"

"We could arrange for you to appear by video conference."

"Yes, please. The sooner we begin, the sooner this will be over. And after arraignment?"

"Not much for a while," Casey said. "I'll mostly be pushing for access to evidence and witnesses. There will be a preliminary hearing in about a month, where both sides get to argue legal points. Mostly about what evidence will or won't be admitted at trial."

"And what happens to me during that time?"

"At some point you'll be transferred to a correctional facility, probably Inverness. They have a hospital ward there, but it's pretty basic, so you'll be staying here until your condition has improved significantly."

"I don't suppose there's any chance of bail?" Elliott said.

"We'll fight for it at the arraignment, but like I told you before, I doubt it'll be granted."

Elliott nodded slowly. "What about the trial? When will that be?"

"Hard to say. Probably three months from now at the soonest, but it could take up to a year."

"And I'll be inside the whole time. Great. Anything you can do to get it moving would be good."

Casey took a legal pad and a pen out of her briefcase. "Can you tell us what happened on the night you were arrested?"

Elliott tensed. "Yeah. It happened after Mick dropped me

off. As soon as I left the office, there was a cop car in my rearview mirror. I took it easy, but he pulled me over after maybe a quarter mile."

"Were there any other cars around?" I asked.

"No. I pulled over and wound down my window, and the cop just shouted at me."

"What did he say?"

"He told me to get out of the car and put my hands up." Elliott's face darkened. "Then he shot me."

"What? Immediately?" I could hear Casey's surprise.

"Almost. I got out of the car and put my hands on my head. He had his gun out and he shot me. He didn't even ask me my name."

Casey and I looked at each other. Elliott's story was beyond strange.

"Was there another officer there?" Casey asked.

"I don't know."

"And the guy who shot you. Did you see his name badge?"

"No. It was dark."

"Can you remember any other details?"

"No. I vaguely remember being in the ambulance, and then I was here." Elliott winced. "I think I'll take a hit of that morphine now."

He squeezed the morphine pump a couple of times. Almost immediately, the tension flowed out of his face.

"I know what you're thinking, Mick. That I should have run. But I'm going to beat this."

"I know you are, buddy," I said. "And we're going to help you do it. Get some rest. I'll come see you tomorrow."

We left Elliott and went for coffee. Neither of us spoke as we walked. I was in shock about Elliott's story and I expected Casey was too. You hear a lot of crazy things when you're a defense attorney, but I'd never heard of a cop shooting someone as soon as he got out of the car.

When we got to the cafeteria, the boiled vegetable smell was worse than on our previous visit. We got drinks and sat at a table.

"What did you make of all that?" Casey asked.

"Something doesn't add up. I mean, what with Andre Gladen and all the others, we've all seen stories about cops killing Black guys. But shooting Elliott before he's had a chance to say or do anything makes no sense."

"Do you think he's being straight with us?"

"On the shooting? Yeah, I do. I think that's how it went down."

"Me too," she replied. "How did they find him so fast?"

"They must have followed us from the council meeting."

"That still doesn't explain why Elliott got shot. Why didn't they just arrest him?"

"Because somebody wants this whole thing tied up with a neat little bow. Somebody knows Elliott didn't do it and shooting him was their way of shutting him up." I banged my fist on the table. The brawler in me wanted to find the person responsible and rip their fucking throat out, but I'd settle for kicking their ass in court.

"So you still think it's a gang thing?" Casey said. "Even after a cop shot Elliott?"

"I do, especially given the Mexican cartel connection. The cop could be on the gang payroll. It wouldn't be the first time a uniform took a few bucks to do some dirty work." I paused. "Although now you mention it, there might be another answer. When we first found the body, Elliott said the cops could be behind it. They've been hassling him because he organized the Black Lives Matter protests. Maybe some cop got the bright idea to whack Betts and dump the body at Elliott's place. Kill two birds with one stone, so to speak."

"That's pretty far-fetched, Mick. Like you said, we've seen cops do some dark shit lately, but it's usually on the spur of the moment. Premeditated execution of one man to frame another is next-level stuff."

"Okay, what if someone else killed Betts, and when the cops found the body they decided to use it to frame Elliott?"

"That's more likely, but still deep left field. Let's keep on the gang angle for now. Meanwhile, I'll push hard on discovery from the arrest and shooting. Demand that the DA turns over any recordings, in-car video, investigation reports, the works. If there's anything in there to back up your theory, we can pursue it."

"Right." I sat back and ran a hand through my hair. "You know, if the discovery backs up Elliott's story, things could get ugly. The BLM protests are still going on every night. If video of a Portland cop shooting an unarmed Black guy got out, this city would explode."

"You're right, but we should probably plan a press conference anyway. Things have been tense enough, since word spread that Elliott has been shot. If we control the narrative, hopefully we can keep a lid on things and claim the moral high ground at the same time."

"Sounds like a plan. How can I help?"

Casey fidgeted with her coffee cup. "Mick, there's no easy way to say this. I don't want you at the press conference."

"What are you talking about?"

"You know why. Like I said, we're trying to claim the moral high ground."

I felt my face grow hot. "Oh, I get it. Having Mick Ward the disbarred lawyer in the picture isn't the image you're looking for."

"Don't take it personally. You know how the game is played. We want the story to be about Elliott, not you."

"Yeah, fine. Whatever."

She was right, but that didn't mean I had to like it. For a while, we sat in silence. Eventually, she leaned forward and put her hand on mine.

"You're okay with this, right?"

There was a look in her eye I couldn't quite place. Something personal, enough to take me down a notch.

"Guess I have to be," I said. "You're the boss."

She squeezed my hand and sat back. "I know it's tough. I wish it didn't have to be this way."

"Thanks." I managed a smile. "Now get out of here."

Casey nodded and smiled back at me, then got up and left.

I sat there, finishing my coffee and thinking about the case. I was relieved to see Elliott doing better. Hopefully, removing the bullet would save him from being paralyzed. But whatever happened, he had a tough road ahead. He'd be spending time in jail—at least until we got through the trial, and possibly a whole lot longer. Looking after yourself in jail was tough enough at any time. Doing it in a wheelchair would be a nightmare.

Meanwhile, I had to get ready for a capital murder trial, starting with the arraignment, and I felt uneasy. At first, I couldn't work out why. Then it hit me. I hadn't been in a courtroom since I was disbarred. How would I respond? How would the judge react to my presence? Or the prosecutor, for that matter? I thought about not going, or just sitting in the public gallery. But I couldn't help Elliott if I was sitting in the cheap seats. I had to get back on the horse.

NINETEEN
NOBODY'S PERFECT

I got to the hospital as early as I could on Friday morning. Elliott was awake when I arrived. He still looked fragile, but his eyes were clearer and the morphine pump was looped around his bed rail, rather than clutched in his hand. He smiled when he saw me come in.

"Hey, buddy," I said. "How are you feeling?"

Elliott sighed. "Okay, I guess. Tired." He waved a remote control at the TV. "Basic cable sucks."

"Amen to that." I sat by his bed. "You feel up to talking about a few things related to your case?"

"Definitely. What's up?"

"I've been investigating who could be behind this, and I've got a couple of questions for you."

"Okay, what can I tell you?"

"Let's start with this. Was Betts still dealing?"

Elliott hesitated. "Why do you ask?"

"Your old Crip buddies seem to think he was."

"What did you talk to them for?" he snapped.

"Why do you think? I told you before that's the most likely

answer. So I tracked down DeAngelo Kennedy and asked him about it."

"I'm guessing he wasn't too happy when you mentioned my name."

I rubbed my eye. The swelling and discoloration were gone, but it still felt tender. "You could say that."

"Mick, I've got history with those guys," he said. "Last thing I need is to give them a reason to come after me."

"Don't worry, you're fine as long as you stay off their turf. What about Betts? Was he dealing?"

"Yeah." Elliott paused, his breathing heavy. "I got word a while back that Betts was still in the game."

"Did you hear this before or after your fight with him?"

"After. I got a call from one of his Deuce Mob brothers. Told me not to fuck with Betts because he was protected. I knew what that meant."

I knew, too. Gang members wouldn't waste a second on a small-time argument unless the guy involved was important. It also confirmed what Billy Hinds had discovered: it was unlikely the Bloods had killed Betts.

"I have to ask. Why didn't you tell me about this when we found the body? Or when we met with Casey?"

"I don't know. Does it matter?"

"Of course it matters," I said. "We're trying to figure out who set you up. If you want us to help you, you've got to be straight with us."

Elliott closed his eyes and slowly shook his head.

"Come on," I said. "The time for fucking around is long gone."

Elliott took a deep breath. "I took money," he said.

"What? From Betts?"

"Yeah. I took money to turn a blind eye to him dealing."

"Jesus Christ. Why?"

"It's a long story. But he came to me after we fought at the NNC meeting. Said we should be working together, not against each other. He said he'd kick me a cut if I looked the other way. It was right after I got the call saying Betts was protected, so I knew I couldn't stop him dealing. Meanwhile, the after school computer club at Albina Community Center was running out of money, and I couldn't find a sponsor to keep it going. So I took the money from him. His drugs hurt plenty of kids. This way, his money could help a few. I put it all into the computer club, I swear. I never kept a dime for myself."

"How much are we talking?"

"Maybe ten grand, all up."

I rolled my eyes. "Well, there's the connection."

"What do you mean?"

"Between you and Betts. It all fits now. Your Crip buddies already hated you. They knew Betts was dealing again and they find out you're taking a cut from the Deuce Mob Bloods. So they whack him and dump the body on you."

"I don't buy it."

"Why not?"

"It's too complicated. If the Crips wanted me gone, they'd just whack me themselves. They wouldn't fuck around burying a body in my yard."

"You better hope you're right."

"Why?"

"If my theory is correct, we can't go to the cops with it. You'd have to admit to taking money from Betts, which means you'd go down for dealing. Not quite as bad as murder, but you still won't see daylight for a long time."

"Great. Now I gotta worry about that too."

"Look, it's not the end of the world," I said, "but I need your help."

"What do you mean?"

"The plan stays the same. We need to figure out exactly who killed Betts and serve him up to the cops. But if it wasn't the Crips, we need an angle, a way to figure out who pulled the trigger. Help me out."

"I'm trying. Really, I am."

I looked at my friend, lying in a hospital bed and surrounded by all kinds of medical equipment. He looked like a dried-out shell of his former self.

"I know you are, buddy," I said. "And I'm sorry for pushing you. I'm just trying to help."

"Thanks, Mick. I appreciate it."

I stood up. "I'll let you get some rest. Hang in there."

I clapped Elliott gently on the shoulder and left.

The drive home passed uneventfully. I passed the time half-listening to the radio and mulling over what Elliott told me, trying to figure out what it meant. I couldn't believe that son of a bitch took money from a dealer. After all those years of getting his life back on track, too. But then, what could he do? Betts had protection, so Elliott would be putting his life on the line if he tried to stop him. He couldn't go to the police for the same reason. Maybe he could have ignored it; let the dealing happen, but not taken any money. But are any of us that pure? With the money going to help keep the computer club alive, this way, some good came of it.

Would I have stood by him if I'd known? Definitely. Sure, I was pissed at him, but more for holding out on me than for what he did. And I still owed the guy my life. Besides, I was already in it up to my neck, and it was too late to change that now. I just hoped we could come up with some way to move the investigation forward.

TWENTY
SECONDS OUT

The next few days felt like a decade. After my meeting with Elliott on Friday, we couldn't do anything until the following week. I called Casey a couple of times on Saturday morning to run some ideas past her, but she kept telling me to save it for Monday. I'd say yes reluctantly, then call her a few minutes later with another suggestion. Eventually, she switched off her phone. I spent the rest of the weekend wrapping up my work on Kristen's civil case. I didn't find anything else useful in the documents, but it was almost interesting enough to keep me occupied, and I needed the money.

On the Monday morning Casey had me research grounds for bail in murder cases, so we could argue for it at the arraignment. I spent three days digging and the results weren't promising. I only found bail granted in seven murder cases in the last five years, and each time the charges were lower and the defendant had no prior record. Still, we had something to take to the arraignment.

Elliott's surgery would take place on Friday, so the DA's office agreed to set the arraignment for Thursday, with Elliott appearing by video conference. Casey scheduled the press conference for straight after. She fed Joe Gorman at the *Willamette Week* some inside information for a lead-up piece, in return for a couple of friendly questions at the conference. The *Willamette Week* was a free local newspaper with a staunchly liberal perspective. Although its coverage was sometimes skewed, it had broken some big stories in recent years and was widely read. Plus, Gorman was an outspoken critic of the Portland Police Bureau. It would be a good place to start, especially if Gorman's lead-up piece could get some of the network news crews to show up.

We visited Elliott on Thursday morning to prepare him. He looked more energetic, his voice was clear and strong, and he didn't need the morphine pump at any point in the hour-long meeting. We walked him through the arraignment process and how the video conference would work. He took it all in, a look of quiet determination on his face, and I felt encouraged when we left.

Casey headed back to her office to prepare for the arraignment. I stopped by Bunk Sandwiches and grabbed a pork belly Cubano for lunch, then went home and changed into a suit and tie. Looking at myself in the mirror was like looking back in time. For years, this had been my uniform. Unlike a lot of lawyers, I'd never been too picky about where I got my suits. Being a big guy, it took me a while to find a brand that would fit across my shoulders without expensive alterations. Once I did, I'd buy two or three a year in neutral dark shades and rotate the older ones out. I had fun with my ties, though. I liked to go for something colorful. It was my way of brightening up what was often a very dark place to be.

Today, given the circumstances, I wasn't in the mood for levity; I chose a charcoal-gray suit and one of my plainer ties. I put them on, adjusted my cuffs, and left.

The arraignment was taking place at the Multnomah

County Justice Center. The Justice Center was an ugly postmodern building in downtown Portland, close to the river. As the home of the Portland Police Bureau, it had been at the epicenter of the Black Lives Matter protests since they started. In the early days, demonstrators had smashed their way into the building and ransacked the lobby, overturning metal detectors and other security equipment, lighting fires, and spray-painting anti-police slogans on the walls. The protesters still gathered outside every night, but temporary chain-link fencing and a heavy police presence kept them from doing further damage.

Despite the heavy security, all the ground-floor windows were still boarded up. But then, these days, so was most of downtown Portland. Another reminder that we had to be careful with the information about Elliott's shooting.

When I arrived at the courtroom, a technical team was setting up the video conference equipment, but otherwise the room was empty. Justice Center Courtroom 3 was used for arraignments and other preliminary hearings, and was specifically designed for criminal cases. The room had light blue walls and a raised bench for the judge. To one side, there was the clerk's desk. The defense and prosecution tables sat in the middle of the room, with the jury seating to the left and a small public gallery behind where the lawyers sat. The technical team had set a monitor on a stand to the left of the defense table, with a webcam on top. On the other side of the judge's bench, the defendant's stand had a steel door in the back and was surrounded on three sides by bulletproof glass. There were nine small holes in a square pattern in the glass to allow attorneys to confer with their clients.

I took a seat at the defense table. A moment later, a short, harried-looking woman in a baggy pants suit bustled into the room and dumped an armful of files on the prosecution table.

She patted her pockets, pulled her phone out of one, then looked at me and did a double-take.

"What the hell are you doing here?"

"Hello, Nicole," I replied. "Nice to see you."

Nicole Astert was Chief Deputy District Attorney for Multnomah County. She headed up the major crimes team. During her rise to the chief deputy role, she'd become known for over-charging cases to bully defendants into taking bad plea deals. Over the years, we'd gone up against each other many times, and I'd come to conclude she didn't have a decent bone in her body. Nevertheless, I was surprised to see her. Normally one of the deputy district attorneys on her team would be first chair on a homicide case. For Nicole to be there meant this case must be the DA's top priority.

"No, really. Why are you here, Ward? You're not a lawyer anymore."

"Why do people keep saying that to me?"

"Because it's true."

"I hadn't forgotten," I said. "I'm on the defense team."

"Oh good. That's going to make winning this case even more fun."

Before I could reply, Casey walked in and sat next to me. She looked me up and down.

"You clean up well," she said with a smile.

"Thanks." I jerked a thumb over my shoulder at the prosecution table. "You see who we drew?"

"Could be worse," she said, loud enough for Nicole to hear.

Nicole ignored the comment, but her face reddened.

The court clerk came in and opened the door to the public gallery. It filled up quickly, with several reporters in the crowd, including Joe Gorman. Detectives Buchanan and Malone sat in the front row, so I waved. Buchanan pretended not to notice, but I was pleased to see Malone sneering back at me.

A technician turned on Elliott's monitor, then ran through some quick tests to make sure Elliott could see the courtroom and hear what was being said. As usual, an awkward few minutes passed before the judge entered and the proceedings began. I sat back in my chair, readjusting to the experience of being back in a courtroom. An arraignment was no big deal, but it served to remind me of so many past battles. It wasn't a good feeling.

When the crowd was settled, the bailiff told us to rise, and the judge entered. The case had been assigned to Judge Eric Obrecht, which was no surprise. Judge Obrecht had been the presiding judge in the criminal courts for several years, which made him responsible for assigning major criminal cases. He had a reputation for saving the highest profile cases for himself, especially in an election year. He never let politics get in the way of his job though, and was known for being even-handed. All in all, we could have done worse.

Judge Obrecht instructed us to be seated, then addressed Elliott's monitor.

"Before we proceed, I would like to confirm that the technology is working. Mr. Russell, can you hear me?"

"Yes, Your Honor," Elliott replied.

"And can you see the proceedings?"

"Yes, Your Honor."

"Good. In that case, let us begin. Mr. Russell, it is charged by indictment that in violation of section 163 of the Oregon Criminal Code, on or about the fourteenth of June, you willfully and with malice aforethought murdered Malik Betts."

Judge Obrecht then had the clerk read the special circumstances alleged by the prosecution: murder for hire, and murder in furtherance of a broader criminal enterprise. When he was done, the judge looked at Elliott's monitor again.

"Mr. Russell, do you understand the charges against you?"

"Yes, Your Honor."

"And how do you plead?"

"Not guilty, Your Honor."

"All right." The judge looked at some papers. "Since the charge is aggravated murder, bail will be denied. Ms. Raife, do you have a comment?"

Casey stood up. "Yes, Your Honor. I realize that bail is rare in a murder case, but it can be granted. Just last year, bail was granted in the Willie Mitchell case, on the grounds that the prosecution lacked clear and convincing evidence. The circumstances in this case are highly unusual. Mr. Russell is gravely injured and cannot safely be held in custody. And as in the Mitchell case, the prosecution lacks any evidence to support the aggravated murder charge, let alone to meet the clear and convincing standard required."

Nicole Astert was immediately on her feet. "Your Honor, Malik Betts was found executed in Mr. Russell's backyard. How much evidence do we need?"

"And Mr. Russell was the one who called the police!"

The spectators stirred and Judge Obrecht banged his gavel. "All right, calm down, everyone. Counselors, please approach the bench."

Casey and Nicole walked up to the judge's bench. I followed a few steps behind Casey, hoping the judge wouldn't send me back. He didn't.

Judge Obrecht leaned forward and spoke in a low voice. "Before we go any further, I will remind you that this is a court of law, and I expect decorum. Are we clear?"

Casey and Nicole both nodded.

"Good. Now, Ms. Astert, please explain why you think I should deny bail in this case."

"Your Honor, while Ms. Raife is correct that bail has been granted in some murder cases, it cannot be granted in an aggravated murder case as a matter of law. Moreover, Malik Betts was shot between the eyes, execution style, which is typical of murder for hire—and compelling evidence of a broader criminal enterprise."

"But you don't have any evidence connecting my client to this alleged criminal enterprise," Casey countered.

"Oh, come on, we found his body in your client's backyard! And besides, Mr. Russell is clearly a flight risk."

"Your Honor, calling my client a flight risk is absurd." Casey gestured at the monitor. "Look at him. He's lying in a hospital bed, paralyzed from the waist down. How the hell is he going to flee?"

"All right, that's enough," Judge Obrecht said. "Ms. Astert, I'm not convinced by the aggravated murder charge. We will have a pretrial hearing to determine whether it can proceed. For now, though, the law is clear. Bail is only granted in murder cases in extraordinary circumstances, and this one doesn't rise to that level. While I agree Mr. Russell is not a flight risk, the aggravated murder charge compels me to deny bail at this point. If the charges are reduced after the pretrial hearing, or other evidence emerges, I will reconsider."

Judge Obrecht leaned back and we returned to our seats. I flashed Elliott an apologetic look.

The judge banged his gavel again. "Bail will be denied in this case. My clerk will be in touch with preliminary hearing and trial scheduling. This hearing is adjourned."

We all stood as Judge Obrecht rose and left. I waved to Elliott again, as the technician switched off the monitor. We waited for the crowd to leave, then walked out of the courtroom. Casey put a hand on my arm.

"Remember what I said at the hospital?"

"Yeah, we're good."

Outside, there was a crowd of reporters waiting on the steps.

They were arranged in a rough horseshoe shape around the top of the steps. A TV cameraman stood at the front of the crowd and his colleague held a boom mike over his head. The other reporters all held microphones, smart phones, or other recording devices. Several members of the public milled around too, clearly curious about what was happening.

As we emerged, Casey tapped me on the shoulder.

"Meet me at my office in an hour."

I made my way around the crowd to the bottom of the stairs. Nicole Astert was walking right in front of me.

"Hey, Nicole," I said, "you might want to hang around for this."

She stopped and turned around. "What are you talking about?"

"Wait and see." I smiled and nodded at Casey as she approached the crowd of reporters. Nicole stood next to me, an angry frown on her face.

As soon as Casey made it to the top of the steps, she was bombarded with questions. She held up her hands and waited for the noise to subside, then she began to speak.

"Ladies and gentlemen," she began, "thank you for being here. I know you have a lot of questions, but before we begin, I'd like to make a short statement. As you know, my client Elliott Russell has been charged with the murder of Malik Betts. You also know that Mr. Russell is in the hospital, having been shot at the time of his arrest. Given everything this city has endured in the past month, we urge you to reserve judgment on his shooting. However, I can assure you that my client did not kill Malik Betts, and the truth will come out in this case. We will show that the police have consistently ignored evidence that would've led them to the guilty person. Instead, they chose a narrow-minded pursuit of my client that resulted in him being arrested and shot while a killer walks free."

Casey paused as the crowd bombarded her with questions. It was impossible to make out a single voice in the din.

I turned to Nicole and smiled. She scowled at me and stomped off, clutching her pile of files to her chest.

Casey waited for the noise to subside, then she raised her arms again, beckoning the reporters to be silent.

"I'll take a couple of questions now," she said.

Again, there was a flurry of waving arms and shouting voices.

"Joe Gorman," she said, "you first."

I saw the look in her eye and Gorman's nod. His payback for getting the crowd of reporters to be there.

"Ms. Raife," he said, "your client was running for City Council. Do you think his shooting was politically motivated?"

Perfect. Gorman got to grind his personal axe, and he made Casey's point for her. The two of them should have been on Broadway.

"We don't know the motive for this shooting yet," Casey replied, "and as I said, in the circumstances, we must be cautious. But we will be exploring every angle. Next?"

"Why was your client in hiding?" a woman I didn't recognize yelled before anyone else could speak.

Casey didn't even blink. "Mr. Russell was not hiding from anyone or anything. He was going about his lawful business when he was stopped by the police and shot. Are there any more questions?"

Another flurry of shouts and waving arms followed. Casey pointed to a TV news reporter standing next to a cameraman. "Mr. Hardy?"

"Why would the police shoot your client if he was innocent?" Hardy asked.

"That's what we intend to find out," Casey replied. "No more questions."

She marched down the steps, her forceful manner enough to part the crowd before her. I couldn't help but admire her performance. She had done a masterful job of getting our story out and then leaving before anyone could poke holes in it.

I watched her go. When she was out of sight, I texted her. *Nice job. That will keep them guessing.*

Her reply came back immediately. *For now. But if we can't back it up, they're going to hit us with both barrels.*

TWENTY-ONE

GIFT HORSE

To kill time before meeting Casey, I went to the Red Star and had a beer. Normally after a hearing like that, I'd head straight to the Lotus to yak it up with other lawyers, but I figured Casey's press conference would be the talk of the bar. She wanted me to keep a low profile, so that's what I did.

Casey's office was just around the corner from the Red Star. When I got there, she looked up from her pile of paperwork.

"What did you think?" she said.

"Bravo, maestro."

"Thanks." She sat back and sighed. "I just hope Elliott isn't bullshitting us."

"Speaking of Elliott, we should call him."

Casey called the hospital and asked the duty nurse to take the phone to Elliot's room. While we waited, she laid her phone on the desk and hit the speaker button.

Elliott answered a moment later. "Hey, Casey."

"Hello, Elliott, you're on speaker. Mick is here too."

"How are you feeling?" I said.

"Okay, I guess." His voice was strained, as though every word took enormous effort. "Disappointed about bail, but it was inevitable. What happened when the judge called you to the bench? I couldn't hear."

Casey leaned forward. "We argued about the bail issue some more. Like you said, denial was inevitable, but I planted a seed in the judge's head that the DA is going too far with this case. I think it worked."

"Well, that's something." He paused. "Hey, I need you to do me a favor."

"Sure, anything," I said. "What is it?"

"Can you get Billy to put out a press release on my behalf? I want an announcement that I'm suspending my election campaign to focus on proving my innocence. Maybe also mention that the charges are obviously politically motivated, and that I intend to resume my campaign as soon as possible. Billy can come up with the exact wording. He's good at that stuff."

"Of course. I'll call him today. That should play well alongside news of Casey's press conference."

"Thanks," he said. "You think we'll be done by November?"

"Hard to say," Casey replied. "You have a right to a speedy trial, but it's not always a good idea to rush a case like this."

"Yeah, I know. But damn, I want this to be over."

I could hear the weariness growing in Elliott's voice. "You sound tired. Why don't you rest up for the surgery tomorrow? I'll come see you over the weekend and we can talk about the case."

"Okay. Thanks, Mick."

I hung up the phone and sighed. "Poor bastard. We've got to help him."

"There's not much we can do right now," Casey said. "We've got nothing until we see discovery and talk to witnesses."

Casey's phone rang. She looked at the display. "It's

Buchanan. I'll put him on speaker. Keep quiet." She pressed a button on the phone. "Hello, Detective. What can I do for you?"

"What the hell was that stunt you just pulled?" Buchanan said. He sounded mightily pissed.

"I read the papers, Detective. I watch the news. Every statement your department has issued about my client has painted him as a killer," Casey replied. "I know you haven't come out and said it. But you've damn well implied it at every opportunity. So don't complain when the shoe is on the other foot."

"Never mind that crap. Thanks to you, I've got four uniforms stationed at the hospital just to keep the reporters out."

"Not my problem. Is that the only reason you called?"

"No. When you see your so-called investigator, tell him to call me. I want to talk to him."

Buchanan hung up. I had switched my phone off for the arraignment. I took it out and switched it on. There were three missed calls and two voicemails from Buchanan. I held it up to Casey.

"I guess he wasn't kidding," I said.

"You better call him."

"I know." I stood. "I'll call you later, tell you what he had to say. Shall we meet tomorrow? Say 2 pm?"

"Yeah. I'll call you if anything comes up before then."

Outside Casey's office, I listened to Buchanan's voicemails. Two variations on the theme of *Call me right now, asshole*. I felt like blowing him off, but that was only delaying the inevitable, so I made the call.

"Where have you been?" Buchanan snapped.

"Good afternoon to you too, Detective."

"We need to talk. Get your ass over to the station."

"Not going to happen." I paused and looked around,

thinking about where we could meet. "If you need to talk to me, I'll be in the Yamhill Pub for the next hour or so."

"The Yamhill? Do you ever go anywhere that isn't a shithole?"

"Don't bad mouth my people, Detective."

I hung up and walked the three blocks to the Yamhill. To be fair, Buchanan was right. It was a shithole. The windowless bar was dimly lit, with Pabst Blue Ribbon neon signs on the walls and pinball machines over by the toilets. The walls were covered in graffiti and patrons were free to add more at any time. The sticky carpet smelled of stale beer. They usually played good music, but today I walked in to Blink 182. Still, the noise would prevent any conversation from being overheard.

Most of the barstools were occupied, so I grabbed a pint and sat at a corner table. Buchanan arrived ten minutes later. He saw me right away.

"Nice place," he said, frowning at the graffiti on the walls.

He was alone, which surprised me. "Are we waiting for your trained monkey?"

"This conversation is just you and me."

That was interesting. Portland Police Bureau policy requires two detectives to be present for any interview, so they can both testify to the conversation later. Which meant Buchanan didn't want anyone else hearing what he said.

"Have it your way, Detective. What's so urgent that you're willing to meet me here?"

"You were building a fence at Elliott Russell's house?"

"You know I was," I said carefully. "He's my friend."

"When did you start?"

"I don't know. Maybe a couple of weeks before the big night. I'd been fitting it in around other jobs."

"And how did you know where to build the fence?"

"It's a fence," I said. "I don't know if you noticed, but they usually go around the edge of the lot. It's not hard."

Buchanan blew a hard breath out through his nose. "Don't fuck me around. We found the blueprints. We know the driveway was supposed to go where Betts was found."

"Okay. So what?"

"You don't think it's troubling, that your friend was planning to put a big old concrete slab over where the body was buried?"

"What's troubling is that a cop shot him while he had his hands up."

Something dark flickered across Buchanan's face, but he recovered quickly. "Here's the thing," he said. "We had an anonymous tip saying Russell kept a gun in his nightstand, but we didn't find one when we searched the house. What do you say about that?"

So that's why Malone had been surprised when they didn't find the gun at Elliott's place. "I'd say you need a better class of informant."

"Maybe. Or maybe someone familiar with defense law told Russell to get rid of the gun."

I leaned back, deliberately keeping my expression blank. "Stop dancing, Detective. Tell me what you want."

Buchanan paused and rubbed a hand over his bald head. "Look, Mick. Elliott Russell is going down. And the DA still hates your guts, which means you're going down too. Unless you help us out, that is."

I laughed. "I thought that's where you were headed. You're going to lock me up and throw away the key unless I rat out my buddy, right?"

"I'm not asking you to break attorney–client privilege here." Buchanan leaned forward and tapped a finger on the table. "Just tell us what happened before Russell lawyered up. The DA has authorized me to offer you full immunity from prosecution, no questions asked."

Something wasn't right. I looked Buchanan up and down. "Question for you. Have you, at any point in this case, considered a suspect other than Elliott Russell?"

Buchanan shifted uneasily in his seat. "It's obvious Russell is guilty. Why would we waste our time on anyone else?"

"I thought not. Next question. You've got a chief deputy DA personally taking a case she'd usually farm out to a junior member of her team. You've got so many cops involved that you could afford twenty-four-hour surveillance on Elliott. Normally you guys wouldn't put down your donuts for a dead gangbanger. Why all this firepower for Malik Betts?"

"Look, since the BLM riots started–"

I held up a hand. "You mean the BLM protests."

"Since the BLM riots started, I've been absolutely fucking buried. When help comes along, I'm not going to stop and ask why."

"And now you're offering me immunity from prosecution. But you know accessory liability requires that I intended to help commit the crime and actively participated in doing so. Good luck meeting that standard. And besides, if the case against Elliott is as tight as you say, the DA doesn't need my testimony. So why are you here? I'm smelling desperation, Detective. Someone up high is getting nervous. Why?"

"Are you going to testify, or not?"

"Here's what I think. You know something isn't right about this case. And you knew damn well what I'd say to your offer before you made it. But you made it anyway, because a big cheese told you to. Who?"

Buchanan shifted in his seat again. "I take it that's a no?"

I stood up and left.

I wandered around for a while, too confused to have a

destination in mind. So, the cops knew about the gun. Whoever was behind this must have called in the tip. Hanging on to it no longer seemed like such a good idea. I'd had visions of pulling the real killer's prints, but we had no fingerprint matching capabilities, or chain of custody, for that matter. And I had no way of getting it tested without revealing that I had it, which would put me back in the crosshairs for accessory liability. No, the gun had to go.

And what of Buchanan's expression when I talked about Elliott being shot while he had his hands up? I'd seen that look before—Buchanan was an expert at keeping his cool, but when he eventually blew up, you didn't want to be anywhere nearby. And he'd come close to blowing his stack today. He wasn't happy about what went down at Elliott's arrest. What did he know that we didn't?

A few minutes later I found myself back outside the Justice Center. Crowds were gathering for tonight's BLM protest, mostly younger Antifa types, dressed in black with bandanas on their faces. Spreading out in a line between the protesters and the heavily armed riot police forming up outside the chain-link fence, was a knot of middle-aged women in yellow T-shirts. They were known as the Wall of Moms, a group that had come together in response to Portland Police's violent treatment of the demonstrators. The first night they did it, the police teargassed them too, which made for national news Mayor Alioto could have done without. Now, the police trod carefully around them, but you still got the sense that more than a few cops wanted to crush some skulls with their batons.

I gave the crowd a wide berth and kept walking toward the river, unsure what to make of my conversation with Buchanan. Why would he expect me to flip on Elliott, especially when the accessory case against me was so weak? He had to know I'd refuse, and he clearly wasn't comfortable when I called him on it. Which meant my guess was right. Someone powerful had forced him to do it. But why?

I called Casey.

"Hey, Mick, what's up?"

I told her about the conversation with Buchanan.

"So they know about the gun?" she said.

"Don't worry; I'm getting rid of it tonight."

"Good," she said. "The immunity offer is weird, especially coming from a straight shooter like Buchanan. He has to know they have no leverage on you."

"I know. I've never known him to act that way."

"Maybe Elliott wasn't crazy after all when he said the cops were involved. Sure sounds to me like Buchanan's getting grief from above."

"Yeah. Tony's got some back door connections at the police bureau. Want me to see what he can find out?"

"It can't hurt."

"Okay, I'll call him. I'll get back to you later, okay?"

"Sounds good."

I hung up and called Tony.

"Hey, Mick. How did things go today?"

"The arraignment went as expected. No bail, but we did get a pretrial hearing on the ag murder charge. Casey gave a great press conference afterward, yanked the DA's chain a bit, which was nice. Oh, and Buchanan offered me immunity to flip on Elliott."

"What? That's crazy."

"Yeah. Which is why I'm calling. Do you still know someone inside PPB?"

"Yeah," he said warily, "but I need to tread carefully there. My guy can't just go ask Buchanan what the fuck is going on."

"I know, but right now anything we can get would be an improvement."

"Okay, I'll see what I can do."

"Thanks. You want to get some dinner?"

"Normally I'd love to, but it sounds like I gotta go make some calls."

"Fair enough. Then let's grab lunch before we go to Casey's office tomorrow."

"Sounds good. I'm in."

TWENTY-TWO

BAD BOYS

I did as I'd promised and threw the gun in the river that night. It didn't feel right, but the risks were too great. Our anonymous tipster could come up with something to give the cops probable cause to search my lockup, and if that happened, Elliott and I were both in big trouble.

The next morning, Tony and I met up at Pine Street Market, an indoor food hall in an old carriage house a couple of blocks from Casey's office. Pine Street was set up like a European food market, with vendors around the outside walls, and a combination of counter seating at the stalls and communal tables in the center. The exposed brick walls gave it a rustic, continental feel, and the smell of food cooking in a dozen different kitchens made for a mouthwatering atmosphere.

Tony had steamed buns and kimchi from Kim Jong Grill, and I went for a bowl of ramen from Kinboshi. We ate at a bench in the center of the hall, content to talk sports and soak up the air conditioning. After the craziness of the past forty-eight hours, we both needed a breather.

As we left, Tony took an envelope out of his pocket and handed it to me. "By the way, Kristen asked me to give you this.

Payment for the rest of your work on the construction defects case. She said there could be more jobs coming your way."

I stuffed it in my jeans. "Thanks, man."

We made it to Casey's office a little before two. The three of us sat at her small conference table and Casey rubbed her hands together.

"Okay, Tony, tell us what you've been up to."

"My guy hasn't had much time, but he got something interesting about the cop who shot Elliott. His name's Sam Kavanagh. Only been on the force just over a year, but he's already raised some eyebrows."

"How so?" Casey asked.

"He's had a bunch of disciplinary reports already. Apparently, he's been in more trouble than most cops with ten years behind the badge. Ugly stuff, too. He was one of the guys who fired rubber bullets at the BLM protesters when everything kicked off back in May."

"Okay, so we got a cop with a taste for violence. This is my surprised face," I said.

"Here's the thing," Tony replied. "My guy says most cops with a rap sheet like Kavanagh would have been kicked out. Especially since he's on probation for the first two years."

I shrugged. "So he's protected. Could be anything. An uncle in the command ranks."

"Maybe. But it doesn't smell right. My guy is going to dig deeper, but like I said, he's gotta be careful. Especially if this guy has juice."

"You're right, it's worth exploring," Casey said. "Our discovery demand included everything the PPB has on our shooter. I'll call over to the DA this afternoon, make sure they know we mean *everything*, especially his disciplinary record."

I leaned forward. "The more we talk about this, the more I think we're onto something with the cop angle. They've been acting weird from day one. I knew they'd come after Elliott, but I figured they'd treat it like any other gang murder. Token investigation, assign it to any DA from violent crimes, lock Elliott up. Instead, they shoot Elliott, Nicole Astert takes point on the case and Buchanan offers me immunity if I flip. Now there's something going on with the shooter. All of which means this isn't just a couple of beat cops going rogue."

"That may be so, but all we have right now is speculation," Casey replied. "We need a credible alternate theory for Betts's murder. Saying 'the dude who shot Elliott was a bad cop' is a long way from being a home run."

"Okay," Tony said, "I'll see if I can work some other angles. Mick, I might need some help from you."

"You got it. Casey, when do we get the first round of discovery? Does the DA still jerk us around on timing?"

"Yeah. I'm guessing ten days to two weeks if we're lucky."

"Great. At least then we'll have a better idea of their case. Maybe we can poke some holes in it."

Casey nodded. "Yeah, that's when it gets real. I want to go over it with a fine-tooth comb. Every witness, every report, every exhibit—we dig and dig until we find the holes. And pray that holes are there to be found, because right now we don't have a defense."

"Then maybe we need to shake a few trees," I said.

"Got any trees in mind?"

"No, but I'll think of something." I paused. "There's still Betts's business to explore."

"Okay, so now we need to investigate that too. You realize we're not exactly running a big team here?"

"Tony and I will make it work." I looked at Tony and he nodded back.

"Fine. But be smart about it. Don't knock yourselves out.

We've got a lot of work to get ready for trial and I need you guys at your best. Take the weekend to recharge, okay?"

I hadn't thought about rest until Casey mentioned it. Six weeks had passed since we found Malik Betts's body in Elliott's backyard. Six weeks that felt like a lifetime. I was exhausted.

"Yes, boss." I stood up to leave and threw Casey a mock salute. She flipped me off as I headed for the door.

"What now?" Tony asked when we got outside.

"You heard the lady. Take the weekend off."

"You're not going to do that, are you?"

"Probably not, but I'll keep it lowkey. Maybe poke around a bit on Sunday. Tomorrow, I want to go see Elliott." I looked at my watch. "He should be out of surgery by now."

"Give him my best. Take care, Mick." Tony clapped me on the shoulder and walked away.

I stood there for a moment. What could I do now? I wanted to keep working, pushing, digging, doing anything I could to help Elliott. But I had nothing left in the tank.

It was brutally hot again and I didn't want to sit in my sweltering living room. I decided to go to Holman's for a drink and some dinner. Jeremy would probably be behind the bar and their burgers were okay.

Another thing I liked about my apartment was that it was so close to Holman's. My place was on Southeast Ankeny, just west of 28th, in a 1950s redbrick building called The Strand. There were plenty of Portland's hot new eateries nearby, but I didn't care about them. Holman's was only a few hundred yards away. I parked outside my place and walked over there.

Holman's was busier than usual. There was an empty seat by me at the bar, but the rest of the joint was full. A dive bar like Holman's was the perfect refuge from the relentless summer heat. Dark wood, red leather, faded carpet and industrial strength air conditioning. After a session there you still went home smelling of cigarettes, even though the smoking ban had been in place for years.

Jeremy came over as soon as he saw me. He spread his arms and his face lit up with mock surprise.

"Mick Ward! It's been a while!"

"Very funny." I'd been in the night before.

Jeremy smiled and shook my hand. "Want your usual?"

"Yeah. And keep them coming."

"You got it."

Jeremy threw some ice in a glass and poured. I called him Jeremy Jesus. He was a young born-again Christian with a ponytail, unkempt beard and neck tattoos, and he poured some of the strongest drinks in Portland.

Jeremy put a tall glass of clear liquid in front of me, a faint orange tinge visible in the dimly lit bar. He knew how to make a screwdriver just the way I liked it. I didn't always drink screwdrivers, but they were my go-to beverage when I was in the mood. They pack a punch, the clear spirit keeps the hangovers manageable, and you get a shot of vitamin C from the OJ. Although not so much the way Jeremy made them.

There was one other person sitting at the bar, three stools down from me. A dark-haired woman in blue medical scrubs. Her hair was pulled back in a tight bun and her pale skin was almost translucent in the dim bar light. She caught me looking at her, and she raised her eyebrows at me, a half-smile on her face.

"You just solved one of life's great mysteries for me," I ventured.

"What mystery is that?"

"I always wondered whether doctors wore their scrubs home or changed at work. Now I know."

She laughed. "That's a great life mystery?"

"What can I say? I lead a simple life."

She laughed again.

"Can I buy you a drink?"

"Sure, why not?" She drained her glass, the ice rattling as she put it back on the bar. "Rye on the rocks."

I waved to Jeremy. "Rye on the rocks for the lady, please."

"You got it." Jeremy poured the drink and put it in front of her.

I leaned over and held out my hand. "My name's Mick."

"Helen. Thanks for the drink." She shook my hand. I got a better look at her face. Helen looked early thirties, with dark eyes and thin red lips that stood out sharply against her pale skin. She also looked as tired as I felt.

"Was that really a great mystery for you?" Helen said.

"No. But I did wonder."

"You did?" she said, and took a gulp of rye. "Why?"

I couldn't think of anything to say. "Because you look so good in them."

She rolled her eyes. "Yeah, I'm 'Venus in Furs' tonight."

"You like The Velvet Underground?" I said. "Me too."

"I was thinking of the Sacher-Masoch novel," she replied, and cocked an eyebrow at me.

I'd never heard of the book or the guy, so I didn't say anything.

"Oh well," she said with a sigh, and drained her rye. She gathered up her things, grabbed a backpack from beside her stool, and left.

"I see you haven't lost your touch," Jeremy said.

I laughed. "Probably for the best."

He pointed at my glass. "You want another one?"

"No, I'm good." I finished my drink and went home.

TWENTY-THREE
WALK ON

Even though I was exhausted, I only slept fitfully. I kept waking up and thinking of Elliott, racking my brain to figure out who could be framing him. Eventually, a little after five, I gave up and got out of bed.

I made coffee and toast for breakfast and sat at the kitchen table, half asleep and fully brain dead. The caffeine slowly dragged me out of the fog, but I could tell today was going to be tough. Thankfully, I didn't have much on the agenda beyond going to see Elliott. I cleaned up my breakfast things and took a shower.

Then I remembered something else I meant to do today. I patted my jeans pocket and was relieved to find the check Tony gave me was still there. I deposited it with my bank's phone app. It was just about enough to cover what I owed Sarah in alimony, so I sent her a payment. I was almost two weeks late this month, but it wasn't hanging over my head anymore. The last thing I needed right now was another angry phone call.

I called Elliott to see if he was ready for a visitor. He sounded groggy, but keen, so I headed out.

Press interest must have died down pretty quickly since the

arraignment; when I got to the hospital, only Officer Wittkowski was guarding Elliott's door. He recognized me and let me in without saying anything. Elliott was lying in his bed, no longer hooked up to as many machines. The morphine drip was still there, and judging by the relaxed look on his face, he'd been using it. Hardly surprising given that his chest and back were encased in a rigid white plastic brace that looked like a stormtrooper's body armor.

I sat by his bed. "Hey, buddy, how are you feeling?"

"Probably better than you. But I've got morphine."

"Yeah, I can see that. How did the surgery go?"

Elliott sighed. "Okay, I guess. They got the bullet out, but apparently my spinal cord is damaged."

"What does that mean? Will you walk again?"

"Doctor Ross says maybe, but it's going to take intensive rehabilitation. Three months of inpatient treatment to restore lower limb function, then outpatient therapy a couple of times a week, probably for a year or two, and even then I might need a brace or a cane when they're done."

There was no way in hell Elliott would get that kind of specialist treatment in jail. His expression told me he knew that too.

"Sorry to hear that," I said.

"Thanks. What's happening on the case?"

I told him about Buchanan offering me immunity, and the shooter's disciplinary problems.

"Makes sense," he said. "I told you before, we need to look at the cops. They don't like me, Mick."

"Don't worry, we're working on it. Tony is investigating and we get discovery in a week or so. We haven't given up on the gang angle yet either."

"I told you, that isn't it. This is too complicated for gangbanger stuff."

"Maybe so. We're going to look at Betts's business some more, too. Anything you know about it that might help us?"

"No, I don't think so."

Elliott winced and squeezed the pain pump. I wanted to ask him more about Betts and his business, but that would have to wait. I put my hand on his shoulder.

"Get some rest. I'll come see you again soon."

"Okay." He looked up at me. "Can I ask you something?"

"Sure."

"When Buchanan offered you immunity, were you tempted?"

"Hell no."

"You don't think I killed Malik?"

"Of course not!" I squeezed his shoulder, gently. "Never have. Not once."

"Good," he said, and closed his eyes as the morphine kicked in.

I left quietly, troubled by what he'd asked me. Had I suspected he was guilty at any point? I guess I had. The first thing Tony said was that Elliott did it, and he was skeptical when I disagreed. The same thing happened with Casey. Each time, I'd wondered whether they were right. But Elliott's shocked reaction when we found the body told me all I needed to know. He couldn't fake that. He didn't kill Betts.

My phone rang as I got to my car. I guess I'd been expecting this call.

"Hi, Sarah."

"Hello, Mick," she said. "What's this payment you sent?"

"Alimony. What did you think?"

"I thought you couldn't afford it."

"Yeah, well. I made a bit of money, so there you go."

"Are you sure?"

"First you hassle me when I don't pay, now you hassle me

when I do. Make your mind up!" I took a deep breath. "Sorry. I didn't mean to snap. It's been a shitty time. Thanks for checking."

"Is it Elliott's case? I heard you're working on it."

"Yeah. It's not going well."

"Oh." She paused. "I always liked him, you know. I hope you work something out."

"Yeah, me too. Thanks for calling."

I hung up, unsure what to do next. I hadn't been outside long, and my T-shirt was already sticking to my chest through the heat, so lunch and a pint in the shaded beer garden at the Lucky Lab on Hawthorne seemed like a good option. Lunch, then home to rest up for the big weeks ahead.

TWENTY-FOUR

BE CAREFUL WHAT YOU ASK FOR

D iscovery arrived almost two weeks later, on a Thursday morning. Tony was already there when I arrived at Casey's office to help review it. There was a stack of documents on the table, close to two feet high. Casey had a smaller pile in front of her. She looked up as I walked in.

"Morning, Mick. I've got something to show you."

She stood and made her way to the copy room, opened the door, then gestured inside. A small folding table had been wedged in between the printer and supply cabinet, with a battered black office chair parked by it.

"It's your new office. What do you think?"

The table was barely four feet wide and the chair looked like it had been pulled out of a dumpster.

"Wow. I'm overcome with excitement."

Casey laughed. "It's not the executive suite, but it's all the space I have. Now that discovery is in, you're going to be working here full time until we're done with the trial. You'll need a desk, and that's the best I can do."

Back when I'd had my own practice, I'd rented a suite of office space. My desk had views out over the river and to Mount

Hood beyond. Now I'd be squeezing into a makeshift workspace in a closet.

"I'll make it work," I said.

Casey sat back down at the conference table. "Great. Right, let's review what they sent us."

I took a seat. Casey gestured at the stack of paperwork.

"We're not going through all of this today. But I pulled a few things from the response summary that you should see.

"First and foremost, they refused our request for material relating to Elliott's arrest. There's no video, no arrest report, nothing. We got the arresting officers' names and records. That's it. They claim this case is about who killed Betts, and since Betts was already dead when Elliott was arrested, anything related to the arrest is irrelevant."

"That's bullshit," I said. "We're going to move to compel, right?"

"Of course. In fact, that's your first job. Get me legal authority to back us up. I've got the basics on discovery being broad and that pretty much everything is allowable. I need a specific argument that the material is discoverable because it's relevant to the defense theory of the case."

"Shouldn't be too hard. What's next?"

Casey waved a binder at me. "We've got the pathologist's report. It puts the time of death as between noon and midnight on Friday, June 14. That's the night you guys went to the awards dinner, right?"

"It is. I picked Elliott up at his place around seven and dropped him off around eleven."

"I don't suppose you know where he was the rest of the time?"

"Not specifically. When I asked him, he basically said he was either at work or at home all week. We can check the details with him."

"Okay. Speaking of Elliott, next on the list is his criminal record. It's included in discovery under exhibits that may be introduced at trial. I want to exclude it as irrelevant, so that's another legal research task for you, Mick."

So that's why Casey had set up a desk for me. We were barely fifteen minutes into the meeting, and I already had enough work to keep me busy for a week or two. And there was the mountain of discovery paperwork to review. Before I could catch my breath, she took a sheaf of papers that were stapled together from Tony's pile and passed them to me.

"This is what we got on Sam Kavanagh, our shooter. It's supposed to be his full service record. I don't see any mention of disciplinary issues. I would have expected there to be incident reports, along with some bullshit excuse for why he wasn't disciplined, but there's nothing."

"That's weird," Tony said. "My guy is solid. He wouldn't have told me about Kavanagh having discipline issues if it didn't happen."

"Agreed," Casey replied. "If we're going to paint Kavanagh as a bad cop, we'll need evidence to back us up. Tony, you're on that one, right?"

"You got it."

Casey looked at me. "Are you okay, Mick?"

I pointed at the picture of Sam Kavanagh on the first page of his service record. "Kavanagh is a redhead. One of the cops who searched Elliott's place the night we found the body was a redhead."

"Interesting. Do you recognize his face?"

"No, I didn't get a good look at the guy. But I know I saw red hair."

Casey looked thoughtful. "Tony, can your guy find out whether Kavanagh was on duty June 14th?"

"I'm sure he can."

"Good. Now for the bad news. There are a couple of police reports you need to see." Casey grabbed some more papers and slid copies to Tony and me. "Now we know how the cops got probable cause to arrest Elliott."

I looked at the documents. The first one was a witness interview transcript from a woman named Mary Parkinson, who was present for the fight between Elliott and Betts at the NNC meeting. She claimed that Elliott had threatened to kill Betts.

"What a joke," I said, tossing the report on the table.

"It gets worse," Casey replied, pointing to the other document. "Read that one."

It was another transcript, this time from an interview with Donald Wayne Martin, the owner and sole proprietor of Shooter's Armory, a licensed gun store. Mr. Martin claimed that on Wednesday, June 12, Elliott Russell purchased a Ruger SR9 9mm handgun and a single box of ammunition from him.

I jumped up out of my seat. "You've got to be fucking kidding me!"

"You don't think it's true, do you?" Casey said.

"Of course not!" I prowled around the office, fighting the urge to smash everything in sight. "It's complete bullshit. How did they come up with this crap?"

Casey closed her laptop and sighed. "I knew they'd come up with something."

"What do you mean?"

"Remember that gun you removed from Elliott's place?" she said. "Ever since you told me about it, I've been wondering what they would do in response. If someone planted that gun, they would have been pissed when the cops didn't find it. Without the gun, there's no physical evidence tying Elliott to the crime. You put a big hole in their case by disposing of it. So I figured they'd try something else to make the case against him watertight, I just didn't know what. Now I do."

"Yeah, suddenly they have a mystery witness who claims he sold Elliott a 9mm handgun two days before Betts was killed with the same type of weapon. Fuck!" I put my hands behind my head. "There has to be some way we can discredit this guy. Does he have security video showing Elliott there?"

"Probably not, but you know what he'll say," Casey said. "It was months ago, so it's been erased. Unless we can come up with witnesses to say Elliott was nowhere near that store on the date in question, we're screwed. And even if we can, it's down to who the jury believes—us or them."

"We need to talk to this guy," I replied.

Casey frowned. "Do you think he'll take our call?"

"Not if he knows who we are. But I could go to his store and pretend to be a customer."

"That's not a bad idea," Casey said. "But not today. You need to calm down before you go see him."

"Yeah, you're right. I'll do it tomorrow. We can spend today getting background on him."

"Good." Casey sat back and spread her arms. "So where does all this leave us?"

I pointed at the stack of papers on the table. "All this bullshit has me thinking Elliott might be right. We need to look harder at the cops. Starting with Sam Kavanagh, and why his record looks so clean."

"I agree," Tony said. "Let me take that. I can look for any other connections while I'm finding out why Kavanagh has a clean record."

"Okay," Casey replied. "We still need to close the loop on the gang angle, too. Where are we at on that?"

"I think we can park it for now," I said. "We know it wasn't the Bloods, given the meth angle and what Billy said about them being pissed Betts is dead. I thought it might be the Crips, because Elliott took money from Betts, but I poked around some more and they didn't even know that went down. Plus, now we have discovery, I think Elliott was right. This plan is too complicated for them. No way they could plant witnesses like the gun store owner."

"Makes sense. Speaking of Elliott, we need to talk to him about the discovery. Mick, let's head over to the hospital. Tony, I think we can cut you loose. You've got enough to get on with. Call me if you find anything."

"You got it," Tony said. He gathered his things and left.

Casey gestured at the pile of discovery papers. "What do you think?"

"To use a technical term, I think we're deeply fucked," I said.

"Yeah, pretty much." Casey sighed. "That gun store owner's testimony hurts us. If the jury hears that Elliott bought a gun two days before the shooting, it's all over. Any thoughts on what we can do about it?"

"Not at first glance. I can't see any grounds to exclude it. Which means our only option is to find a way to wreck his credibility on the witness stand."

"Easier said than done."

"Yeah. Let me see what I can get when I visit him tomorrow. And we can have Tony poke into his background, see if that turns anything up."

"Okay." Casey went to stand, then stopped. "There's one more thing. Buchanan called me this morning. They're transferring Elliott to Inverness on Monday."

"Could this day get any better?" I said, shaking my head ruefully. "All right. Let's go break the bad news to Elliott."

TWENTY-FIVE

BAD NEWS COMES IN THREES

C asey had parked at the building, so we took her car to the hospital. It was a Subaru Forester, which wasn't a surprise. You can't throw a stone without hitting a Subaru in Portland. Casey's was about fifteen years old, with a snowboard rack on the roof and the clear coat faded off much of its green paint. Given the state of Casey's office, I expected the interior to be covered in paperwork and fast-food wrappers, but when I got in it was showroom clean and tidy. I raised my eyebrows.

"What?" Casey said, as she put her seat belt on.

"Nice ride, Counselor."

"I'm not a complete slob, you know."

"I didn't say a word."

Casey smiled, started the car and drove off.

Elliott was propped up in bed when we got to the hospital. He still wore the stormtrooper body brace, but the morphine drip was gone and he looked much stronger than the last time I'd seen him. There was a wheelchair parked by his bed.

"Is that for you?" I said.

"Yeah, I'm allowed to spend two hours a day out of bed."

I was about to say something positive, but that meant he was closer to being moved to jail, so I just nodded.

Casey sat in the visitor's chair. "How are you feeling?"

"Better," Elliott replied. "Stronger."

"Good." Casey opened her briefcase. "We got discovery materials from the prosecution today and there are a few things we need to discuss. First, we got the pathologist's report. It puts Malik's time of death as between noon and midnight on Friday, June 14. That's the day of the awards dinner, so we know you were with Mick from about seven to eleven. Where were you the rest of the time?"

Elliott put his head back and stared at the ceiling. "Let me see. I worked until about two or so, then I had a meeting with a couple of donors and a campaign planning session later that afternoon. I'd have to check my calendar for exact times, but I think I was home at around four. Then I hung out and worked on my speech until Mick picked me up."

"Three hours," I said. "Plenty of time to find Malik Betts, shoot him and bury his body."

Elliott glared at me.

"Sorry, buddy, but that's what the prosecutor will tell the jury."

"Mick's right," Casey said. "You didn't have any visitors? Make any calls?"

"No, not that I remember. But that's a good point. Wouldn't my cell phone show I was at home the whole time?"

"It'll show your cell phone was at home the whole time. Which is why you left it at home when you went to kill Betts." I held my hands up. "Again, that's just what the prosecutor will say."

"We'll pull your phone records, just in case," Casey said. "Maybe you sent a text, or did something else that puts you in the same place as your phone."

"It's worth a shot," Elliott replied, without much conviction.

"We'll interview your neighbors too. See if anyone saw you coming and going, or saw your car parked out front."

"Okay. What's next?"

"There are a couple of witness statements I want to ask you about," Casey said. "The first one is from a woman who saw your fight with Betts at the NNC meeting. She said you threatened to kill him. Did you?"

Elliott tried to shrug, then winced in pain as his body brace hitched up. "I don't know. Maybe. It was a fight."

"Okay, let's leave that for now. The other one is more important. A gun store owner claims you bought a 9mm handgun from him two days before Betts was killed. I'm guessing that's not true?"

"No way!" Elliott snapped. "That's bullshit. I never bought no gun."

"I thought not," Casey replied. "We're working on how to deal with that."

"Phone records," I said. "While we're checking them to see if Elliott was at home at the time of the murder, we can check whether he was anywhere near the gun store on that day. Like I said before, it's not perfect, but it could help."

Casey nodded. "Good idea. Now, Elliott, there's one more thing. Detective Buchanan called this morning, to inform me that you're being transferred to Inverness jail on Monday."

"It just ain't my day, is it?"

"I know it's small consolation, but there are worse jails than Inverness," Casey said. "It's mostly nonviolent offenders. And we're still working on our investigation. Something will come up."

"Easy for you to say, Counselor. You ain't the one going to jail on Monday."

Casey found something to busy herself with in her briefcase. I reached out and put my hand on Elliott's arm.

"Is there anything we can do for you?" I said.

Elliott looked at me sheepishly. "Yeah, there is. I need to go to the bathroom."

"You want me to help you into the wheelchair?"

"It's more than that," he said. He rapped his knuckles on his body brace. "I can't reach below my waist." He looked up at me, eyebrows raised.

I shook my head and smiled. "Oh man, if I'd known this was in the job description I'd have run a mile."

I helped Elliott into the wheelchair and pushed him down the hall to the bathroom. He was able to lift himself onto the toilet using the wall bars. We managed the rest of the process without making a mess or looking each other in the eye, then washed up and went back to his room.

"Thanks, Mick," he said. "I owe you one."

"Any time, buddy. You know that." I smiled, trying to look calm. But all I could think about was Elliott in a body cast and wheelchair at Inverness jail. I thought about our bathroom visit. Good luck getting a prison guard to help. How else would he manage? No doubt about it, life for my friend was going to get a whole lot worse.

We said our goodbyes and left. Casey and I didn't speak on the way to the car, both lost in our thoughts about Elliott's predicament.

We left the parking lot and headed back to the office.

"I know what you're thinking," Casey said, "but Elliott will be fine."

"No, he won't. Being in jail in his condition is going to be dreadful. But I'm more worried about keeping him safe. Think about it. Someone's trying to frame him for murder. A cop shot him for no good reason. Whoever is behind all this wants Elliott out of the way real bad. What's to stop them paying some Aryan Nation goon to shank him in the shower?"

"I know. I'll talk to Buchanan and make sure Elliott has vulnerable population status. In fact, I'll petition Judge Obrecht for it tomorrow. Make it official."

"Thanks." I wasn't convinced it would help, but I didn't know what else we could do. Elliott was going to jail and once inside, he'd be beyond our reach. I stared out the window and said a silent prayer for my friend.

TWENTY-SIX
NEIGHBORHOOD WATCH

The next morning, I got up early. Shooter's Armory didn't open until 11, so I dived into online research on Donald Martin and his store. It was on Northeast Sandy Boulevard, out past 82nd Avenue in the Roseway neighborhood. Roseway was a rundown part of town where trailer parks sat side by side with used car lots and pawn shops. The store's website had an American flag and a "Thin Blue Line" banner at the top, but I didn't read too much into that. After all, it was no surprise to see a gun store owner on the right of the political spectrum, especially when that same owner had come forward to testify against the local Black Lives Matter organizer. According to its website, the store sold a wide range of guns and ammunition, and had an indoor shooting range at the back. They offered discounts to serving and former members of law enforcement and the military.

Donald Martin the individual wasn't exactly a surprise either. He was active on social media and had recently posted pictures of himself at Proud Boys rallies and other white supremacist events. He didn't have a criminal record. The store's information page mentioned he was ex-military, but that was all I could find. Everything was consistent with him wanting to testify against Elliott, but it wasn't enough to provoke him into fabricating a gun sale to do so. Especially when his witness statement identified exactly the type of gun that had been planted at Elliott's house. There had to be some connection between Donald Martin and whoever was framing Elliott. I called Tony and asked him to see whether he could find anything.

I'd unearthed all that I could by poking around on the internet, so I decided to hit the road. I figured Donald Martin might not respond well to lawyer attire, so I changed into jeans, work boots and a flannel shirt, then drove out to Shooter's Armory.

The gun store occupied a squat brick building, with a pothole-filled parking lot out front. Its tan paint was faded and stained, and heavy iron bars had been fitted over the windows and door. A brass bell jingled as I entered.

The man behind the counter matched the photos of Donald Martin I'd seen online. "Hi there. Can I help you?"

"Uh, yeah, I hope so," I said, trying to sound nervous. I looked around the store. There were racks of gun bags and accessories in the middle, and boxes of bullets filled a couple of shelves on the right wall, under a sign saying 'Please don't open the ammo.' A couple of AR-15 assault rifles hung on the wall behind the counter, and the glass display case was full of handguns. Between them stood the man who had greeted me. He looked about fifty, shorter than average, with a salt and pepper goatee and a paunch that stretched the buttons on his red plaid shirt.

I walked over to the counter, which had several "Thin Blue

Line" stickers on the glass.

"I, uh, I think I need to buy a gun."

"Well, you came to the right place," he said. "My name's Don. What kind of gun are you looking for?"

"Hey, Don, I'm Gary," I replied. "Um, I'm not sure what I need. Some kind of handgun, I guess. I want to be able to protect myself and my family, you know? I mean these riots, it's terrifying. This shit's been going on too long."

"Yeah. Drives me crazy to see those punks tearing up our town. I got a lot of cops as customers. I can't believe they have to deal with that crap."

"I know," I said. "It's getting so this town isn't safe for regular folks anymore. Hell, the whole country is going that way. I wish we could do something about it."

Martin lifted his chin. "Yeah, well, I'm gonna do what I can."

"What do you mean?"

"You know that punk Elliott Russell? The BLM guy who killed that gangbanger? Well, he bought the gun he used from me. And the cops want me to testify at his trial."

"No way! Are you gonna do it?"

"Damn right I am. Like you say, we all have to do something to make that shit stop."

"Wow, that's crazy. When did he come in here?"

"Two days before he shot that guy."

I continued playing dumb. "No way! How did you know it was him?"

"I saw his picture on the news." He nodded slowly. "I reported it right away. Anyway, tell me again what kind of gun you're looking for?"

"Uh, something for protection. I don't know much about guns, but my buddy has a SIG Sauer and he says it's awesome. You carry those?"

"Sure." He opened the back of the display case, took a couple of handguns out, and laid them on the counter. "Either of these should be good for what you need."

"Can you tell me about them?"

Martin launched into a sales pitch about the two SIG Sauer models he'd chosen. I tried to look interested while at the same time fighting the urge to climb over the counter and choke him out.

"I can do the P938 as a package with a bag and two boxes of ammo for six fifty. The P365X will run you a hundred bucks more, but the magazine holds more shells and honestly, it's a simpler weapon for a beginner like you. No offense."

"None taken," I said. "Let me think about it. What time do you close today? I can come back later this afternoon."

"No problem, take your time. We close at five every day."

"Great, thanks." I turned to leave.

I got in my car and called Billy Hinds to check a couple of things, then called Casey.

"Hey, Mick, what's up?"

"Not much," I said, eyeing the door to Shooter's Armory to make sure Donald Martin didn't emerge. "I just got done with our friendly neighborhood gun store owner."

"What's your take on Mr. Martin?"

"He's pretty much what we expected. Middle-aged white bread guy, lots of cops for customers, big time Thin Blue Line supporter. He'll come across well when he first gets on the stand, but you can go after him on cross. I found a bunch of hardcore right-wing stuff on his social media. And Oregon requires background checks for a handgun purchase. There's no way he ran one on Elliott, because it would have flagged his felony conviction."

"He'll probably just say Elliott used someone else's ID."

"So, you ask him how he recognized Elliott from TV, but

didn't recognize that the ID Elliott used wasn't his. Better still, let's subpoena all the background checks he ran on June 12th. I wouldn't be surprised if there isn't a single African American customer among them."

"Good thinking," Casey said. "Anything else?"

"Yeah. I called Billy Hinds and had him check Elliott's calendar for June 12th. He had a couple of meetings, but there are gaps in there big enough for him to be able to drive out to Shooter's and back. Billy says he'll get witnesses who can testify Elliott was at work all day, though."

"Okay. It would help if they were telling the truth. Much harder for the DA to make them look stupid on the witness stand that way."

"That's exactly what I said."

"Good. Maybe this guy won't be so bad for us after all." Casey sighed. "Are you coming to the office?"

"Yeah, I'm on my way."

Casey and I spent the rest of the day doing legal research and drafting our motion in response to the discovery. We wanted the judge to force the prosecution to turn over material related to Elliott's arrest and Sam Kavanagh's disciplinary record, and to prevent them from bringing up Elliott's criminal record at trial. The hearing would be a good opportunity to get a read on Judge Obrecht and how he viewed the case. We felt good about the first point—as far as we could tell, the DA had no good argument for not turning over material on Elliott's arrest and shooting. But the other two points would be interesting. The DA said Kavanagh's file didn't exist, and excluding Elliott's record would be tough. Where the judge came down on those questions would tell us a lot about likely future rulings and help us plan our strategy accordingly. We wrapped up about eight. Casey told me to go home and get some sleep. I said I would, but I knew I wouldn't catch a wink.

TWENTY-SEVEN
STRANGER DANGER

Monday afternoon, we drove out to Inverness jail to see Elliott. We'd spent the morning finalizing and filing our motions to force the DA to turn over the material on Elliott's shooting and Kavanagh's disciplinary file, and to exclude Elliott's criminal record. Around the time we finished, Buchanan called to tell us Elliott had been transferred and was now in protective custody. Rather than trust him, we decided to make sure the protection was adequate ourselves.

Inverness jail was a Multnomah County facility, just off of Interstate 205 up by the Columbia River. It mostly housed first-time offenders and people awaiting trial on a variety of charges. It was relatively modern, and not as overcrowded and cramped as many other jails. But it still had its share of violence, so we needed to know Elliott would be safe.

Casey turned off the Interstate at Airport Way. A couple of quick right turns had us in the Inverness parking lot, where she pulled into a visitor's space. The jail looked like a pile of giant concrete boxes stacked on top of each other. The gray walls were almost entirely blank, broken up only by a few narrow windows. We went inside, signed in and took a seat in the waiting area.

I'd spent a lot of time in this room, waiting for meetings with clients. It usually took about an hour and today was no exception. I killed time flicking through an old copy of *Sports Illustrated*. Casey worked her phone, her heel tapping idly on the floor.

Eventually we were called for our turn. A corrections officer led us through to the visiting area. Unlike many state and federal prisons, Inverness hadn't switched to video- or phone-only meetings with inmates. It still had a series of four Perspex-walled rooms, each with a table bolted to the floor and a couple of blue plastic chairs.

The officer led us to the end room, let us in, then closed the door behind us. Elliott was already inside, sitting at the table in his wheelchair. He had on orange jail overalls, and his full-body harness had been replaced by a contraption with a T-shaped brace across his shoulders and a rigid metal rod down the back. Three sets of black elastic straps held it in place, pulled tight across his shoulders, chest and waist. It looked even less comfortable than the stormtrooper outfit had been.

"Good to see you, buddy," I said. "How are you doing?"

"Hey Mick, Casey. Good to see you too." Elliott sighed. "I'm okay. Can't say I'm happy to be here, but I gotta get used to it."

Casey pulled out a notepad. "Tell us about your situation here. Has anyone talked to you about protective custody?"

"Yeah, they put me in the administrative segregation wing. That's all they've got, so I'm in with all the disciplinary cases. Still, it keeps me out of general population. Given my condition, that's a good thing."

"Okay, good to know. We'll stop by the administration office on our way out, see if there's anything we can do to make it better." Casey made a couple of notes on her pad.

"Thanks." Elliott looked at me. "How's life on the outside?"

"Not the same without you. By the way, I talked to Billy yesterday. All the NNC crew were asking after you."

"Yeah, I bet they were. Now I'm gone, they're all upset because they've got to do some work for a change."

I laughed. "Ha, probably. Hey, we filed our motions in response to discovery this morning. Hearing on them should be in a couple of weeks."

"Good," Elliott said, his face hardening. "I want to know what kind of bullshit the cops made up about shooting me."

"Yeah, us too," I replied. "Also, I went to see that gun store owner. Not surprisingly, he's your standard issue racist nutjob. It's early, but I think Casey can destroy him on the witness stand."

Casey frowned at me. "Careful. You don't know that."

"Come on, you got this." I wanted Casey to agree, if only to make Elliott feel better, but all I got out of her was a slight nod.

We talked for a while longer. Elliott told us about the last couple of days. The new back brace gave him a greater range of motion than the body cast. However, he still needed help to use the bathroom. But he was now able to spend most of the day out of bed and using the wheelchair, so that was an improvement.

We stopped by administration when we were done, as Casey had promised. I was pleasantly surprised to hear that Buchanan had made it very clear Elliott was to be protected, with the staff under strict instructions to make sure he was never left alone with other members of the prison population.

We set off back to the office, and my phone rang as we pulled onto the Interstate.

"Hey, Tony, what's up?"

"Hey, Mick. I got some more information on our friend Kavanagh."

"Great. Hold on a second. I'm in the car with Casey, so let

me put you on speaker." I put my phone on the center console. "Okay, what have you got?"

"I found out about Kavanagh's disciplinary record. He's got a file, all right. A thick one. I don't know where the crap we got in discovery came from, but it sure as shit isn't Kavanagh's actual disciplinary record."

Casey's head jerked back. "Are you sure?"

"My guy's never let me down before."

"Interesting," Casey said. "I'm going to amend our motion to compel as soon as we're back at the office. Thanks, Tony. Anything else?"

"No. Mick, I'm looking into Donald Martin, but there's nothing obvious linking him to Elliott or the case. This could take a while."

"I know," I said. "Do what you can. We can take another swing at him after the motions to compel. Maybe we'll get something that connects to him."

"Maybe." He didn't sound confident.

"Thanks, man. Talk to you later."

Back at the office, Casey and I spent a couple of hours beefing up our discovery motion on Kavanagh's disciplinary record and filing the amended version. Casey called Judge Obrecht's clerk, to make sure the judge got it before he left for the weekend. The clerk told us that the hearing on both motions we filed was scheduled for a week from Thursday.

I finished up work and went home. Around eight, I was hungry, so I wandered over to Holman's. The bar was mostly full, but there were a couple of empty stools, so I grabbed one. When Jeremy saw me, he waved the vodka bottle at me and raised his eyebrows. I nodded.

He made my drink and brought it over. "Hey, Mick, how's life?"

"Hey, Jeremy." I jerked a thumb at the kitchen. "Any specials tonight?"

He looked nervous. "Irish stew."

"I'll bet that's selling great in this heat. I'll take a burger, please."

Jeremy smiled and went off to put my order in. I sat there and sipped my drink for a while, then finished it and gestured for another.

I sat there, toying with my drink and trying to think about anything except Elliott sitting alone in his cell. It had been almost two months since we found Malik Betts's body, and we were still no closer to figuring out who set the whole thing up. If anything, we had even more questions now. Who put Donald Martin up to testifying against Elliott? And why choose him? Meanwhile, what happened to Sam Kavanagh's disciplinary record? The answer to any one of these questions might break the whole case open, but we had nothing.

"Are you okay, Mick?" Jeremy put my burger down in front of me.

His voice snapped me out of my reverie. "Yeah, I'm fine. Why?"

"You looked like you were a thousand miles away."

I felt like I was a thousand miles from finding any answers.

"I'm just tired," I said. "Can I get that burger to go?"

TWENTY-EIGHT
ALTERNATE REALITY

T he hearing on our discovery motions was scheduled for
10 am, so Casey and I arrived at Multnomah County
Courthouse around 9:45am. The courthouse was a concrete
and stone structure with Greek-style columns dominating its
imposing façade. It had been in use since 1909 and was due to
close next year. The building needed a comprehensive seismic
retrofit, which the County had determined wasn't cost-effective,
so they built a new courthouse instead. The new building, a
modern glass and steel design four blocks to the east, lacked the
gravitas of the current one and I couldn't help feeling that
something special would be lost when this place closed.

We took the elevator up to Judge Obrecht's courtroom on
the third floor. As the elevator doors opened, Detective
Buchanan was standing outside. He made to get in, then saw us
and stepped aside, not meeting our eyes as we passed. He got in
the elevator and the doors closed behind him.

"Strange for him not to say anything," I said.

Casey nodded. "Yeah."

Unlike the utilitarian Justice Center hearing room used for
Elliott's arraignment, Judge Obrecht's court was a classic old-

style courtroom. All the furniture was dark wood, polished and foreboding. The floors were marble tile and our footsteps echoed off the vaulted ceiling as we made our way to the defense table. Nicole Astert was already in place at the prosecution table. She didn't look up from her files.

Judge Obrecht emerged from his chambers at precisely 9 am. He was a short, rotund man with thinning brown hair and thick wire-rimmed glasses. He pulled back his chair, smoothed his flowing black robe, and sat.

"Good morning, all," he said. "Today we're going to proceed on three motions filed by the defense. I have a motion to exclude Mr. Russell's prior record, and two motions to compel discovery. Ms. Raife, is that correct?"

"Yes, Your Honor," Casey said.

"And are you ready to proceed?"

"I am."

"And you, Ms. Astert? Is the prosecution ready to respond?"

"We are, Your Honor," she replied.

"Good." Judge Obrecht shuffled some papers. "I've read the motions and the prosecution responses. I think the issues are clear in each case. We'll deal with the issue of Mr. Russell's record first, then move on to the two discovery requests. Ms. Raife, you believe that Mr. Russell's record is inadmissible?"

Casey stood up. "I do, Your Honor. It is well established that evidence of prior crimes is not admissible to show that a defendant acted in a similar manner in the current case. Yet the prosecution seeks to use my client's arrest for firearms possession more than a decade ago as evidence that he is a killer. Clearly, such evidence cannot be admitted."

"Ms. Astert?" Judge Obrecht said.

"Your Honor, evidence of past crimes is admissible as proof of motive, opportunity and intent. In this case, the defendant was arrested with a firearm mere days after the deceased killed his brother. The evidence is admissible to show that the defendant is able to obtain firearms, and that he had a longstanding motive to murder Mr. Betts."

"Oh come on, Your Honor," Casey said. "The prosecution is talking about my client's state of mind ten years ago. How can that possibly have any relevance to current events?"

Nicole made to reply, but the judge held up a hand to stop her. He looked at Casey. "Ms. Raife, it's unusual to seek to exclude evidence this early in proceedings," he said. "And the prosecution has a point about relevance as to motive. So I'm going to defer my ruling on this motion. Let's see how things play out and I will reconsider at the pretrial evidentiary hearing."

"Yes, Your Honor," Casey replied.

Judge Obrecht opened another folder on his desk. "Moving on. The matter of Officer Sam Kavanagh's disciplinary record. Ms. Raife, you claim that Officer Kavanagh has an extensive disciplinary record that was not provided to you in discovery, despite your request. Correct?"

"Yes, Your Honor. We have credible information from a reliable source stating that Officer Kavanagh has been the subject of disciplinary action on several occasions."

"And why is Officer Kavanagh's record relevant to this matter? As the prosecution's response states, this case is about the murder of Malik Betts. Mr. Betts was long deceased before Officer Kavanagh entered the picture."

"Your Honor, the defense contends that Mr. Russell is the victim of a conspiracy. The same person or persons who murdered Malik Betts placed his body in Mr. Russell's yard to frame him for the murder. Shortly thereafter, Mr. Russell was the victim of an unprovoked shooting by Officer Kavanagh. Material is discoverable if it is reasonably likely to lead to the discovery of admissible evidence. We have a right to review

Officer Kavanagh's record for information relevant to the defense theory of the case."

Nicole rolled her eyes. "Your Honor, the defense is clutching at straws. This fishing expedition cannot be allowed. And besides, the prosecution turned over all the information made available to us. My office requested Officer Kavanagh's full record from Central Precinct command. If no disciplinary file was provided, I can only assume the file does not exist."

Judge Obrecht raised his eyebrows. "Ms. Astert, as you are aware, this is a capital murder case. As such, you need to do better than just assume. When no file was provided, did you call Central Precinct to check whether they had any disciplinary records for Officer Kavanagh?"

"No, Your Honor."

Judge Obrecht frowned. "I see. Lieutenant Hayes is still in command of Central Precinct, is he not?"

"He is, Your Honor."

"Then you will call the Lieutenant immediately upon leaving my courtroom today. Inform him that Ms. Raife's office is to receive Officer Kavanagh's entire disciplinary record by close of business today. Every last scrap of paper. Make sure he understands that I will be most displeased if it is not delivered."

"Yes, Your Honor. The prosecution has one request, though. We need time to review the file and potentially redact sensitive information relevant to ongoing investigations."

"Very well. You have one week from today. And in future, please do not assume others are complying with their legal duties. As the lead prosecutor on this case, it is your responsibility to ensure that they do so. Is that also clear?"

Nicole bowed her head. "Yes, Your Honor."

"Thank you. Now, our final matter—records related to Mr. Russell's arrest." Judge Obrecht took his glasses off and pinched his nose. "The law in this matter is clear. Discovery is broad and inclusive, particularly where necessary to protect a defendant's rights in a capital murder case. Ms. Astert, you claim the material is not relevant, but relevance is only an issue if Ms. Raife tries to introduce evidence at trial. It does not affect whether it is discoverable, as any second-year law student would know. So, I am going to rule in favor of Ms. Raife and order the material to be disclosed immediately. And I am again going to remind you to comply with your legal obligations to the defendant."

Nicole took a deep breath and nodded. Casey and I smiled at each other.

"Don't get too excited, Ms. Raife," the judge said. "My ruling comes with a strong caution. I have reviewed the material in question. It includes graphic footage of Mr. Russell being shot during his arrest. This city has suffered violent unrest on a nightly basis since the death of Andre Gladen. Should this video be made public, I shudder to think of the chaos that would follow. I thereby order that the material be sealed. Ms. Raife, you and your team are to treat it with utmost confidentiality. Rest assured I will impose the strictest possible sanctions for failure to do so."

"I understand, Your Honor," Casey said.

Judge Obrecht banged his gavel. "In that case, we are adjourned. Good day."

We stood, and the judge left the courtroom. Nicole gathered her files and hurried out, clearly chastened by the judge's criticism.

"That could have been worse," I said.

"Yeah. Let's get back to the office. I want to be there when that video arrives."

We stopped at Bae's and grabbed takeout fried chicken sandwiches on the way back. Once we returned to the office, we set up around the conference table and ate our lunch in silence.

I finished my sandwich, balled up the wrapper and tossed it at the trash can. It bounced off the rim and rolled under Casey's desk.

"Don't give up the day job," she said.

"Yeah, because it pays so well." I reached under the desk for the wrapper, put it in the trash and sat back down. "Sounds like Judge Obrecht won't take any crap from the prosecution. That should be good for us."

"Definitely. But it means we'll have to be sharp as well. He won't take any crap from us either."

"True. Anyway, I'm going to get back to work. Give me a yell when anything comes in from the DA's office."

I went back to my folding desk in the copy room and dived into my legal research task list. I'd been at it for about an hour when a courier arrived at the office. Casey accepted a package and opened it.

"Looks like a USB drive and a note." She unfolded the note. "Says here the arrest material is on the USB, and that it's encrypted and copy-protected to prevent us making duplicates. Want to check it out with me?"

"Of course."

"Okay. Notes from the investigation into his shooting are also enclosed. Oh, and get this for a shock development. Apparently, Officer Sam Kavanagh *does* have a disciplinary file. They're going to do their redactions and get it to us by Wednesday of next week."

"What a shock." I pointed at the USB drive. "Right now, I want to see what's on that."

Casey grabbed her laptop and plugged the USB drive in. It contained a single compressed folder.

"Looks like some PDFs and a video," Casey said. "I think we start with the video."

"Definitely."

Casey opened the video file. It was from a patrol car dashcam, with the date and time shown in the bottom left corner. The video began at 10:13pm on June 18, the night Elliott was shot. The video showed the back of Elliott's car, a ten-year-old red Honda Civic. The patrol car's flashing lights played a red and blue strobe effect on the Honda.

A police officer entered the shot from the left, moving toward Elliott's car, with his gun extended. I assumed it was Kavanagh.

"Get out of the car slowly, hands on your head," he shouted.

Elliott said something in response, but the audio wasn't clear enough to understand him.

"I said get out of the car!"

Elliott's door opened slowly, and he emerged, hands on his head. He stood upright and went to say something. Before he could get a word out, Kavanagh fired three shots in quick succession, the noise startling us both. Elliott jerked backwards as the shots hit him, slammed into his open car door, then slid to the ground.

After the roar of the gunshots, the sudden silence was eerie.

Another officer appeared on screen from the right. He ran toward Elliott. "What the fuck are you doing?" he yelled.

"He went for his gun! I had to fire!"

"His hands were on his head! I didn't see a gun!"

"You were in the car. You can't see anything from back there!"

"Shit, he's fucked up." The officer knelt by Elliott. "He's still breathing. Call an ambulance! Now!"

Kavanagh didn't move. The other officer looked back over his shoulder. "Call a goddamn ambulance!"

Kavanagh still didn't move, so the other officer grabbed his shoulder microphone and radioed for an ambulance, then he bent over Elliott.

"Can I have some help, here?" he yelled. "He's bleeding real bad!"

Kavanagh ignored him and walked back to the patrol car. He leaned in and reached for something on the dashboard. The screen went black.

Casey and I stared at each other, eyes wide.

"Fuck me," she said eventually.

"Play it again."

By the time the second run through ended, I was so angry I could barely speak. I took a deep breath and composed myself. "I don't know about you, but to me it looked like Kavanagh set out to execute Elliott."

"Careful with that word," Casey said.

"What else do you want to call it?"

"It sure as hell wasn't a regular traffic stop. I can see why the judge wants it sealed."

"Open the other attachments. Let's see what they say."

Casey clicked the touchpad a couple of times. "Okay, looks like we have both officers' incident reports and a preliminary investigation file." She clicked again, then scrolled down a few pages. "PPB has initiated a use of deadly force investigation and the shooting has been referred to the DA's office for potential criminal review. Kavanagh is on temporary altered duty pending the outcome of the investigation."

"Temporary altered duty? He should be behind fucking bars!"

"We both know that's not going to happen."

"It's bullshit, but you're right. Why are you smiling?"

"We might just have a winner here."

I frowned. "What are you talking about?"

"Our SOD defense. We've been looking for a plausible Other Dude. Sam Kavanagh, step right up. Think about it. We show the video to the jury. We ask them what type of man would just shoot Elliott like that. Then we put Kavanagh on the stand and make him squirm. It doesn't matter whether he killed Betts, so long as we make the jury think he might have."

"What if Kavanagh was on duty the night Betts was shot?"

"Tony's checking that, right?"

"Yeah."

"Okay, so let's wait and see. And if he was on duty, we can still use it. Make it look like Kavanagh is part of a bigger conspiracy. Someone went for Betts, then for Elliott."

I paused for a moment. "You know, there's something else we can use this for too. Bail."

"Tell me more."

"I don't have the statute in front of me right now, but I'm pretty sure it says that a defendant in a murder case is not entitled to bail if the proof is evident or the presumption strong that the person is guilty. We can use the video to rebut the State's strong presumption argument, and with Elliott in a wheelchair, he's certainly not a flight risk. So there's no basis to hold him without bail anymore."

"I knew I hired you for a reason. See if you can get me some case law and we'll file a motion for a release hearing."

"What do we tell Elliott?"

"I don't want to get his hopes up too high, but we'll tell him about the bail motion."

"He's going to want to see the video," I said.

"We need to hold off on that. Given the judge's order, we can't just whip out a laptop in an Inverness visiting room."

"I know." I checked my watch. "Look, it's too late to go see him today. But let's go out there tomorrow morning. Maybe we can call them beforehand and set up a secure viewing."

"Okay, sounds good. Let's take a look at the officers' reports."

Casey opened Officer Kavanagh's. The first couple of pages

were routine cop speak about their shift that night. Then Kavanagh described seeing a Honda Civic driving erratically on North Rosa Parks Way. When they turned on their lights and told the driver to pull over, the Civic sped off. A chase ensued, but after three blocks the Civic pulled over. Kavanagh claimed he told the driver to exit the car with his hands on his head, but when the door opened, he saw the driver reach for a weapon. Fearing for his life, he discharged his firearm three times.

"Can you believe that bullshit?" I said. "Putting aside the whole load of crap about Elliott going for a weapon, there's no way he would ever run from the cops. He's smarter than that. And besides, he knew he was likely to be arrested soon anyway."

"Probably, but I'll bet any amount you care to name, his partner's statement says the same thing."

Casey opened it, and sure enough, it repeated the same story about Elliott speeding off, almost word for word. As for the actual shooting, Kavanagh's partner Officer Dwayne Wright claimed to have been unable to see anything that happened. Which was interesting, given that in the video he clearly said Elliott had his hands on his head.

Casey pushed the laptop away. "We have to get this video in front of the jury."

"Definitely. If we do that, there's no way they'll convict Elliott."

"We need a strong argument that it's relevant to our SOD theory. You know the DA is going to claim the video is too prejudicial for the jury to see. So we'll need to make it watertight." Casey pointed at my desk in the copy room. "Get me some case law, hotshot."

TWENTY-NINE
FISH IN A BARREL

Casey called Inverness the next morning and they agreed to let us use a secure room for our visit. We arrived right at the start of visiting time, but they still made us wait an hour to see Elliott.

The room they led us to was much the same as the regular room, only instead of being clear, the walls were painted a drab pale brown and the only window was a small opening in the steel door. Elliott was already in the room when the guard led us through. Even though I'd been visiting most days, I still got a shock each time I saw him in a wheelchair and an orange jail suit.

"Hey, guys," he said, "how did the hearing go?"

"Good, for the most part," Casey replied, as we sat down. "The judge isn't going to let the prosecution get away with anything. And we got the material from the night you were arrested."

She paused and looked at me.

"There was dashcam video," I said.

Elliott took a deep breath. "Did you bring it? I want to see it."

"We'll show it to you in a minute," she said. "But before we do, we need to talk about a couple of things. First, the judge ordered the evidence sealed. That's why we're in this room today, and it also means you can't tell anyone about what you see. And that won't be easy. I need you to promise you'll keep it to yourself."

"Why? What does it show?"

"It's not pretty," I replied. "It went down exactly like you said. Looks like Kavanagh took just long enough to be sure it was you, then he pulled the trigger."

Elliott banged his fist on the table. "I told you, Mick. I fucking told you! The cops are behind this."

I held up a hand. "Take it easy, buddy."

"What was it you said to me? 'Cops don't flat out execute people?'" He gestured at his useless legs. "They had a damn good try with me."

"Calm down, guys," Casey said. "Elliott, you may have a point. There's something not right about the video. But what we have is a long way from proof. At this stage, I'm not even sure I can get it admitted as evidence in your trial. But we'll work on that."

"To hell with my trial," Elliott snapped. "Show it to the goddamn world!"

Casey held up a hand. "I told you, the judge ordered it sealed. If I do that, the judge will blow his stack. There's no way we could use it at trial. Hell, I could lose my license. And trust me, the last thing you need is for the judge to be mad at the defense team."

"There has to be a way to get it out there!"

"Casey's right," I said. "We can't. Think about it. I'm telling you the video is bad. If it goes public, the shitstorm will make the Andre Gladen protests look like a Disney parade. Seriously, this town will explode. I know you don't want that."

Elliott rubbed his face, then pushed his wheelchair back from the table. "Yeah, you're right. I don't want a bunch of white kids smashing shit up in my name." He came back to the table. "Anyway, what's gonna happen to the cop who shot me?"

"We don't know yet," I said. "They say they're investigating the shooting, but it already smells like a cover-up."

"Yeah, I'll bet it does. You know his white ass will get away with it. Meanwhile, I'm just another nigger in a jail cell." Elliott spread his arms. "What happens now?"

"We keep working," Casey said. "If we're going to convince a jury that someone other than you shot Betts, we need a strong story about why. And I'm going to keep pushing the DA's office to turn over information. They've done the minimum possible so far, but the good news is the judge isn't happy with them. We can use that to our advantage."

"Meanwhile, I just sit and wait?"

"Maybe not. We're going to use the video to argue for reconsideration on the bail issue. We might be able to convince the judge that it casts serious doubt on the prosecution's case."

Elliott's eyes went wide. "Oh man, if you got me out of this place, it would be like all my Christmases came at once."

"Don't get your hopes up," Casey said, "but we'll give it a shot."

"All right," Elliott replied. "That's a start."

Casey pulled the police statements out of her briefcase. "Now on to the other thing we need to discuss. I know we talked about this already, but what do you remember about when the cops pulled you over?"

"What I told you before. I was leaving the NNC office when I saw flashing blue lights behind me. I thought they were just going to hassle me again, so I pulled over. Then I saw the guy with his gun out, so I was real careful when I got out of the car. Made damn sure he could see my hands were on my head. Fat lot of good it did me."

"Before you stopped, you didn't try to get away from them? Accelerate, or lead them on a chase?"

"Hell no! I ain't stupid."

"I know. And I believe you. But both cops claim you did, in their statements. So we'll have to deal with that at trial."

"All right. Let's see that damn video, then."

Casey took her laptop out and set it up with the screen facing away from the small window in the door.

"Okay," she said, "but remember what I said. It's graphic. If you want to stop at any time, just let me know."

Elliott positioned himself in front of the laptop. "Play it."

Casey started the video. I went and leaned against the wall, watching Elliott's face. When the shots rang out, his eyes widened, but he kept looking at the screen. He made it as far as Officer Wright telling Kavanagh to call an ambulance, and Kavanagh not doing it. Then he reached over and slammed the laptop shut.

He glared at me. "You tell me that motherfucker didn't want me dead!"

"Sure looked like he did," I said. "But why? Still doesn't make any sense to me."

"I told you. It's about the protests. I've been a thorn in PPB's side for years. Guess I finally pushed them over the top."

"That doesn't explain how Betts got shot."

"I'm not even sure it matters," Casey said.

"What are you talking about?" Elliot snapped.

"I'm talking about defending you in a murder case. Maybe the cops came up with a plan to kill you on their own. Maybe there's some bigger conspiracy. But that's not the case we need to worry about. You'll be on trial for the murder of Malik Betts.

My job is to prevent you from being convicted. That's all I'm focused on."

"Okay, so how are you going to do that?"

"Same approach we've had all along," Casey said. "Convince the jury someone else shot Betts. This video helps, but it's still too loose. I need to connect it to Betts, somehow, and right now I have no idea how to do that."

Elliott threw his hands up. "Oh great! PPB is trying to kill me and my lawyer doesn't know what she's doing."

"That's not what I meant. Don't worry, I'll be ready for trial. I just meant that I need to be a hundred percent focused on that. I can't be doing an OJ Simpson impersonation, chasing around after the real killers. And Mick, that goes for you too."

She looked at me and I nodded.

"Elliott, I know it's difficult," she continued, "but we have to take it one step at a time. Our next move is to use that video to get the judge to reconsider bail. Then, Mick and I will be working through every aspect of the prosecution's case, looking for cracks. I don't know where that's going to take us, but our focus will be on getting you acquitted. Do you understand?"

Elliott sighed. "Yeah, I do. Look, I'm sorry I got mad at you." He waved his hand at the laptop. "That shit is hard to take, you know? Especially sitting here in a goddamn wheelchair."

"We know," I said. I stood. I wanted to clap Elliott on the shoulder, or shake his hand or something, but physical contact with inmates was strictly prohibited, so I made an awkward kind of half bow. "Don't worry. We'll give it everything we've got."

THIRTY
FUN IN THE SUN

"Where are you going?" Casey said.

I stopped at the office door. "I need to make some calls. I'm trying to meet with one of Betts's former customers."

"That's not the priority right now. I need you working on legal research for the bail petition."

"We still need to find out who killed Betts."

"No, we don't. Look, we had this conversation already. For now, Kavanagh is our Other Dude. And even if he isn't, we can still use him to make it look like there was one."

"Elliott deserves to know who set him up," I said.

"And once we've made sure he isn't convicted of murder, we can figure that out. But our job is to win at trial. I need you focused on that, Mick."

"I'll do your research, but let me talk to this guy."

"Only when the research is done. The sooner we file, the sooner Elliott gets out."

I felt like a scolded child, but she had a point. "Okay, fine. I'll get on it."

I went back to my desk. I had to turn sideways to squeeze past the photocopier and get to my chair. Thank God everything I needed was online. There wasn't room for the stacks of law books that used to be necessary for researching prior cases.

I began with the statutes themselves. In Oregon, a defendant is entitled to bail unless they're a flight risk or a danger to the public. In murder cases, the defendant is presumed to be dangerous, so bail is denied if the proof is evident or the presumption strong enough that they're guilty. Elliott had been denied bail at the arraignment because Betts being found executed in his backyard was more than enough to pass the strong presumption of guilt test. But back then, we didn't have the video. Now, I needed to find previous cases we could use to argue that with Kavanagh in the frame as a potential killer, the State's case no longer met that test.

Fortunately, plenty of other defendants had tried similar arguments before. After a couple of hours, I'd compiled a list of cases that could help us. But now came the tough part—reading through each of them, looking for a nugget of reasoning we could use to support our claim. It was late Friday afternoon and I had a solid couple of days' work ahead of me. Good thing I didn't have plans for the weekend.

Around six, Casey came and stood in the doorway.

"I'm heading out," she said. "You should probably wrap up, too. You need a break."

"I want to get through a few more cases. I'll give it another hour or two. You go. I can lock up when I'm done."

"Suit yourself." She turned to leave, then stopped. "Look, I'm sorry I got mad at you before."

"Don't worry about it," I said. "You were right."

Casey smiled and left. I waited a couple of minutes, then picked up my phone and dialed.

"Is this Toby Burke?"

"Yes. Who's calling?"

"Mr. Burke, my name is Mick Ward. I'm an investigator. You purchased a condominium in Northeast Portland in March of this year, correct?"

"Yes."

"And your realtor was Malik Betts?"

Burke hesitated. "Yes. But why are you calling me? What's this all about?"

I had to tread carefully. I wanted Burke intrigued, but not afraid. "Were you aware that Malik Betts is deceased?"

"What? No! What happened to Malik?"

"I'm afraid he was the victim of a crime."

"You mean he was murdered?" Burke hesitated again. "Wait, are you with the police?"

"No, sir. I'm a private investigator. And you're not under suspicion, or in trouble in any way. I'm just talking to some of Mr. Betts's former clients, to gather background information to assist my investigation."

"I'm not sure I can help."

"You'd be surprised. Even the smallest detail might help us find out who killed Mr. Betts." I threw in that last line to hook him, and sure enough, it worked.

"I'd like to help, but I can't talk to you right now. I have to go meet my girlfriend. Maybe we could meet on Sunday?"

"Thank you, Mr. Burke. Sunday would be fine."

We arranged to meet at Stormbreaker Brewing on Sunday afternoon. With that done, I worked through the first few cases on my list for an hour or so without finding anything useful, so I called it a night as well.

It took me all day Saturday and a few hours Sunday morning to get through the rest of the cases. By the time I'd finished, I had a screaming headache and blurred vision, but I'd found enough to make a solid argument. I used them to write a passable first draft of a motion for the judge to reconsider bail in Elliott's case. When I arrived for my meeting on Sunday afternoon, I was ready for a beer.

Stormbreaker Brewing was nothing more than a giant tin shed with a five-barrel craft brewery in it, but their beer was good, and their beer garden had comfortable seats and a nice breeze blowing through. On a warm Sunday afternoon, it was a very pleasant place to pass some time. I got there an hour early so I could savor some brief downtime.

I had just finished my second pint of Stormbreaker's superb Right as Rain pale ale when, five minutes after our appointment time, a guy walked in and scanned the crowd as though he was looking for someone. I held up my hand and he made a beeline for me.

I stood. "Toby Burke?"

"Yes. You're Mick Ward?"

"I am." I offered my hand and he shook it, then we sat down.

Toby Burke was in his early thirties, with unruly short blond hair and a crooked smile. He wore a Nike branded tee and hoodie jacket, short pants and slides.

"Thanks for meeting me," I said.

"I almost didn't come." He tapped his index finger on the table. "You told me you're investigating who killed Malik. But I did some research. The police have already arrested someone. So tell me why I shouldn't leave right now."

"They've arrested someone, but not the guy who did it. The man they arrested, Elliott Russell, is innocent. He's being framed and I'm part of his defense team. That's why I'm trying to find out who really killed Malik Betts."

Burke's eyebrows shot up. "Framed? That sounds like a bad movie."

"Believe me, I wish it was. But it isn't, and I need your help to prevent an innocent man going to jail for the rest of his life."

"Okay, good enough. Let me get a beer and we can talk." He gestured at my empty glass. "You want another?"

"Sure. Pale ale."

Burke headed for the bar and returned a couple of minutes later with our beers.

"So how can I help?" he said.

I took a sip of my drink. "Tell me about Malik. Did you know him before you bought the condo?"

"No, I only came to Portland seven months ago. I moved here from Denver, because I got a job at Nike headquarters. I looked around online for a realtor, and Malik had a couple of listings in the neighborhoods I was interested in, so I called him. Long story short, he found me this condo in Northeast Portland that looked good. Crappy commute from there to Nike, but it's a cool area and the price was right."

"How was he as a realtor?"

"Fine, I guess. It was a pretty simple transaction. Cash purchase, so he didn't have to do much."

"And personally, what did you think of him?"

Burke paused to take a drink, then answered. "A bit flashy for my taste, to be honest. He wore shiny suits and gold jewelry. I'm more of a jeans and tee guy. And when we went to look at properties, he'd insist on picking me up. He had this brand new Porsche SUV, a Cayenne S, I think. And he liked showing it off."

"A Porsche? Not a Bentley?"

"Definitely a Porsche. I know the difference."

"I'm sure you do. I'm just surprised because I was under the impression he drove a Bentley."

"Maybe he had both. I hear there's a lot of money in real estate."

"There must be. Speaking of which, you mentioned the price. He got you a good deal?"

Burke nodded vigorously. "Oh yeah. The condo was brand new. Never been lived in before, and the price was ten grand less than a couple of other new units in the same complex."

"Wow. Do you remember who the seller was?"

"Some property investment company, I think. I can't remember their name." He laughed. "I guess my place wasn't a very good investment for them."

"I guess not." I took another drink. "And did you see Mr. Betts again after the purchase?"

"Yeah, glad you asked. It's a crazy story." Burke ran a hand through his hair. "When the condo sale closed, Malik invited me to a Trail Blazers game to celebrate. I thought we'd just be in regular seats, you know? But it turns out he had one of those fancy luxury suites. He'd invited a few other customers too and he had everything laid on: real French champagne, great food, the works. He had this sweet sound system in there and he even had the Blazers dancers come through the box at halftime and put on a show! It got pretty wild. To be honest, I don't even remember who the Blazers played."

"Sounds like quite the night," I said.

Burke leaned forward, warming to his subject. "That's not even the best bit! We pissed off the mayor!"

"What?"

"Yeah, the guys in the suite next to ours weren't happy about the racket we were making. Bunch of old dudes in suits. A couple of them came over to our suite and got into it with Malik, and it turns out one of them was the mayor."

"Okay, now I'm interested. Tell me exactly how it went down."

"Well, I remember someone banging on the door to our suite. We could barely hear them over the music. Anyway,

Malik answered the door and there were two guys in suits standing there. They obviously knew Malik and they were pretty pissed. This one guy, I'm guessing he owned the suite next door, because he did most of the talking. He was pissed. He kept saying something about how he'd warned Malik before about attracting so much attention. Eventually, Malik agreed to tone it down a bit and the guys left. The next day I saw a picture of the mayor on the cover of *The Oregonian*, and it was the other dude who'd been at the door, the one who didn't say much. It was kind of funny. Here I am, new in town, and already I'm on the mayor's shit list!" He laughed again and shook his head.

"Tell me more about the guy who was arguing with Malik. Can you describe him?"

"Sort of. White guy. Tall, thin, gray hair, gray suit. Oh, and his name was Charles."

"How do you know that?"

"When they were leaving, the mayor said something like, 'Come on, Charles, let's go.'"

"Interesting. Did Malik say anything to you or the other guests about what happened?"

"I don't think so. But I was pretty loaded at that point, so I can't be sure."

"Did you see Malik again, after that night?"

"No. He never called me again and I had no reason to contact him." Burke drained his pint and looked at me expectantly. I smiled and nodded.

"Be right back," I said. "What are you having?"

"Pale ale, same as you."

I went to the bar and ordered our drinks. I thought about what Burke had told me while I waited for the beers to be poured. Something occurred to me about the incident he'd described. I did a quick search on my phone and found what I was looking for.

Back at our table, I put our beers down, took out my phone and showed a picture to Burke. "That guy Charles who was with the mayor. Is this him?"

Burke peered at the screen. "I can't be a hundred percent sure, but that sure looks like him."

I put my phone away and we talked for a while longer. Burke kept pressing me for information about my investigation, but I made excuses about how it was too early to know anything meaningful. When we finished our beers, he offered to get me another, but I declined. I had work to do. Specifically, research about the man whose picture I'd shown to Burke. The same man who'd threatened Elliott at the City Council meeting right before his arrest.

Charles Sinclair.

THIRTY-ONE
BACK TO SCHOOL

I was excited to see Casey at the office on Monday, but I knew I'd have to be careful about the Sinclair revelation. So I made sure we went through the draft motion for a release hearing before I mentioned anything about him. I walked Casey through my reasoning and she made notes on her copy as we went. When we were done, she sat back and waved the memo at me.

"It's a shame you blew up your legal career. This is good work."

"Gee, thanks. I think."

"Seriously, it's good. I'm going to make a couple of minor tweaks and then file it pretty much as-is. I think we've got a good shot at getting bail for Elliott."

"I hope you're right," I said. Casey appreciating my work felt good. Maybe I still had some lawyer chops after all. But it meant nothing if Elliott was still locked up when we were done.

Casey started to stand, but I held up a hand. "Wait. I have something else to tell you about."

"What?"

"After I got done with the motion, I met with that guy I told you about. Betts's former client."

"Mick–"

"No, listen. This is important."

Casey rolled her eyes. "This better be good."

I told her Burke's story about the incident at the Blazers game.

"Okay, so the mayor and some developer dude were pissed at Betts. So what?"

"A couple of things. First, Sinclair was pissed because he didn't want Betts attracting attention. Attention to what? And second, do you remember that City Council meeting I told you about? Right before Elliott got shot? They were debating a new ordinance that would effectively shut down condo developments in established neighborhoods inside the city limits. I did some digging last night and it looks like Sinclair has about half a dozen planned developments in the works."

"I still don't get it."

"Things got pretty heated at the debate. Sinclair was seriously pissed at Elliott. At one point he said something like, 'You've interfered where you're not wanted for the last time.' It sounded weird at the time, but I had no idea what he meant. Think about it now. What if he and Betts were involved in some way and the deal went bad? Wouldn't killing Betts and framing Elliott for the crime be perfect for him?"

Casey's eyebrows shot up. "Wow, that's a big leap from an argument at a basketball game."

"Maybe. Or maybe we've finally found someone with a motive to want both Betts and Elliott out of the way."

"You're killing me, Mick. You come in here with the best damn legal reasoning I've read in a while and now you want to go off and chase down some left-field theory about Charles Sinclair, a pillar of the Portland community, being a murderer."

She pointed at the motion I'd drafted. "What I need—no, what Elliott needs—is more of this."

"I know. And don't worry; you'll get it. Elliott's defense is my top priority, guaranteed. But I want to poke at this Sinclair connection some more too. You said it yourself; we need a credible theory, if we're going to get the shooting video admitted as evidence. If there was some kind of questionable deal between Sinclair and Betts, it might lead us to our connection."

Casey gave me a wry smile. "If I told you not to waste time on this, you'd do it anyway, wouldn't you?"

"You know I would."

"Okay. So what's your next play?"

"Good question. I want to talk to Sinclair, confront him with some of this information, and see how he reacts. But I'm guessing he's not going to take my calls."

Casey smiled again. "You crack me up, Mick. You came in here today with some great legal analysis and now you've forgotten lawyering 101. What does an attorney do when they want to talk to a witness?"

I groaned. "I'm an idiot. We subpoena him. I'll draw it up now, so you can sign it and get it served."

"Attaboy! You do that and I'll get the motion filed. We're making progress. Good progress."

I was back at my desk later that morning when Casey shouted at me from her office.

"Hey, Mick, you might want to come and see this."

I squeezed past the copy machine and went into Casey's office. She was making her way to the conference table, laptop in hand.

"I just got an email from Nicole with Kavanagh's disciplinary record. Let's see what they didn't want us to know."

We sat at the table and read the document Nicole Astert had provided. Kavanagh's file started with a summary of his performance at the Academy. He'd graduated towards the bottom of his class. Apparently, he had the aptitude and aced the physical tests, but he hadn't shown much motivation to learn the principles of actual police work.

Kavanagh's first disciplinary note came about a month after he joined the force. He and his partner had responded to a disturbance outside a liquor store. The store's proprietor had called to say there was a guy harassing customers in the parking lot. When they arrived, they found a drunk homeless guy trying to get customers to buy him booze. Kavanagh's partner, who had been on the force for five years, tried to calm the guy down and get him to move on. The guy kept refusing and that's when things turned ugly.

Two customers had seen what went down and both filed complaints. They each stated that Kavanagh tried to shove the guy out into the street. According to them, when the guy refused to move, Kavanagh took out his truncheon and whacked him across the knees, then kicked him twice, in the stomach and the face, while he was down. He was going in for another kick when his partner stopped him. They bundled the guy into the back of the patrol car and left.

There was no mention of the victim's ethnicity, but his name was Jamarcus Watkins, so it wasn't hard to guess.

Not surprisingly, both Kavanagh and his partner claimed that Watkins had taken a swing at Kavanagh before any force was used against him, which directly contradicted the onlookers' statements. The incident resolution noted that unprovoked use of force was a firing offense, but since the evidence was inconclusive as to whether Kavanagh's use of force *was* unprovoked, there were no grounds for termination. Instead, Kavanagh was ordered to take remedial training on handling encounters with impaired persons.

"Wow, he got off to a hot start," I said.

"Yeah." Casey scratched her chin. "I've seen cops fired for less, you know."

"Given the size of his file, it's a miracle he's still on the force. It takes more than a relative in high places to protect you from this crap. He's involved in something."

We continued reading through the file. There were other inappropriate use of force reports with largely similar patterns. And each time, the resolution stated the evidence was inconclusive, and recommended additional training for Kavanagh.

Also, as Tony had told me, Kavanagh was one of half a dozen cops who had complaints filed against them for firing rubber bullets at civilians during the BLM protests that erupted after Andre Gladen was killed. This time the force closed ranks around all six of the accused, with multiple officers filing statements to the effect that protesters had charged at the police brandishing Molotov cocktails and other weapons, and no disciplinary action was taken against any of them.

Then we came to an incident towards the end of the file, about two weeks before Elliott's arrest. In some ways it continued the pattern of prior incidents; Kavanagh had used excessive force in dealing with an altercation at a party. But there were two important differences. First, the incident had taken place while Kavanagh was off duty and working as a private security guard. Second, other than Kavanagh, the names of everyone involved in the incident were redacted. Wherever a name would have appeared, the text had been replaced with solid black blocks.

"What do you make of that?" Casey said.

"I'm not sure. Plenty of cops work security gigs on the side."

"True, but why redact names in this case? They didn't in any of the other incidents."

"Good point."

"Besides, those redactions stop us following up on that one event. Kind of defeats the purpose of discovery." Casey made a note on her pad. "I need to go to the judge, get him to order the cops to give us the unredacted version."

"It might not matter," I said.

I grabbed the laptop and scrolled back up to the top of the incident report. The date and time weren't redacted, and nor was the location: Paley's Place restaurant.

"Now, that is interesting." Paley's Place was one of Portland's finest restaurants, with prices to match. It was also in constant high demand, with the wait time for reservations running at two to three months. Whoever booked the place out for a private party had a lot of influence as well as money.

"I don't think they'd go to the trouble of redacting names just to spare blushes." I jabbed a finger at the screen. "There has to be more to this. I'm going to dig into it and see what I can find."

"Okay, it can't hurt. What's your plan?"

"I'll go to Paley's. Talk to some staff, see if I can find someone who worked that night. It might take a few days. I need to prep for Sinclair's deposition and the bail hearing. Plus, Tony and I are going to see some guy who can get us information on Betts's business dealings on Wednesday."

"Fine, but don't leave it too long." Casey leaned forward. "I think you might be onto something here."

THIRTY-TWO
DIGGING IN THE DIRT

"Who's this guy we're going to see?" I asked Tony.

"He's my go-to guy for computer searches. Kind of paranoid, but if you want information that's in a database somewhere, he's the man."

I stared out the window as Tony drove us up into the hills behind downtown. A thunderstorm had blown through town Tuesday night, soaking Portland with a couple of inches of rain, and bringing the brutally hot summer to an abrupt end. By the afternoon, the rain had eased back into the usual northwest drizzle that hung over the city like a damp blanket.

"Where does he live?"

"Out past Cornelius Pass, on a couple of acres in the hills." Tony tapped a hand on the steering wheel. "Oh yeah, I meant to tell you. My guy checked Sam Kavanagh's schedule. He was working the night Betts was shot, and when you found the body, so that probably was him at Elliott's house."

"Shit. So much for him being the shooter."

"Yeah, sorry about that."

"Not your fault," I said. "I guess that would have been too easy."

Tony nodded and kept driving.

We drove around the back of the Mount Calvary cemetery and up Skyline Boulevard, then cruised along the winding two-lane road, passing hobby farms and horse ranches. Traffic was light, mostly BMW and Audi SUVs, with the occasional shiny new pickup truck. Playthings of the wealthy urban hobby farmers who lived up there. We passed a group of Lyra-clad cyclists, challenging themselves against the long, undulating hills. The road was still wet, with frequent blind corners, so Tony kept to a reasonable speed.

A couple of miles past Cornelius Pass Road, Tony turned off onto a dirt driveway. It wound through a stand of tall cedars, then opened up in front of an old sky-blue ranch-style house that was invisible from the road. Paint was peeling from the house's siding and much of the roof was covered in moss. There were two large satellite dishes mounted on poles behind the house, visible above the roof.

We got out of the car and Tony knocked on the door. It opened right away. A guy peered out from behind the door.

"Come in, quick," he said, waving us inside.

Tony and I went in and the guy closed the door behind us quickly.

"Did anyone see you coming?" he said.

"I doubt it, man," Tony replied. "There's not much traffic out here at this time of the morning."

"Can't be too careful. Come sit down, guys. I'll make coffee, then we can get started."

He ushered us over to an old chrome and Formica dining table at one end of the living room, then left for the kitchen. I raised my eyebrows at Tony. He shook his head and made calming hand gestures at me. I shrugged and didn't say anything.

The rest of the living room was furnished in thrift shop

fashion, shabby mismatched furniture on battered hardwood floors that hadn't been refinished in more than a decade. Mediocre watercolors of rural scenes hung on the yellowing walls. Jesus, where did Tony find this guy?

The guy came back, holding three mugs of coffee. He was tall, maybe six feet two, but thin as a rail. He had long dark hair, streaked with gray and tied back in a ponytail, and a scraggly salt-and-pepper beard. With his tie-dyed tee, and denim cut-offs, he looked every inch the aging hippie. But there was something cold and sharp in his eyes, something very far from peace and love.

"Come with me," he said. He handed us a coffee each and turned away from us.

"Wait, how about some introductions first?" I said.

He turned back and glared at me. "I don't know who you are. I don't want to know who you are. And I sure as hell am not going to tell you who I am."

He turned away again and headed through a door into a darkened room. Tony frowned at me and followed.

I trailed along behind, standing at the back of the room. At first, I couldn't make out much in the darkness. As my eyes adjusted, I found it hard to believe what I was seeing.

The room had heavy sheets hung over the windows to prevent anyone from seeing inside. Long desks lined two sides of the room, each loaded with computer gear. I counted three laptops and two desktop computers. Each of the desktops was paired with giant twin monitors. There was a printer on each desk, too. Even a Luddite like me could tell this setup was for much more than video games or surfing porn.

"Right, let's make this quick," the guy said, as he sat in an office chair by one of the desktops. "Tony says you need information about a business. Give me names, dates, anything you've got."

"Start with Malik Betts and his real estate agency Phoenix Realty. I need a list of all their transactions in the past five years. I'm looking for dates, property addresses and details, buyer and seller details, prices and so on. Can you get that?"

The guy made some notes. "Yeah, that's easy. What else?"

"Start there and we'll see."

He went to work, hands dancing on the keyboard. After a couple of minutes, he frowned at something on the screen.

"That's interesting," he said.

"What?"

"Malik Betts doesn't own Phoenix Realty."

"Then who does?"

"Not who. What. It's owned by another company, Pacific Holdings." He typed some more. "Which is in turn owned by another company... Ah, here we go. Three layers down, there's our friend Mr. Betts."

"So what are we talking about here?" I said. "Shell companies or something?"

"Exactly. Someone doesn't want to be identified as the owner of Phoenix Realty."

"Why? Tax evasion?"

"No, when I come across this sort of thing there's usually some fraudulent trading going on. Price fixing, no-bid contracts, that kind of thing."

"So that means Betts was involved in some other businesses too?"

"Most likely." He hammered away at the keyboard again. "Yes. At least two more, and again there are a couple of shell companies between him and the store front."

He worked for a minute or two more, then pushed his chair back from the desk. "Guys, this is a complicated web. Whoever set it up knew what they were doing. I haven't seen a setup this convoluted for a long time. It's going to take a while to untangle."

"No problem," I said. "Take all the time you need. But I want to know every company linked to Betts and ideally get transaction histories for all of them. Oh, and can you pull real estate closing records too? The official county recorder ones."

"No problem. Give me a couple of days. I'll dump the transactions, and I'll run some pattern analysis for you, see if I can flag anything interesting or unusual." He looked at Tony. "I'll put what I find in the usual place and ping you when I'm done. You can show yourselves out."

He went back to the keyboard, not even looking to see whether we left.

I was still shaking my head when we drove away.

"What?" Tony said.

"Interesting dude."

"You don't know the half of it," Tony replied. "He's not even supposed to be online."

"What do you mean?"

"He's on parole for some pretty serious cybercrime. Hacked a National Security Agency black site and posted reams of classified information on an open whistleblower website. He served two years and he's on parole for five more. One of the parole conditions is that he has to stay off the internet. So, officially he lives in a studio in John's Landing, with no wifi. But he spends most of his time out here. I helped set him up in this place and in return he does me some favors when I need information. That's why he's so hush-hush."

"You keep interesting company, my friend."

Tony smiled. "What do you make of the shell company stuff?"

"Betts was doing a lot more than just selling condos. But what, I don't know. I guess we'll see when we get the details.

Your guy said he'll get us the details in a couple of days. Is he likely to be on time?"

"He works fast. I'll be surprised if we don't get the data tomorrow."

"Good."

"Why do you ask?"

"We're deposing Sinclair on Monday. I'd love to have a connection to Betts to throw at him, see how he reacts." I sat back. "See if the fucker squirms."

THIRTY-THREE
IT'S JUST BUSINESS

"This should be fun."

I stared up at the forty-two stories of the US Bancorp Tower. Known to locals as Big Pink, because of its pink granite and tinted glass façade, it was one of Portland's tallest buildings. Charles Sinclair's company, CDS Development, occupied the top three floors.

Tony's cyber expert had, as promised, come through with volumes of data about Betts's business dealings. So much so, that it had taken me almost a week to work through it all. But the effort was worth it. The data showed strong connections to Sinclair and now we had a chance to see where that led.

We took the elevator to the fortieth floor, where a receptionist met us and led us to a conference room with stunning views of downtown, the Willamette River and the Cascade Mountains off in the distance. The court reporter was already in the room, setting up his equipment at one end of the oval-shaped conference table. He did a double take when he saw me.

"Mick, I wasn't expecting to see you here today. I thought you were..." His voice trailed off.

"Hello, Scott. You're right, I was disbarred. Three years ago, in fact. But I'm helping Casey out on this case. She's the star of the show today."

"Oh, okay. Well, it's good to see you, dude. Hi, Casey, good to see you too." He turned away awkwardly and went back to working on his equipment.

I wasn't surprised to run into Scott Dukes here. He used to be my go-to court reporter for depositions. Most defense lawyers used his services at one time or another. He was fast, accurate and affordable.

Sinclair hadn't arrived yet, but he'd staked out his territory by placing a monogrammed black leather folio and gold pen on the table, in front of a chair looking away from the view. We set up facing his seat, poured ourselves coffee from the silver service, and waited.

Sinclair arrived fifteen minutes after the scheduled 10 am start time, accompanied by a man he introduced as Gerald Whitehead, his lawyer. I hadn't come across Whitehead before, and judging by Casey's puzzled look, neither had she. Sinclair himself wore a dark blue suit, white shirt and red tie. He nodded to us as he sat down.

"Let's begin, shall we? The sooner this farce is over, the better."

Casey didn't rise to the bait. She began the deposition in an expressionless voice, providing the case details for Scott to take down, reminding Sinclair that his testimony was under penalty of perjury, and asking some basic questions to establish his identity and ownership of CDS Development.

Since I wasn't a lawyer anymore, Casey was the only one who could ask Sinclair questions, but I'd prepared a list for her in advance. Casey kicked off at the top.

"Let's start with your relationship with the deceased, Malik Betts," she said. "How long had you been in business with him?"

"I wouldn't say I was in business with him," Sinclair replied.

Casey made a show of running her finger down one of the documents in front of her and frowning.

"You sold him five condominiums in the North Forty development in January 2016, for a total of $1.35 million, didn't you?"

"It's quite possible," Sinclair replied. "I can't recall exactly."

"And you sold him a further ten condominiums in the same development in July of that year, didn't you?"

"Again, I don't exactly recall."

"Mr. Sinclair, over the subsequent four years, you sold over fifty condominiums to Malik Betts, usually in lots of five or ten, from four other condo complexes built by CDS Development here in Portland. The total value of these transactions was in excess of $12 million. Is that not correct?"

Sinclair frowned. "You seem to know a great deal about my business. Where did you get this information?"

Casey kept her face deadpan. "Please answer the question, sir."

"Look, Miss Raife," Sinclair said, a sharp edge to his voice, "I build and sell a lot of properties. I don't remember every individual transaction."

"And Mr. Betts usually sold the condos shortly after purchasing them from you, didn't he?"

"I don't know. I'd say you should ask him, but..." Sinclair spread his hands.

"Yes, quite. But you were no doubt aware that the condos you sold to him were often on the market again shortly thereafter, sometimes while you still had other new units for sale?"

"Yes, I was aware of that."

Casey slid a sheet of paper across the desk to Sinclair. "Good. This is a list of condominium sales in your three most recent developments, sorted by price. As you can see, Malik Betts usually sold those condominiums for less than other real estate agents. Sometimes by as much as ten percent. Why was that?"

"I have no idea."

"It wasn't because he wanted to sell the condominiums quickly?"

"I'm sure he had his reasons. I don't know what they were."

"And yet, despite making such small profits on those sales, Malik Betts drove a Bentley and a Porsche and he kept an expensive hospitality suite at Portland Trail Blazer games. Doesn't that strike you as odd?"

"Maybe he had other business interests. Maybe he was better at them than he was at selling condos."

"I suppose that could be the explanation. But isn't it true that no one else bought more condos from you, or sold more condos in your developments, in the last four years?" Casey looked at Sinclair innocently. "And before you answer, I remind you that you're under oath."

He scowled at her. "So he bought a lot of condos. So what?"

"Okay, let's move along," Casey said. "Are you familiar with a company called Starlight Supply?"

Sinclair pretended to think for a moment. "I believe so. They sell construction supplies, don't they?"

"They certainly sell supplies to CDS construction," Casey replied. "Over fifty million dollars worth in various materials in the past two years, in fact."

"Is that a question?"

"No, but this is. Do you know who owns Starlight Supply?"

"I do not."

"Neither did we, at first. You see, Starlight Supply is owned by a shell company, which is in turn owned by another shell company. But when you peel back the layers, the principal owner was Malik Betts."

"Interesting," Sinclair said. "Maybe that's how he could afford the fancy cars."

"Are you sure you didn't know that Malik Betts owned Starlight? And again, I remind you that you are under oath."

"Objection," Gerald Whitehead said. "Asked and answered."

Casey looked at Sinclair, but he gave no indication of wanting to change his answer.

"All right," she said. "I would assume that, as a businessman, you had a close relationship with your biggest customer. After all, you would want him to keep buying properties from you. Did you interact with Malik Betts outside of a business setting?"

Sinclair folded his arms. "No, I didn't."

I scribbled something on my notebook and slid it in front of Casey. She read it, then looked up at Sinclair again.

"Isn't it true that Mr. Betts leased the hospitality suite next to yours at the Moda Center?"

"I believe so, yes."

"And you had a confrontation with Mr. Betts at a Portland Trail Blazers game earlier this year, didn't you?"

"Quite possibly. He occasionally got rowdy at Blazer games. I'd have to go over there and tell him to quiet down."

"But on this occasion, you said that you'd 'warned him before about attracting attention'. Attracting attention to what?"

"I don't recall using those words."

"Be that as it may, despite your earlier evasion, I think we've established that you have known and done business with Malik Betts for several years now, yes?"

"I suppose so."

"And how would you characterize your relationship with him?"

"I'm not sure I'd even call it a relationship. Yes, I sold him some condos. But outside of that, we saw little of each other." Sinclair raised his eyebrows. "I'd say he wasn't to my taste."

"Interesting," Casey said. She took her time over making some notes, then looked up at Sinclair expectantly.

Sure enough, he took the bait. "Miss Raife, you're clearly implying that I had a hand in Malik Betts's demise. But as you yourself pointed out, I sold him a lot of condominiums and made a large amount of money doing so. Why on earth would I want him dead?"

"I'm not implying anything, but thank you for the clarification." Casey turned a page in her notes. "Okay, let's move on to your relationship with the accused in this case, Elliott Russell. When did you and he first cross paths?"

"Hard to say, exactly. Does it matter?" Sinclair turned to his lawyer. "How much longer do I have to put up with this?"

Whitehead didn't look up from his notes. "Not much longer, I expect. Answer their questions and we'll be done soon."

"Let me ask the question a different way," Casey said. "Mr. Russell and the Northeast Neighborhood Coalition have been spearheading the campaign against large condominium projects in those neighborhoods."

"If you could call it a campaign. More of a bunch of rabble-rousers."

"But those 'rabble-rousers', as you call them, have successfully shut down three of your proposed developments in the past five years. Correct?"

"I'll take your word for it," Sinclair replied. "We have many project proposals that never get off the ground."

"You're awfully calm about it, considering what it cost you."

"What do you mean?"

Casey picked up some glossy folders and waved them at Sinclair. "Well, according to these annual reports, the developments you have built in the past five years have earned your company anywhere between three and ten million dollars in profit each. Is that correct?"

"Yes. So?"

"Based on those numbers, each project the NNC shut down cost you a minimum of three million dollars in profits. That's a lot of money, don't you think?"

Sinclair pointed at the folders. "As those annual reports show, CDS Construction makes a lot of money from the developments we do build. I don't lose any sleep over the ones we don't."

"In addition to costing you around ten million dollars in lost profits, the NNC succeeded in getting the City Council to vote on an ordinance to limit the number of new multi-unit developments in a given neighborhood. A proposal that would have effectively prevented you from building any new developments within Portland city limits, correct?"

"They got it on the agenda for a council meeting. But anyone with a leftie lawyer and too much time on their hands can get Portland City Council to vote on some socialist ordinance. Doesn't mean it will pass, or survive a legal challenge if it does."

"Was that the ordinance that was on the agenda at the City Council meeting on Tuesday June 18 of this year?"

Sinclair shrugged. "Was it? I don't know."

"But you were at that meeting, sir," Casey said. She pointed her pen at him. "In fact, you and Mr. Russell became engaged in a heated confrontation at that meeting."

"We may have disagreed. I wouldn't call it a heated confrontation."

"At that meeting, didn't you tell Mr. Russell he 'had interfered where he wasn't wanted for the last time,' or words to that effect?"

"I doubt I used those words, but I expect I made reference to the fact that he was under suspicion of murdering Malik Betts." Sinclair leaned back and gestured across the table at us. "A suspicion that, judging by your presence here today, will soon be confirmed."

"And you're aware that Mr. Russell was shot later that evening?"

Sinclair put both hands on the table and leaned forward. "Ms. Raife, I've been in this industry for thirty-five years. I've built more projects than you've had hot meals. Every single one of them has been challenged by someone or another. Lawyers, politicians, activists, you name it. I've even had environmentalists strip naked and chain themselves to a bulldozer to stop a site from being cleared. Yes, Mr. Russell objected to some of my recent developments. But if I killed everyone who ever opposed me, we'd be looking at a trail of bodies a mile long." He stood up and grabbed his leather folio. "I've had enough of your stupid questions and insinuations. Gerald, we're done here."

Sinclair stalked out of the room without looking back. Gerald Whitehead gathered up his things and hurried after his client.

"Nice guy," I said.

"Yeah, isn't he?" Casey replied.

"Should we get him back? We still have more questions."

"Let him go. We can follow up with an interrogatory."

"Fair enough." I sighed. "That asshole made some good points today. If Betts was such a big customer, it's not going to be easy to convince a jury that Sinclair wanted him dead."

"I know. Still, we've got time to figure that out. Let's focus on the bail hearing."

"Thursday, right?" I said. Casey nodded. I picked up my stuff and stood up. "Yeah, we need to win that one. The sooner we get Elliott out of jail, the better."

THIRTY-FOUR
WARMUP BOUT

We arrived at Multnomah County Courthouse on Thursday, an hour before the bail motion hearing. Elliott was in the holding cell off to the side of Judge Obrecht's courtroom, along with an armed Sheriff's Deputy who was guarding the door. He sat at a small table that was bolted to the floor. His prison-issue wheelchair was a basic steel-framed model with flaking red paint. He wore a suit I'd picked up from his house yesterday and taken out to Inverness for him. He'd lost weight since his arrest and the suit hung loosely on his skinny frame. With the metal back brace holding him upright, he looked like a rag doll tied to a post.

I looked at Elliott in his poorly fitting suit, with his legs hanging loose and useless, and tried not to imagine what it took to get him changed out of his prison overalls and into his court attire.

"Hey, buddy," I said. "How are you doing?"

"Pretty good," he replied, his voice low and quiet.

Casey put her briefcase on the table. "Hello, Elliott. Did Mick explain to you how the hearing works?"

"Yeah. The judge will ask you why I should get bail, and then the prosecution gets to answer, and he makes his decision."

"Pretty much. It's important that you stay calm. The prosecution is going to accuse you of all kinds of things. A big part of our case is establishing that you're not dangerous, so if you react or get angry, it hurts our case. Are you ready for that?"

Elliott gestured at his legs. "Do I look dangerous?"

"That's not the point. It's going to be tough enough convincing the judge to grant bail to a murder suspect, without you giving him an excuse not to."

"Don't worry, I'll stay calm. I'm not going to be the one that blows my chance of getting out of that shithole."

"Good." Casey spread some papers on the table. "Now I want to walk you through our position, and the prosecution's likely response, so you know what to expect."

Casey led him through our motion a step at a time. Elliott followed closely, asking questions and nodding his head. It took about fifteen minutes, and when they were done, he wheeled himself back from the table.

"So, what are our chances today?"

Casey shrugged. "Hard to say. I think we have a good argument, but like I told you, judges don't like granting bail to murder suspects. It's only happened six times in the last five years. We'll do our best, but don't get your hopes up too high."

"Okay." Elliott's head slumped. "Man, I want out of that place."

I wanted to cheer him up, but I couldn't think of anything to say. We were spared a lengthy awkward silence when the judge's clerk opened the door to the holding cell and leaned in.

"Can you take your places in the courtroom, please?" she said. "The judge will be ready soon."

The Sheriff's Deputy moved toward Elliott's wheelchair, but I held up a hand to stop him.

"I'll do it," I said.

I grabbed the wheelchair's handles, then leaned forward and whispered in Elliott's ear. "Are you okay? You don't sound great."

"People keep fucking with me, man. At Inverness."

"What do you mean? Aren't you in protective custody?"

"It ain't enough. There's a couple of guys, you know the type. Big meathead white dudes, probably Aryan Nation. They don't like Black Lives Matter much and they know who I am. So they do shit just to mess with me."

"Like what?"

"Like sometimes when I shower, they move my wheelchair so I gotta crawl across the bathroom floor to get to it. The guards are no help. They just stand there and watch, don't lift a finger to help. Hell, half the time they laugh at me."

I pushed Elliott over to the defense table, my knuckles white on the wheelchair's handles. I knew bad shit happened in jail, but hearing about Elliott being on the receiving end set me on fire. Right now, all I wanted to do was drive out to Inverness, find those jumped-up steroid babies and kick their pasty white asses.

Casey sat down next to me. She did a double take when she saw my face.

"What's up with you?" she said. "You're bright red."

It took all my strength to keep my voice low. "We need to get Elliott out. Don't fuck this up."

I'd never spoken to Casey like that before, and her face told me she didn't like it. But I held her gaze and eventually she looked away.

We were spared further confrontation when the judge's clerk emerged from chambers and stood at her desk.

"All rise for the Honorable Judge Eric Obrecht."

I stood and looked around the courtroom. Nicole Astert sat

alone at the prosecution table and there were a few people on the polished wooden benches of the public gallery. Billy Hinds sat with a half dozen NNC members and Tony was just to their right. I recognized a few reporters, too. The possibility of Elliott getting parole must have been newsworthy. I was surprised to see Detective Buchanan in the gallery as well, sitting on his own at the far side.

Judge Obrecht made his way to the bench, gathered up his black robe, and sat. "Please be seated." He opened a folder on his desk as we sat down. "We are here today, in the matter of State versus Russell, to examine the defendant's motion to reconsider bail in this matter." He glanced at Casey, and Nicole Astert. "Counselors, are you ready to proceed?"

"Yes, Your Honor," they said in unison.

"Very well. Ms. Raife, in your motion you presented two arguments as to why this court should grant Mr. Russell bail. We will begin with your claim that the State's case is insufficient to support denial of bail. Please summarize your position for the court."

Casey stood, rested the tips of her fingers on the table, and began to speak. "Certainly, Your Honor. Under Oregon's bail statutes, and the Oregon Constitutional Provisions providing for bail, a person who is charged with murder can be released on bail if the State does not establish that the proof is evident or that there is a strong presumption the person is guilty. The State's case fails that test.

"First of all, the proof in this case is seriously lacking. The State has offered no evidence connecting my client to this crime beyond the mere location of Mr. Betts's body. There is no witness testimony placing my client at the scene of the crime, nor for that matter any evidence as to where the scene of the crime was. There's no murder weapon, or any other physical evidence. Oregon case law establishes that multiple items of direct evidence are required to establish that proof is evident, and the State has not provided any.

"Second, in its rush to prosecute my client, the State has ignored other avenues of inquiry and plausible suspects. Your Honor, it is crucial to note that my client was the one who notified the police that Mr. Betts's body had been placed in his yard. He made every effort to co-operate with the police and yet, two days later, the police pulled him over for no reason and shot him the moment he opened his door. These actions demonstrate that there is more to this case than meets the eye. With so many unanswered questions, there can be no strong presumption that Mr. Russell is guilty."

Casey stopped, her back straight and her chin lifted defiantly. Judge Obrecht turned to Nicole.

"Ms. Astert, how does the State respond?"

"Your Honor, the defense is clutching at straws. Mr. Russell and Mr. Betts have been sworn enemies since they were rival gang members a decade ago. Mr. Betts shot and killed Mr. Russell's younger brother. Shortly thereafter, Mr. Russell was arrested in the vicinity of Mr. Betts's house. He was in possession of an unlicensed handgun. As recently as a month before the murder, Mr. Russell and Mr. Betts had a fistfight at a public meeting, during which Mr. Russell threatened to kill Mr. Betts. Then we find Mr. Betts's body, executed, in Mr. Russell's backyard."

Judge Obrecht looked thoughtful. "And yet, as Ms. Raife points out, the State has not proffered physical evidence linking Mr. Russell to the crime."

"Not yet, Your Honor. But our enquiries are ongoing, and we expect to have that evidence shortly."

"Thank you, Ms. Astert. Ms. Raife, what do you say to that?"

Casey stood up quickly. "Your Honor, as I mentioned

before, the law requires the State to provide direct evidence of guilt, and mere speculation as to what they may find in the future does not meet that test."

"Very well," Judge Obrecht said, "let's move on to the second argument. Ms. Raife?"

"Your Honor, Oregon law establishes two reasons for denial of bail: first, that the defendant represents a danger to the public; or second, that they are a flight risk." Casey turned and held her hand out toward Elliott. "It is self-evident that my client is neither. He has no history of violent conduct, he is physically incapable of violent acts, and he certainly can't run."

Casey sat down again.

"Ms. Astert?" the judge said.

"Your Honor, the defendant absolutely is a flight risk. He was arrested when he tried to flee from police performing a routine traffic stop."

Casey shot to her feet. "Your Honor, that is not true. Nothing in the evidence provided indicates that my client tried to flee. He was stopped a few blocks from his office. And even if that were the case, he can no longer drive a car, so he certainly couldn't try it again."

Nicole made to respond, but the judge held up a hand to stop her. "Thank you, counselors. Ms. Astert, how do you respond to the contention that Mr. Russell is not a danger to society?"

"Your Honor, the mere fact that the defendant is confined to a wheelchair doesn't mean he isn't dangerous. He can still shoot a gun, and as I already mentioned, he has a prior conviction for illegal firearms possession. He absolutely is a danger to society."

I could tell Casey wanted to respond, but she remained seated. It was a good move—Nicole's point was accurate, and to challenge it would only give it more emphasis in the judge's mind.

"Thank you, both. I believe I understand your positions." The judge read through his notes, scratching his chin thoughtfully.

He put his notes down and looked up. "All right, I have reached a decision in this matter. As you are aware, there is a strong presumption against bail in a capital murder case. And I agree with Ms. Astert that the defendant's physical condition does not preclude him being dangerous."

He paused. I stole a glance at Elliott. He was watching the judge and his face was expressionless, but his eyelids were trembling ever so slightly. He looked like he'd collapse if the ruling didn't go our way.

"That being said, defense counsel has raised some compelling points. In my opinion, it is highly unlikely the defendant would make the decision that he'd rather live underground on the lam for the rest of his life as opposed to coming to court to face the charges, given the gaps in the prosecution's murder case and his severely limited physical state. Moreover, I agree with Ms. Raife that the video of the defendant's arrest and shooting raises troubling questions.

"I thereby set bail in this matter at $150,000. He will be released upon posting of the appropriate bond. Bail conditions are as follows. The defendant will surrender his passport and must report his whereabouts to this court daily. Bail will be revoked immediately, if the defendant is arrested for any potential felony offense. This hearing is adjourned."

He banged his gavel and stood.

"All rise," the clerk said.

We stood as the judge left the courtroom. I put my hand on Elliott's shoulder and squeezed. He put his hand on top of mine. I could feel it shaking.

"Thank you both so much."

Casey shook his hand. "Thank Mick. It was his idea to move for bail and his legal work that built our argument."

Elliott grinned at me. "Thanks, man. What happens now?"

I squeezed his shoulder again. "You're welcome, buddy. It will probably take a day or two to get the bond posted, but we'll have you home soon."

"I can't tell you how much this means to me."

Casey and I looked at each other over Elliott's head. I could tell she was thinking the same thing I was. Getting Elliott out on bail wouldn't matter a damn in the end if we didn't win at trial.

THIRTY-FIVE
HOMECOMING

"You might notice a couple of things look different," I said, as I parked the rented wheelchair-accessible van outside Elliott's house.

I reached across and slapped my hand on Elliott's leg.

"You know I can't feel that shit, right?" he replied, a smile on his face.

"Yeah, whatever. Take a look at the house."

Elliott leaned forward and looked past me. "Holy shit, a ramp! Thank God. I'm gonna need that. Did you build it?"

"No, Ray and G-Dog did that for you. But never mind the ramp; take a look at the side of the house."

He peered out the window again. "You're shitting me. The fence is done?"

"Yeah. Once we got the idea to try for bail, I came over on weekends and worked on it. Finished it yesterday. I only had time to get one coat of stain done, but I'll do the rest next week."

"Mick..." Elliott's voice trailed off and I felt awkward.

"Never mind that," I said, "let's get you inside."

I helped Elliott out of the van and he rolled himself up to

the house. He smiled as he pushed himself up the new wooden ramp.

As expected, it had taken us two days to gather up the ten percent bond on Elliott's bail, pay the court clerk, and arrange for his release from Inverness. Now it was approaching noon on Sunday and Elliott was home. I hadn't had many happy moments since the day we found Malik Betts's body, but this was definitely one.

I unlocked the front door, then tossed him the keys to his house.

"Thanks, man," he said, and wheeled himself inside.

Not surprisingly, Elliott had become very adept at maneuvering a wheelchair. He spun a quick 360 in the space where the kitchen, living room and dining room met.

"Oh man, you even cleaned up. Mick, this is too much."

The cops had trashed Elliott's place when they searched it, and putting it back together had been a major pain in the ass. But I couldn't bring him home to a junkyard.

"No problem" I said. "Not sure I put everything back where it belongs, but I tried. Anyway, don't worry about that. It's a nice day. How about I grab us a couple of beers and we head out back so you can admire my fence-building skills?"

Elliott smiled and nodded. "Sounds good to me. Sounds real good to me."

I grabbed two beers from the fridge and followed Elliott to the back door. He stopped when he got to the deck.

"Surprise!" Casey, Tony, Billy Hinds, Ray and G-Dog yelled in unison, then raised their beers to Elliott.

Elliott turned back to me. His eyes wanted to kill me, but his smile was as big as I'd ever seen it. I tilted my beer at him, then took a long pull on it.

Elliott wheeled himself out to join the crowd. I stood back and drank in the smiles, handshakes and back slaps, as he did the rounds. Casey and I hadn't been sure about having a welcome home party, given that Elliott still had to face trial, but in the end we decided a small gathering with close friends would give him a much-needed lift. Seeing his face light up as he caught up with people told me we made the right call. Maybe all the shit I'd put up with since I got back in the game was worth it after all.

We hung out for a while, enjoying each other's company and the autumn sun. Billy had brought his grill over. He fired it up and set some burgers to cooking. They smelled great and I had a hard time waiting my turn to get one when they were done.

Ray and G-Dog helped me clear up and carry the plates inside when we were done eating. Ray rinsed and I loaded the dishwasher. G-Dog leaned on the kitchen door.

"How's he doin', Mick?"

"Why do you ask?"

He gestured at the backyard. "Out there, every time I asked him about bein' in Inverness, he changed the subject. But I could see from his face that it wasn't good."

"You did a stretch there, right?"

"Yeah, almost two years."

"Imagine doing it again, only in a wheelchair and a back brace."

G-Dog pursed his lips and nodded, slowly. "Yeah, I thought so."

Ray handed me another plate. "How's his case looking?"

"Hard to say. Trial starts in mid-October. A lot has to happen between now and then."

"Case is bullshit, man," G-Dog muttered.

"Yeah, it is. Grab us some more beers and let's rejoin the gang."

My phone rang as we went back outside. It was Kristen Campione. I stepped out into the yard and answered.

"Hey, Kristen, what's up?"

"Hi, Mick. I've got a case you might be interested in. Racial discrimination against a major grocery chain. A bunch of Hispanic employees at their warehouse out in Hermiston filed suit. In a shock development, the defendants have sent a gazillion boxes of discovery documents, and I could use some expert help reviewing it."

"When do you need it? I'm kind of busy right now."

"Is that the Elliott Russell thing? I heard you were helping out on that."

"Yeah."

"Are you sure you can't squeeze this in? It's a solid case, and there are statutory attorney's fees, so I can pay you more than last time."

Kristen's offer sounded good. I was behind on my rent again, and I loved the idea of sticking it to some racist corporation. But as I watched Elliott enjoying a beer with his friends, I knew where my focus had to be.

"Sorry," I said. "I'd love to help, but I just don't have the time to do it justice right now."

Kristen sighed. "Okay, I understand. You can't blame a girl for trying."

I went back to the deck and rejoined the crew. We hung out for a while longer, enjoying the fresh air and being back together. As the sun dipped below the horizon, Billy packed up his grill. He nodded at Ray and G-Dog.

"Give me a hand with this, guys," he said. "Elliott's looking tired. Let's let him get some rest in his own home tonight."

The three of them packed up the gear, said their goodbyes, and left.

"It's cooling off," I said. "Let's go inside. I'll make coffee and we can talk about the case."

Casey, Tony and Elliott sat in the living room while I made the coffee. I brought the mugs through and passed them around.

Elliott raised his mug to us. "Thank you all so much for doing this. I can't tell you what it means to me."

"You're welcome," Casey said. "And if you're too tired to discuss the case now, we can do it tomorrow."

"No, I'm fine. I want to do it now. What's happening?"

"Still working on gathering information," she said. "Mick and Tony have found some interesting stuff about Betts's business that we need to explore further. And we got Kavanagh's disciplinary record. It raises some questions too, so we need to chase a few leads there."

"What about the prosecution? At the bail hearing they said they should have 'evidence linking me to the crime soon'. What the hell does that mean?"

"To be honest, I don't know. But whatever they find, they have to turn over to us in discovery, and we'll deal with it then."

"What if they make up some bullshit?"

"Then we have to show the jury that it's bullshit." Casey put her coffee mug on the table. "I know it's hard to wait, but cases like this one take time, and there's always new information coming up. It might not seem like it to you, but we're getting close to finalizing the defense strategy."

"Does that mean you know who set me up?"

"Not yet," I said. "Like Casey said, we're still looking at a couple of possibilities. We've ruled out the gang angle. The Bloods didn't want Betts dead, because they were making big money off him dealing. And if the Crips wanted to come after you, they'd have just shot you themselves."

"Yeah," Elliott muttered, "and those fools ain't smart enough to come up with a scheme like this one. What about the cops?"

"That's one of the angles. They're involved somehow, but we don't know how yet. There's the fact that Kavanagh shot you, and Buchanan offering me immunity if I'd rat you out was pretty damn unusual, too. But I still find it hard to believe they'd come up with a complex plan like this just to get at you. They could've just pulled you over and shot you."

"They *did* just pull me over and shoot me!"

I held my hands up. "I know. But why would they pull all that other shit with killing Betts and dumping the body on you first? I don't buy it. Like I say, they're involved somehow, but I still don't think they're behind it."

"Where does that leave us, then?'

"That's the other angle," I said. "It *has* to be something related to Betts's business. We know he was the middle man for a Mexican cartel. And we know he was dealing in real estate. But most of his transactions were duds—buying condos and then selling them below market price. We need to figure out how he did that and still made so much money. Unfortunately, that kind of digging is going to take time."

"What about that Sinclair guy? You deposed him, right?"

"Yeah. To be honest, we didn't get a lot out of him. We know he didn't like you, but Betts was his best customer, so it's hard to believe Sinclair would want him dead."

Casey's phone buzzed. She looked at the screen, then hit the kill button. "Joe Gorman," she said, looking at Elliott. "He's been running regular articles about your case in the *Willamette Week*. Probably wants a quote on your release."

She put her phone back in her pocket, but it buzzed again right away.

"Gorman again," she said, and took the call.

"Hey, Joe, what's up?"

She listened for a moment, then frowned and held her

phone to her chest. "Mick, grab your phone and pull up Facebook. Find the BLM Portland group."

She went back to her call and I did what she said. The group popped up right away. The most recent post was a video, and my whole body clenched when I saw what it was.

Casey hung up her call and looked at me. "Did you find it?"

"Yeah," I said, and held my phone out to the group. Their eyes widened as they saw the video—the dashcam recording of Sam Kavanagh shooting Elliott.

Casey took my phone and scrolled down. "That's what I was afraid of," she said. "The comments are blowing up. All kinds of threats against the police, and calls for riots. Gorman is outside Portland Police Bureau right now. He said there's a crowd gathering and it's getting ugly. This could be the Andre Gladen riots all over again."

Elliott grabbed the remote and turned the TV on, then switched to KOIN News. A breathless blond reporter gestured at the crowd gathering in Chapman Square, the park opposite the PPB Central Precinct. There were already at least two hundred people there, and more people were flooding in from all directions, while a line of cops in gas masks and riot gear locked arms outside the chain-link fence.

"No way," Elliott said. "Not gonna happen on my account. I gotta go down there. Mick, get your keys."

THIRTY-SIX

IT TAKES ONE

"Are you out of your mind?" I said. "You just got home."

He waved a hand at the screen. "Look at that shit! People are going to get hurt."

"If you go down there, you're asking for trouble."

"I don't care. If those idiots keep throwing shit at the cops, you know what's going to happen. No one is getting killed on my behalf."

When the Andre Gladen riots kicked off back in May, the police came at the protesters with every supposedly non-lethal weapon they had. They were particularly vicious with the rubber bullets. Two people had lost an eye to direct hits, and worst of all, a nineteen-year-old woman died when she was struck under the heart at close range.

"I know you want to protect people, but I don't see how you can." I gestured at the seething mob on the screen. "Look at that crowd. Do you think you can get them to listen?"

"Speaking to crowds is what I *do*. Hell, I got a megaphone in the hall closet."

"Casey? Tony? Help me out here."

"Mick's right," Casey said. "If the crowd sees you in a

wheelchair, they'll just get more riled up. Besides, if you violate your bail conditions, you'll be back in Inverness before you can blink."

"I know that. And trust me, I don't want to go back inside." He jabbed a finger at the TV. "But those people are there because of me. And look at them. Shit is gonna kick off soon. There ain't no way I'm letting anyone die because of me. You're right, it's a bad idea, but I can't sit on the sideline and watch. I gotta do something. If you're not going to drive me down there, I'll call a cab. Either way, I'm going."

I shook my head. "Fine, I'll take you. But we're bailing at the first sign of trouble, okay?"

Elliott was already pushing himself towards the door. "We'll see. Now grab that megaphone out of the closet."

I tried to talk Elliott out of it as we drove downtown, but after a while he stopped acknowledging me. I parked in a lot on Fourth Avenue, a couple of blocks north of PPB.

"Let's do this," Elliot said.

I got him out of the van and we set off for Central Precinct.

By now, night was falling. A police car raced past us, lights flashing and sirens blaring. More flashing red and blue lights reflected off the plate glass windows towering above the street. Shouting and screaming could be heard above the sirens.

A sharp crack rang out, and a cloud of smoke billowed out past the building on the corner. A group of about a dozen people ran past us, heading away from the smoke and noise, bandanas tied around their faces.

We reached Chapman Square. The crowd had grown and almost filled the park. The line of cops in riot gear was still there, and the road between the park and the precinct was blocked by several parked police cars, their lights flashing. The crowd was heaving, with rainbow banners and BLM signs waving in the breeze. Someone in the middle was setting off fireworks, filling the air with colored smoke. The people at the front were screaming abuse at the police. A knot of protesters rushed the cops, but the cops beat them back with batons and plastic shields.

A robotic voice boomed out from a speaker outside the precinct.

"Please disperse! This is an unlawful gathering. Please disperse! If you do not disperse immediately, we will deploy chemical agents."

I leaned down and yelled in Elliott's ear to be heard above the racket. "Let's get out of here, buddy; there's nothing you can do."

"I gotta try," he yelled back.

Before I could stop him, Elliot wheeled himself towards the front of the crowd and shouted into his megaphone. "Everybody, it's me! Elliott Russell! Please don't do this. Please!"

A few heads turned in his direction, but most people couldn't hear him. Meanwhile, the robot voice kept repeating the order to disperse.

I jogged over to Elliott and added my voice, yelling as loud as I could. "People, it's Elliott! Listen to him!"

More heads turned our way. Recognition hit, and people started shouting.

"Hey, everyone, it's Elliott Russell! The guy they shot!"

"He's here!"

"Where?"

"The dude in the wheelchair. It's Elliott Russell!"

More heads turned our way and for a moment it seemed like Elliott might be able to get the crowd's attention. But then a flame arced through the darkness, and a Molotov cocktail shattered on a police car windshield, spraying burning gasoline on a line of cops.

All hell broke loose. The cops charged the crowd, truncheons swinging. Sharp cracks rang out as tear gas canisters sailed into the sea of people. Those nearest to them tried to flee, but couldn't get through the throng. The police were grabbing everyone they could, cuffing them with zip ties and hauling them away. People swarmed around us, running from the chaos.

The wind blew the tear gas in our direction and I caught a lungful. It stank of vinegar. An overwhelming tightness gripped my throat and chest, and my eyes felt like they were on fire.

I grabbed Elliott's wheelchair, acid tears streaming down my face, barely able to see.

"Buddy, we gotta go!"

Everyone was running now. I pushed Elliott as fast as I could, praying that my blurred vision wouldn't make me ram him into something. We turned a corner to head downhill toward the river. Elliott's chair rose up on one wheel. I heaved at it and managed to keep it from tipping. Elliott dropped the megaphone and grabbed the wheelchair's handrails. More explosions boomed through the night, followed by screams. People swept by us on both sides. I pushed as fast as I could, but we couldn't keep pace with the crowd.

At the next intersection I turned left, heading to where we'd parked, but there was a line of cops advancing toward us. I dug my heels in, and managed to bring Elliott's wheelchair to a halt, then spun him around and took off back down the hill.

"Shit! Where are we going?" Elliott yelled.

"To the waterfront! If we make it there, we should be able to cut through the park to evade the cops."

Elliott lowered his head and gripped the wheelchair tightly. I stumbled and almost fell, as we bounced across the light rail lines, but I managed to catch myself. We were only a block from the park, but the crowd was getting larger and more cops were coming in from our right. I leaned left and pushed as hard as I could.

I heard boots pounding the pavement behind me, then something cracked into the back of my head and the world went black.

THIRTY-SEVEN

THE MORNING AFTER THE NIGHT BEFORE

C asey picked me up around three in the morning.

"You look like shit," she said, as the desk sergeant led me out.

"Gee, thanks."

I rubbed the back of my head, then winced as my hand brushed the egg-sized lump in my skull. I had regained consciousness in the back of a police van, with my hands zip-tied behind my back, along with several other people. Elliott wasn't one of them. The van took us to the North Precinct, where we were placed in a holding cell. A cop came by and took us one at a time for processing and a phone call, which I used to contact Casey.

The desk sergeant handed me some paperwork and my belongings. "You're free to go," he said.

I looked at the papers. I was charged with misdemeanor criminal mischief and failure to obey a lawful order, and released on my own recognizance, with a court date to be determined.

Casey grabbed the papers and scanned them. "Looks like you're going to need a lawyer."

"Know any good ones?" I muttered.

Casey gave me a sardonic smile.

"Where's Elliott?" I said.

"They took him to Central Precinct. He's being held there. That's all I've been able to find out so far."

"Shit. I *knew* we should have stayed away."

"Never mind that. You need to go home and get some rest. Judge Obrecht wants us in court at nine. He's not happy about the video leaking."

"I'm sure he isn't," I said. "You got any idea how it got out?"

"No. I was going to ask you the same thing." Casey's eyes narrowed. "Mick, you didn't—"

"Hell no!"

"Good. I didn't think so, but I had to ask."

My eyes still stung from the tear gas and my head felt like it was being jackhammered open. There was a row of plastic chairs against the far wall, so I went and sat down. All the happiness and relief I'd felt yesterday had disappeared, replaced with a deep sense of dread.

"What happens now?" I said.

"Like I said, we go home and get some rest. There's nothing else we can do between now and 9 am."

"Yeah, okay." I hauled myself to my feet. "Let's go."

Casey drove me home. She told me again to get some sleep, but I knew that wasn't going to happen. I took a long hot shower, letting the water cascade over my face while the burning in my eyes slowly faded to a tolerable level. The clothes I'd been wearing smelled like they'd been soaked in vinegar, so I threw them in the washing machine and pulled on some sweatpants.

I turned on my TV and flicked through the channels. All the domestic networks had live coverage from downtown. My worst fears had been realized. After the police charged the crowd, the protesters had turned violent. Pretty much every window within a ten-block radius that wasn't already boarded up had been smashed, and looters made off with everything from sneakers to high-end cookware. A City of Portland trash truck had been set alight and every channel had footage of protesters dancing around the blaze.

To make matters worse, several protesters and one of the cops hit by the initial Molotov cocktail had been hospitalized. No one knew how bad their injuries were.

I made coffee. As I came back to the couch, a 'Breaking News' alert flashed across the screen and the report cut back to the studio.

A serious-looking news anchor I didn't recognize sat at a desk and held a sheet of paper.

"I've just been handed an update," he said. "Elliott Russell, the Portland activist and community leader whose shooting sparked tonight's unrest, is among those arrested. Mr. Russell, who is awaiting trial on the charge of murdering Malik Betts in June of this year, had been released on bail earlier in the day. At this point police have not specified what additional charges Mr. Russell may face."

My phone buzzed. It was Casey.

"You watching this?" she said.

"Yes. Charging Elliott isn't going to calm things down. We could be looking at months of this shit."

"I know. And Judge Obrecht will know it too. It's going to get ugly."

"Maybe we can have Elliott release some sort of statement asking people for calm?" I said. "If nothing else, it might win us some points with the judge."

"That's a great idea, but it could be tough to do. Thanks to this, we're going to be plenty busy as it is." Casey sighed. "I'm not going to get any more sleep tonight and I'm guessing you aren't either. Want to meet me at the office, see what we can do to prepare for the ass-kicking Judge Obrecht is going to give us?"

THIRTY-EIGHT
HOLD OUT YOUR HAND

"Remain standing, counselors."

Judge Obrecht had entered the courtroom with a face like a thundercloud and he wasted no time getting down to business. His head swiveled back and forth slowly as he glared at Casey and Nicole.

"Now, who's going to explain to me how sealed evidence ended up on Facebook?"

"I have no idea Your Honor," Casey said. "The only version in the defense's possession is on an encrypted and copy-protected USB drive that's locked in my safe."

Nicole shook her head. "Your Honor, this is clearly an attempt by the defense to prejudice the jury pool. The State will be making a motion for appropriate sanctions."

Judge Obrecht looked at Casey. "Ms. Raife, I confess that was my initial reaction as well. What do you have to say for yourself?"

Casey bristled. "Your Honor, that is a serious accusation and I reject it entirely. I would never do anything so unethical. I have an unblemished disciplinary record. As I said, the only copy we have is locked in my safe. Besides, the video's release hurts my client, rather than helping him. Less than a day after his release, he is back in jail–"

"Where he will remain," Judge Obrecht interjected. "I signed an order revoking bail prior to the commencement of this hearing."

"Your Honor, before you revoke bail, my client is entitled to a hearing."

"Ms. Raife, your client has violated every condition of his bail—and then some. Given the chaos our city is facing today, I strongly suggest you don't waste the court's time trying to argue otherwise."

Casey went to reply, then stopped and took a deep breath. "Yes, Your Honor. But that just proves my point. The footage being out in public harms my client immeasurably. There is simply no reason for the defense to have released it. And moreover, I object strongly to the prosecution's mention of sanctions when there is no evidence of wrongdoing on my part!"

"Well, the only people who have the video are the defense and the prosecution, and it certainly wasn't leaked by our side, Your Honor," Nicole said. "And while I agree that Ms. Raife has an exemplary record, the same cannot be said of Mr. Ward. I would point out that he was amongst the rioters last night and, like the defendant, was arrested."

I stood up slowly, leaning my clenched fists on the table. "Your Honor, may I address the court?"

"Your Honor, I object!" Nicole snapped. "Mr. Ward is not an attorney and has no place speaking in court."

"While I agree it is irregular," Judge Obrecht replied, "you have made a serious accusation against Mr. Ward, Ms. Astert. Since he is here, I will allow him to speak for himself."

"Thank you, Your Honor." I took a deep breath. "Last night, Ms. Raife and I were with Mr. Russell at his house when we learned the recording had been made public. As soon as we saw that crowds were gathering, Mr. Russell went downtown to try to defuse the situation. Ms. Raife and I did our best to convince him not to go, but he insisted, despite the obvious danger he faced in doing so. He did everything he could to get the crowd's attention, pleading with them to stand down, but to no avail. When the violence erupted, we fled, like most other people. I was knocked unconscious and arrested, and as you observed, Mr. Russell is back in jail. If I had leaked it, do you honestly think we'd have gone anywhere near downtown last night?"

I paused for a moment, an idea nagging at me. Then I remembered Detective Buchanan and how furtive he'd looked when we saw him leaving Judge Obrecht's courtroom before the discovery hearing. "I just thought of something, Your Honor. Ms. Astert says the only people who have the video are the prosecution and the defense. But she's forgetting something. Portland Police Bureau has it, too."

Nicole shot to her feet. "That's absurd, Your Honor!"

Casey stood as well. "No more absurd than the accusation that the defense are behind the leak." She took a breath. "Your Honor, Mr. Ward has a point. I know you're angry about the video going public, but believe me, we are too. There are some serious unanswered questions around PPB's conduct in this case. As we have seen from the footage, a PPB officer shot Mr. Russell without provocation. Now the dashcam recording has been released, and as a result, Mr. Russell is back in jail."

Nicole began to respond, but Judge Obrecht banged his gavel to stop her.

"Everyone be seated," he said. He took off his glasses and rubbed his eyes. "The video's release is a serious matter, but today's discussion has raised more questions than it's answered. I will take no further action at this time, but be assured that when I discover who is responsible, there will be serious consequences. Now, are there any questions?"

"No, Your Honor," Casey said.

"Nor from me," Nicole replied. "However, at this point the State moves to exclude the video from evidence at trial. Last night's violence demonstrates that it is highly prejudicial, and it is in no way relevant to the murder of Malik Betts."

"Your Honor, I object!" Casey said.

"Yes, I'm sure you do," Judge Obrecht replied wearily. "Ms. Astert, the court will consider your motion when it is appropriately submitted in writing. Ms. Raife, you will be given adequate time to submit a reply, and there will be oral argument on the motion. That is all."

He banged his gavel and left.

Casey and I headed to Starbucks for large coffees, then went back to the office. I was dead on my feet by the time we got there, and judging by the way she dumped her stuff and slumped into her chair, Casey was too.

"That could have been worse," she said.

"Yeah. I'm pissed about Elliott's bail, but it was inevitable."

"It was. We should have tried harder to stop him."

"He wouldn't have listened. He's the most stubborn guy I know. It's how he's been so successful at NNC. Doesn't matter what the campaign is, he keeps pushing until he gets his way."

Casey nodded distractedly. She took out her phone, turned it on and listened to her messages.

"Speaking of Elliott," she said, "that was Buchanan. They're transferring him back to Inverness today."

"We should go see him."

"Yeah." She listened to another message. "That's interesting."

"What?"

249

"Officer Sam Kavanagh has been arrested and charged with attempted murder for shooting Elliott."

"Good."

"I'm guessing Mayor Alioto is behind it. He's probably hoping it will calm things down. Last thing his campaign needs is more national news coverage of riots in Portland."

"I don't care why it happened, as long as that fucker Kavanagh gets what's coming to him. You know he would have skated otherwise."

Casey looked at me, eyebrows raised.

"Look, I told you I didn't leak the video," I said. "Do you think I wanted Elliott back in jail?"

"I know. Sorry, Mick. I'm just tired."

"Yeah, me too. But you've got me thinking. I'm going to go poke around the web a bit. Maybe whoever's responsible for the leak left a trail."

I went to my desk, fired up my laptop and checked out some news sites. Kavanagh's arrest was the top story, but judging by the comments, it wouldn't do anything to calm the protests. There were all kinds of demands for retribution and threats of violence against the police.

I went on Facebook and found the original shooting video entry. It had been posted by a user named BlueBoy88. Not surprisingly, it was a private burner account. BlueBoy88 hadn't made any other posts before or after. But a couple of things about the username bothered me. First, there was the 'BlueBoy' part. Was that a reference to the Thin Blue Line police support movement that arose in response to Black Lives Matter? And the '88' looked familiar for some reason too. A quick Google search confirmed my suspicions. 88 was a white supremacist recognition code. H is the eighth letter of the alphabet; 88 represented HH, an abbreviation for *Heil Hitler*.

I tried all the other social media platforms I could think of, but I couldn't find a user called BlueBoy88 on any of them. I tried some more Google searches with variations on the handle, but they didn't help much either. The only 'Blueboy' that showed up was an English indie pop band from the nineties.

Maybe my suspicion about the cops releasing the video was off base. Sure, they probably wanted Elliott locked up, but cops got hurt last night too. If the violence kept up, who was to say that more police officers wouldn't be injured?

My coffee was cold now, but I drank the last of it anyway. I felt like I had a head full of glue, and chasing my tail around the internet wasn't helping. I went back to the Facebook post. It had over two hundred comments now. Most of them were angry diatribes against the police and calls for immediate action. Some comments had been deleted by the Admins—I assumed they were the usual racist junk that inevitably cropped up on these sites. But one post caught my eye. It was a link to a news article about Kavanagh's arrest, with a comment attached.

'Thrown to the wolves. Same old story—soldiers are expendable.'

This user's profile was public, though not particularly helpful. He only had a few posts, mostly pictures of a bunch of large white dudes on fishing trips. Although there were no uniforms in the pictures, the guys all had the unmistakable cop look about them.

So, at least one cop wasn't happy about the video being released and Kavanagh's arrest. But who was 'throwing him to the wolves', and why? Was it related to his bad record? Maybe some officer was upset at Kavanagh's constant disciplinary problems and the fact he kept getting away with them, so decided to act? But releasing the video was a drastic course of action.

Still, it made me think. Maybe Elliott being shot was the

final straw for someone. There weren't many Black cops in Portland, but it only took one.

I took out my phone and made a call. Detective Buchanan answered immediately.

"Mick Ward. Jesus Christ, what do you want?"

"Who released the video?" I asked.

"What?"

"You heard me."

Buchanan sighed. "I have no idea what you're talking about and it might shock you to know that I'm really fucking busy right now."

"I'm trying to help you, Detective. Who was it? Who wanted Kavanagh to pay for shooting Elliott?"

"Oh, I get it. Because I'm a Black cop, I'm part of some secret pro-BLM police conspiracy. Please."

He hung up.

I tossed my phone onto my desk and stared at it. Maybe Buchanan was right. I'd been knocked out cold last night and I hadn't had any sleep. Maybe my addled brain was seeing conspiracies where none existed. But I was convinced that whoever released the video wasn't interested in Elliott. They did it to get at Sam Kavanagh.

THIRTY-NINE

BACK HOME

I went out to the office to talk to Casey, but she had fallen asleep in her chair. Her head lolled back and she was snoring lightly. I wrote a note telling her I was going out to Inverness to see Elliott, then left as quietly as I could.

It was raining again as I headed east on I-84, the fat drops slapping on the windshield helping to keep me awake. Rush hour hadn't begun, so traffic was light. I was still wearing my suit from court that morning, so when I parked at Inverness, I pulled my jacket up over my head and ran to the public entrance.

I told them I was there to see Elliott and went to the waiting area, where I sat down and hung my wet jacket over the chair next to me. My phone buzzed with a text from Casey.

Sorry. Want me to come out there?

I sent my reply. *No need. Get some rest. I'll see you tomorrow.*

I poked around the BLM Facebook page for a while, but I hadn't found anything useful when a guard came to get me an hour later.

Elliott was waiting for me in the visiting room, back in his orange jumpsuit and prison-issue wheelchair. His eyes were more red than white, probably from the tear gas. He looked as exhausted as I felt, but I didn't see any fresh bruises.

"How are you feeling, buddy?" I asked.

"Like shit. How about you? That cop hit you hard."

I rubbed the back of my head and winced. "I'll survive. What happened? I don't remember anything after I got hit."

"When the cop whacked you with his night stick, you let go of my chair and went down. Took me a moment to get stopped and turned around. By the time I did, you were cuffed and two cops were dragging you away. Two more wheeled me to a black and white, then cuffed me and took me to Central."

"Did they treat you okay?"

"Pretty much. They put me in a cell on my own. I just sat there until the morning, when one of them came back and told me the judge had yanked my bail." He waved his arm at the interview room and grimaced. "And here we are again."

"Yeah. I talked to Casey and I don't think there's much we can do about that."

"Yeah, I figured. Serves me right for being a dumbass. Did anyone get hurt last night?"

"Last I heard, five people were in hospital, including one of the cops hit by the Molotov cocktail. But I don't know how bad any of them are."

"Shit." Elliott shook his head. "Five more minutes with that crowd, man. That's all I needed. They were *listening* to me."

I didn't think it would have mattered. Too many people in that crowd came wanting blood, and Elliott couldn't have turned them back. But he was in a bad enough situation, so I wasn't going to tell him that.

"Maybe so," I said. "We'll never know."

"What's it like out there?" Elliott waved a hand loosely. "In the city."

I knew what he meant. "Looks like it's only going to get worse. You saw what the video provoked and people are even more pissed now that you're locked up again. Tonight is going to be a mess."

"I was afraid of that. Any new developments in my case?"

"Yeah, Kavanagh has been arrested and charged with attempted murder. I think that's why the video was leaked. Someone wanted to take him down. Damned if I can figure out who, though."

"Doesn't matter now, I guess. Now that the riots have started up again, they're just going to fuck with me more."

"We'll see about that," I said. "I'll talk to the warden on my way out, see if he can do anything."

"No, he's as bad as the rest of them. It will only make things worse." Elliott sighed and put his head in his hands. "I'm sorry, Mick. I fucked up."

Seeing Elliott so upset brought the weight of the last twenty-four hours crashing down on me. Once again I felt powerless, unable to do anything to help my friend when he needed me most.

"Hang in there, buddy," I said.

"Yeah, I will. Thanks for coming to see me."

I left, this time not bothering to use my jacket for shelter as I walked through the rain to my car. I got in and sat there, water dripping from my hair. Two guys walked past me, to the public entrance. One of them had long gray hair tied in a ponytail, and that gave me an idea. I grabbed my phone and dialed.

"Hey, Sonny, it's Mick."

"Mick! I heard you and your guy Elliott got caught up in that shit last night. You okay?"

"That's why I'm calling. To call in that favor. Do you have any contacts at Inverness? Staff or inmates, I don't care."

"Can't help you on the staff side. We don't do uniforms. But a couple of the Brothers are in there, doing a stretch for a little disagreement we had with the Mongols a while back."

"They got any influence?"

"Some. What do you need?"

"Elliott is back in there and people have been fucking with him. I need it to stop."

Sonny laughed. "Oh, my boys can take care of that. Consider it done."

"Thanks, Sonny. I appreciate it."

"You're welcome. And Mick?"

"Yeah?"

"Still not enough. I still owe you one."

I hoped Sonny's guys would come through for me. The last thing Elliott needed was more trouble inside.

My phone rang soon after I drove off. It was Sarah. I thought about ignoring it, then answered.

"Hi, Mick," she said, then hesitated.

"What is it? Are you calling to bug me about alimony again? I know I still owe you some for last month."

"No, it's…" Her voice trailed off.

"Sarah, I'm having a shitty day. What do you want?"

"It's Ryan. He's asked me to marry him."

"I'm guessing you wouldn't be calling me if you'd said no."

Sarah didn't answer.

"Good," I said.

"Are you sure you're okay with this?"

"I am. Not that I have any say in the matter."

"Thanks, Mick. That means a lot to me."

"I'm still going to send him the thank you cards though," I said.

Sarah laughed. "Of course you are. Maybe we could get coffee some time?"

"Sure, I'd like that," I said, and hung up.

Jesus, how many more hits were coming? I'd said I wanted Sarah and Ryan to get married, but the churning in my guts told me how big a lie that was. Still, now I could stop worrying about alimony. I'd managed to squeeze in a few handyman gigs to supplement the pittance Casey was paying me, but it was still all I could do to keep my head above water.

My phone rang again a few minutes later. I checked to see if it was Sarah, ready to kill the call without answering, but it was Tony.

"Hey, Mick, how are you doing?"

"I've had better days. What's up?"

"A couple of things. First, I got Elliott's phone records. The good news is that positioning shows him either at the office or at home on the day Betts died. The bad news is there aren't any calls or texts that afternoon to confirm he was in the same place as his phone."

"Could be worse. What else?"

"I found something interesting about that gun store owner."

"What about him?"

"I think I've found his connection to the case. His brother's a construction foreman. Works for CDS."

At first, what Tony said meant nothing to me. But then my addled brain made the connection. "You're shitting me. Sinclair's company."

"Yeah."

"Thanks, Tony. This could be huge." I hung up.

Wet roads and rush hour traffic doubled my drive time home. Night was falling when I finally made it to my apartment. I was dead on my feet, so I took off my suit, had a quick hot shower, then lay down to snatch some sleep. I set an alarm for three hours later. Thanks to Tony, I had things to do.

FORTY
PARTY CRASHERS

The alarm blasted me out of a deep sleep at 9 pm. It was all I could do to get up, fighting my overwhelming desire to switch off the alarm and put my head back down. I went to the bathroom and splashed cold water on my face. It woke me up a little, but I still felt like shit. I got dressed, downloaded some pictures from the case file onto my phone, and headed outside.

I drove over to Northwest Portland, skirting downtown on the south side to avoid the chaos of the riots. As I crossed the river on the raised span of the Marquam Bridge, I saw flashing blue and red police lights reflecting off skyscraper glass and illuminating clouds of smoke drifting up into the night. I took the Everett exit, ducked back under the freeway and parked a block down the street from Paley's Place. The restaurant was in an elegant pale blue Victorian mansion. It backed onto a small parking lot, with a dumpster just outside the rear door. Judging by the overflowing ashtray on the top step, I'd found the place I was looking for. I leaned against the dumpster and waited.

About ten minutes later, a guy in a chef's jacket and pants came out and lit a cigarette. He flinched when I emerged from the shadows.

"Shit, you startled me, dude. Not cool," he said.

"Sorry about that," I replied, holding up a calming hand. "I need your help. I'm an investigator and I'm looking for information about an incident that took place here on June first this year. It was a Saturday night and there was a private event taking place. Apparently, there was some sort of disturbance and the police were called. You know anything about that?"

The guy took a thoughtful drag on his cigarette. "Doesn't ring a bell, but then I'm usually off on Saturdays."

"You think you could ask around inside? Find me someone who was there and I'll kick a few bucks your way."

"Sounds fair. I'll see what I can do." He took another drag on his cigarette, then stubbed it out on his shoe and put the unfinished half back in the packet.

He went back inside and I resumed my wait by the dumpster. A couple of minutes later, he stuck his head out of the door. "One of the servers was there that night and she saw the whole thing go down. She said she'll meet you when she gets off shift in an hour. Her name's Hayley. I told her what you look like. You know Joe's Cellar? It's a couple of blocks that way." He pointed north, up the street.

"I'm sure I can find it." I fished a couple of twenties out of my pocket and handed them to him. "Thanks, man."

He tucked them into his pants without looking at them. "No problem. Good luck."

He went back inside and I set off up the street. Joe's was easy to find, thanks to the large sandwich board out front with the name in flowing script and daily specials written in chalk. It was an older corner bar, with cedar siding and neon Pabst Blue Ribbon signs in the windows.

Inside, there were a couple of pool tables, both in use, and half a dozen tables with knots of people around them. The bar was mostly empty, so I took a stool by the far end, where I had a good view of the door.

I had almost finished my second pint when a young woman walked in an hour later. She looked around, saw me wave, and headed over.

I stood up and held out my hand. "You must be Hayley?"

"Yes, that's right." She shook my hand, her grip warm and firm.

"My name is Mick Ward," I said, and gestured at the stool next to mine. "Thanks for coming. Can I get you a drink?"

"Sure. A gin and tonic would be nice, thanks." She sat down, and I flagged down the bartender and ordered her drink, plus another pint for me.

"So, what do you want?" she asked.

"Your colleague told me you were working when an incident took place at a private party on June first of this year. I'd like to ask you some questions about it."

"Why? Am I in trouble?"

"No, nothing like that. I just want to know what happened that night."

"Are you a cop?"

I laughed. "Do I look like a cop?"

The barman delivered our drinks before Hayley could answer. She took a long gulp of hers, then sighed.

"No, I guess not," she said. "Okay, ask your questions."

"Let's start at the beginning. What was the occasion for the event?"

"It was a fundraiser for Mayor Alioto's campaign."

"And was Mayor Alioto there?"

"Yes, but he wasn't involved in the incident."

I took a sip of my pint. "Speaking of that, can you tell me what happened?"

"It was near the end of the evening. We were serving dessert and coffee. Some guy turned up at the door and tried to get in. He looked pretty loaded and he had a woman on each arm. Both of them had big hair and short dresses, which didn't exactly go with the fundraiser crowd.

"Anyway, this guy was really loud. He kept saying something about his buddies being inside. The security guard tried to calm him down, but the guy wasn't having it, so he grabbed him and tried to move him away. Before I knew what was happening, the guy took a swing at the guard, who tackled him and they went rolling down the steps. A couple of us ran out front to see what was happening. The two of them were fighting on the sidewalk. The security guard took him down easily—he got the guy down on the ground and pinned him, with a knee in his back and his arm across his neck.

"Right about then, the cops showed up. Someone from inside must've called them. I didn't see how it ended because I went back in to keep serving, but someone told me later that the cops took both of them away. It was crazy. That kind of stuff never happens at Paley's. We don't even usually have security."

She paused and took another drink.

Something about her story was ringing bells with me. "If I showed you some photos, could you tell me if you recognize the people in them?"

"I can try."

I took out my phone and pulled up a photo of Kavanagh. "Was that the security guy?"

"Yeah, the redhead. That was him."

"And the guy causing trouble," I said. "Was he a white guy? African American?"

"African American. So were the women with him."

I pulled up a photo of Malik Betts. "Was it him?"

"I think so." She took my phone and enlarged the picture. "Yeah, that's him."

"Thanks." A thought occurred to me. "One other thing—who hosted the fundraiser?"

"Some old white dude in a suit. I don't know his name."

I took my phone back and pulled up another picture. "Him?"

"Yes, that looks like the guy. He was kind of an asshole. Arrogant, you know?"

"Thanks. You've been very helpful." I reached into my pocket and pulled out a hundred bucks.

Hayley raised her eyebrows at the five twenties. "Thanks!" She finished her drink. "I hope you don't mind, but I'm going to take off. It's been a long day."

"Go ahead. I appreciate your help."

Hayley headed for the door. I looked at the picture on my phone. Charles Sinclair had hosted a fundraiser for Mayor Alioto. He hired Kavanagh to work security, Kavanagh beat the crap out of Malik Betts, and two weeks later Betts was killed. I'd never believed in coincidences, and this sure as hell didn't look like one to me.

FORTY-ONE
STRIKEOUT

I called Detective Buchanan first thing Tuesday morning.

"Detective, it's Mick Ward. We need to talk."

He sighed. "You're kidding, right? I haven't slept in two days because the whole goddamn city is on fire, and you want to have a conversation?"

"The city is on fire because a cop shot Elliott," I snapped, then took a deep breath. "Look, I know you're slammed, but this is important. I only need ten minutes. I'll come to the Starbucks by the precinct. Surely you can duck out for that long."

Buchanan paused. "All right. If you're willing to meet outside one of your usual shitholes, it must be important. Be there in an hour."

He hung up.

I headed downtown and parked a couple of blocks north of the precinct. As I walked to Starbucks, every street-level window was boarded up and heavily graffitied, with BLM slogans and variations on the theme of 'Fuck the police.' The streets were quieter than usual, as though people were afraid to come out. It had rained overnight and the smell of wet smoke hung heavy in the air.

Starbucks was boarded up too, and an employee was trying to scrub some of the more offensive graffiti off the plywood. I went inside, ordered a large latte with an extra shot and took a seat in the corner.

Buchanan appeared a few minutes later. He didn't order a drink, just came and sat down heavily in the chair opposite me, with a sigh that sounded like the air going out of a slashed tire. He looked terrible. His usually immaculately shaved head was covered with sparse stubble and his dark skin had a strange gray hue.

He rubbed his face. "Okay, you've got your ten minutes. Talk to me."

"It's about Charles Sinclair and Sam Kavanagh. You need to be looking at them for Betts's murder."

Buchanan's head lolled back. "You've got to be fucking kidding me."

"I'm serious,. I've been digging and there's a connection–"

He held out a hand. "Stop. You're going to tell me that Kavanagh worked security for Sinclair on the side and he got into a fight with Betts at a fundraiser two weeks before Betts was killed, right?"

"Yes, but–"

"And that Betts and Sinclair did a lot of business together?"

"They did–"

"You must think we're a bunch of goddamn imbeciles. First thing we did when we heard about the murder was run a search on Betts's name. The Internal Affairs report on the incident between Kavanagh and Betts popped up. We already looked into it and there's nothing there. Kavanagh was working the night Betts died, and besides, Betts bought a lot of property from Sinclair. Do you honestly think one of Portland's most successful businessmen goes around whacking his best customers?"

"Okay, but did you know there's been at least one other recent confrontation between Sinclair and Betts, at a Trail Blazers game?"

"I told you, we investigated and there's nothing there." Buchanan looked at his watch. "Are you done wasting my time?"

"If I brought you information proving there's something weird about the business deals between Betts and Sinclair, would you take another look?"

"No. The Chief raised almighty hell the first time we looked at Sinclair. He's the mayor's biggest donor. You think I'm going to put my pension on the line by suggesting we investigate him again? Christ, I almost liked you better when you were a lawyer." He stood up and left, shaking his head as he went.

I finished my coffee as I walked up to the office. I should have realized that the police would have already made the connection between Betts and Sinclair. Maybe I would have done a better job of selling my idea to Buchanan if I'd led with the unusual business transactions, particularly Betts buying large volumes of condos and selling them so cheap. But I didn't know what was going on there yet. I made a mental note to go back to the data Tony's hacker friend had delivered, to see if I could figure that out.

And what about Kavanagh? I already knew he was working the night Betts died. But his name kept coming up: he shot Elliott, he fought with Betts. Could he be involved? Something occurred to me, so I called Tony.

"Hey, Tony, can you check something for me?"

"Sure, what is it?"

"The night Betts was killed. What time did Sam Kavanagh's shift start?"

"Should be easy to find out. I'll get back to you."

"Thanks, man."

I made it to the office just after nine thirty. Casey looked up from her laptop.

"Working banker's hours now, huh?"

"Yeah, very funny." I sat down in one of the conference chairs and told her about my conversation with Buchanan. Her face darkened as I finished my story.

"So let me get this straight. You found out about this fight between Betts and Kavanagh and you took it to Buchanan before you even talked to me?"

"I wanted to get him on the case. If he'd have turned something up, maybe we could have got Elliott out sooner."

"Jesus, how can you be so stupid?"

"What do you mean?"

"Why don't you just email our whole defense strategy to the DA? You know the first thing Buchanan's going to do is tell Nicole Astert about your meeting. So, now she knows that we're going with a Some Other Dude defense, and that Kavanagh and Sinclair are our other dudes. Which means long before we get to trial, Kavanagh's alibi is going to be watertight and she'll have a line of witnesses a mile long ready to tell the jury what great friends and business partners Sinclair and Betts were. We'll be lucky if we don't get laughed out of court."

I shuffled uncomfortably in my chair. "They had to know already that we'd be trying to paint someone else as the killer."

"Yeah, but they didn't know who!" Casey took a deep breath. "Mick, this case is a pig. We've got to stay tight on communication and strategy if we're going to have any chance of pulling off a verdict for Elliott. Who knows, that information you found out about Betts and Sinclair might still be useful. But promise me that if you find anything else, you'll talk to me before you go off on some wild goose chase with anyone else? Especially the other side!"

"Yeah, you're right," I said. "Sorry. I just want to get Elliott out of that shithole."

"I know. Look, we've got the hearing on the prosecution's motion to exclude the video next Tuesday, and trial starts three weeks after that. The best thing you can do for Elliott is help me win that hearing. Without the video, our case falls apart and we might as well not show up for the trial."

"Okay, where do we stand on that?"

"You remember the test, right?"

I thought for a moment. "Yeah, the judge can exclude evidence if its probative value is substantially outweighed by a danger of unfair prejudice."

"Exactly. The DA will say that this latest round of riots demonstrates the video is highly prejudicial, and we can't argue with that. So, we have to show that its probative value is just as high, if not higher. That means we've got to establish two things: that we have a credible story about how Betts was killed and that the video is essential evidence in proving it."

I grimaced. "And right now our theory has holes in it big enough to drive a bus through."

"Pretty much. I know you like Sinclair as the mastermind behind it all, but it's hard to make a believable argument that he had his biggest customer whacked."

"Yeah, I know, everybody keeps saying that." I paused. "What if we leave him out for now? Just say our theory is that Kavanagh had a fight with Betts two weeks before he was killed, and the video shows he's a loose cannon ready to pull a gun at the slightest provocation?"

Casey thought for a moment, then nodded slowly. "It's speculative, but it might work. I'd feel a lot better about it if you could find me similar cases where a judge ruled that kind of speculation was good enough to meet the test."

"I'm on it." I stood up and went to my desk, then stopped. "Hey, you know we need to add Kavanagh to our witness list, right?"

"Already done," Casey replied.

FORTY-TWO
FRIENDLY CONVERSATION

I spent the next couple of days wading through case law, looking for a hidden gem that Casey could use to convince the judge to let the jury see the video. Legal research can be heavy lifting. There's an art to it, one that I truly believed I had mastered back when I used to do it for a living. But even for an expert like me, this was looking for a needle in a haystack. First, I had to find cases with similar facts, then narrow them down to those where the judge's ruling supported our position.

I stayed at the office until almost midnight both Tuesday and Wednesday, without much success. Casey got there before me on Thursday and there was a steaming hot Starbucks waiting for me on my desk in the copy room when I arrived.

"Thanks," I said to her. "I have a feeling I'm gonna need it."

I logged on and dived straight back into the routine of wading through mountains of case law. A few hours later, I felt like I was going cross-eyed, so I took a break. I called Tony and arranged to meet him for lunch at Pine Street Market.

Summer was well and truly over, replaced all too soon by typically cold and damp northwest weather, so I zipped up my coat and hurried over there. When the rain became heavier, I pulled my hood up. As usual, you could tell the tourists by who was using an umbrella. Portlanders wouldn't be caught dead with one, no matter how hard the rain came down.

Pine Street was emptier than usual when I arrived. More than half of the benches and tables were free. No doubt a good chunk of downtown office workers had decided to stay inside and have food delivered, rather than brave the elements. I looked around and spotted Tony, waiting at the Kinboshi stand.

"Hey, Mick," he said, "I figured some noodles would be good on a day like this."

I shook off my wet coat and draped it over a chair. "Sounds good to me. I'm hungry. Let's order."

We went to the counter, both ordered the tonkatsu ramen, then returned to our seats. We made small talk while we waited for our food. I didn't mind the distraction. There was something I wanted to ask Tony, but I couldn't think of a good way to do it. In the end, I opted for the direct approach.

I took a deep breath. "There's something I need to ask you. You still have an ICS Corrections account, right?"

Tony looked at me warily. "Yeah, why?"

Members of the public couldn't call an incarcerated person directly in Oregon. You had to go through the ICS system and leave a message. The prisoner could call you back using the same system, provided they had money in their account.

"I need to leave a message for Kavanagh. We've added him to our witness list and I want to yank his chain."

"I'm guessing Kavanagh has a lawyer, and more importantly, I'm guessing you know he does. That means you can't contact him directly. Does Casey know about this?"

"No, and I want to keep it that way. I don't want her getting in trouble if there's any blowback."

Tony frowned. "What about you?"

I shrugged. "What are they going to do? Disbar me?"

"That's not the point, Mick. This is a bad idea."

Our noodles arrived, so we waited until the server left. I took a spoonful of the rich pork broth and savored it for a moment. Tony was right. I'd be violating the rules of legal ethics by contacting Kavanagh and it could come back on Casey too.

"Maybe," I said. "But we're running out of options. There's a good chance the judge will exclude the shooting video next week. If that happens, we've got nothing."

Tony poked at his noodles. "All right. You can use my account."

"Thanks, man. I appreciate it."

"What about that information we got from my friend?" Tony said. "Didn't that give you anything?"

"It shows that Betts and Sinclair did a lot of business together. More than we first thought, that's for sure. Those extra shell companies your guy mentioned? The ones Betts owned? They do construction supply and they sell a bunch of materials to Sinclair for his condo developments. But that just brings us back to the same dead end—why would Sinclair whack his business partner when they had a sweet thing going?"

Tony pointed his chopsticks at me. "My advice is to keep digging. Like my guy said, there wouldn't be all those layers of shell companies if the business was above board. It's in there, probably right in front of your face."

"Okay, I'll take another look. I hope you're right."

"One other thing," Tony said. "My guy checked the shift schedules. Kavanagh started at 6 pm the day Betts was killed."

"Plenty of time for him to do the deed before that. Thanks, Tony."

We finished our lunch and went our separate ways. I let Tony leave first, then found a quiet corner of the market and used his ICS account to leave a message for Sam Kavanagh.

"Officer Kavanagh, you've got a big problem, and I can help

you. Call me back, any time after 4 pm today." I left my number and hung up.

I went back to the office and tried to do more research, but I couldn't focus. I felt like I was one break away from figuring out the whole story, but that one break was locked inside a cast-iron safe. No matter how hard I banged on the door, I couldn't get in. Around the middle of the afternoon I gave up, made a weak excuse to Casey, and headed home.

I had just sat down in my apartment when my phone rang. When I answered, a voice that sounded like it had been recorded in a tin shack spoke.

"This is ICS Corrections. You are receiving a call from an inmate in the State of Oregon. Please press one to accept the call. To reject the call, press two, or hang up."

I pressed one.

"Hello?"

A gruff voice answered. "Who the fuck are you and why are you calling me?"

"I can't tell you my name, Officer Kavanagh. But I heard Elliott Russell's defense team is calling you as a witness at his trial."

"Like fuck they are."

"You were added to the witness list today," I said. "They'll get a subpoena if they need it."

"They can get what they fucking like, pal. I ain't saying shit."

"I'm not sure that's going to help you."

Kavanagh paused. "What are you talking about?"

"Let me ask you this. Why do you think you're in jail right now?"

"Because some dumbass punk released a video."

"Exactly. But who? And why?"

"I don't know what you mean."

"Think about it. Before the video was released, you were under internal investigation for shooting Elliott Russell, but everyone knew that investigation was going nowhere. You'd have got a slap on the wrist and life would go on. Same as all the other times you were investigated. Someone probably even told you that."

"It helps to have friends, man," Kavanagh said. I could almost hear the smugness in his voice.

"So who leaked the video? Russell's defense team sure as hell didn't do it. The DA wouldn't have done it, because it hurts their case against Russell. The only other people who have the video are Portland Police Bureau. The police wouldn't have leaked the video directly, because they'd know it would mean another round of riots. But someone with contacts in the bureau, someone with a lot of influence, they could have done it. Why?"

"I still don't know what you're talking about."

"It took me a while to figure it out," I said. "But it's obvious. Who's hurt the most by that video getting out? You. And the people who leaked it are the ones you thought had your back."

"That's crazy," Kavanagh replied, but he didn't sound so cocky now.

"Is it? What if you're expendable now? What if you know something that powerful people want kept secret?"

"Like what?"

"Like who killed Malik Betts."

Kavanagh was silent for a long time. When he spoke again, his voice was almost a whisper. "I told you, I got friends."

"So what? Now you're on the witness list, that means you'll be testifying in open court. One wrong word out of your mouth and your friends go to jail for the rest of their lives. Do you honestly think they'll let you live to take the stand?"

Kavanagh was silent for a while. "Fuck you, man," he hissed eventually, and hung up.

I took a deep breath. My hands were shaking. I'd suspected it for a long time, and at last I knew for sure. Kavanagh shot Betts. It had to be him. Now I just needed to figure out why.

FORTY-THREE

IN THE TRENCHES

I didn't sleep a wink, that night. I'd had a few beers at Holman's to take the edge off, but I still just laid in bed and stared at the ceiling. I kept picturing Sam Kavanagh putting his gun to Malik Betts's head, and Betts looking up at him past the cold steel barrel. Did he struggle? Did he beg for his life? And what were his last thoughts as he saw Kavanagh's finger tighten on the trigger? I had no love for Betts, but it must have been a terrifying way to die.

Eventually, I got up and watched news coverage of the riots downtown. Portland looked like George H. W. Bush's nickname for it—Little Beirut. Crowds of people in balaclavas and improvised gas masks lobbing bricks at riot police, then fleeing the inevitable charge. Breathless reporters ducking at the sound of tear gas canisters being fired overhead. The city I loved was in flames, for all the wrong reasons.

I fell asleep with the TV still on. When I woke up, the riot coverage had been replaced by a depressingly cheerful morning chat show. I turned it off, showered and went to work. The next few days dragged by in a haze of more legal research and drafting. Casey and I worked through the weekend, preparing for the hearing on whether we could use the shooting video at trial. By Monday night, we had a passable argument pulled together, but neither of us felt confident when we finally called it a day.

Tuesday morning dawned cold and damp again, so Casey and I took a cab to the courthouse for the hearing. The general public admission line at Multnomah County Courthouse was usually quite long, but today it stretched halfway around the block. Extra security had been implemented in the wake of the riots. Now, in addition to going through a metal detector, armed police patted everyone down and searched their bags. Fortunately, attorneys and their teams had a separate entrance that allowed us to skip the line, but we received the same thorough search.

Neither of us said much, as we made our way to Judge Obrecht's courtroom on the third floor. We both knew how important today was. If the judge said the video of Kavanagh shooting Elliott couldn't be used at trial, it would blow a massive hole in our defense strategy. We had to convince a jury that Kavanagh could have been the one who killed Betts. Juries love cops, no matter how much they lie on the witness stand. Without the video, we had no chance of making them believe a cop was the killer.

We were the first ones to arrive. Judge Obrecht had closed the public gallery for the hearing, so Billy and the rest of the NNC crew couldn't be there with us. The closure was supposedly another precaution in response to the riots, but Casey and I both took it as a bad sign. A ruling against us wouldn't be well received by Elliott's supporters and Judge Obrecht knew that.

Casey took out her files and set up for her argument, while I leaned back in my chair and stared at the vaulted ceiling. I wanted to be the one arguing the case today. It burned me that I'd never be able to do it again. I trusted Casey; she was as good as any defense lawyer I'd come across, maybe better than I had ever been. But this was a fight for Elliott's life and I desperately wanted to wade in to the fray.

Nicole Astert entered the courtroom, followed by a flustered-looking assistant DA carrying her files. She sat at the prosecution table and looked over at us, a small smile on her face.

"Good morning, counselor. Good morning, Mr. Ward."

Casey nodded briefly. I ignored the greeting.

The court clerk entered from the judge's chambers. "All rise."

We stood, and Judge Obrecht walked into the courtroom. He pulled back his chair and sat down.

"Good morning, all," he said. "We are here on the matter of State versus Russell, and today we're going to hear argument on the prosecution's motion to exclude from evidence the police video showing the arrest and shooting of Mr. Russell, the defendant in this matter. Are both sides ready to proceed?"

Casey and Astert both said that they were.

"Good." Judge Obrecht shuffled some papers. "Ms. Astert, you may begin."

Nicole stood and smoothed the front of her blouse.

"Thank you, Your Honor. It is well established in law that evidence may be excluded if its prejudicial effect substantially outweighs its probative value. The video in question is highly prejudicial and has no probative value in this case."

She gestured toward the courtroom's oak-paneled door. "To understand the video's prejudicial effect, we only need to look at what's happening out there in our city today. Since the video's release, Portland has been subjected to nightly riots and violence. The scale of destruction is staggering. It is blindingly obvious that the video incites raw emotional responses completely lacking in reason, which are entirely out of place in a court of law.

"Moreover, the video has no probative value, because it is in no way relevant to the matter at hand. The question in this case is whether Elliott Russell murdered Malik Betts. The incident captured in the video happened long after Malik Betts was killed, subsequent to a routine traffic stop. While the video may not show Portland Police in the best light, it has no bearing on whether the defendant in this matter shot Malik Betts several days earlier, in an entirely separate location.

"Your Honor, the defense seeks to introduce an incendiary video with no relevance to this case, solely to distract the jury from the mountain of evidence against their client. The rules of evidence exist precisely to prevent that kind of action, and hence the video must be excluded."

Astert sat down, careful not to look in our direction.

"Thank you, Ms. Astert," Judge Obrecht said. "Ms. Raife, your response?"

Casey stood. "Your Honor, the defense does not deny that the video is provocative. But it is precisely for that reason it must be admitted. Another well-established principle of law is that in capital murder cases, the defense should be given wide latitude in introducing potentially exculpatory evidence. In this instance, we have footage that shows a police officer shooting Mr. Russell without provocation or justification. That same officer had a violent confrontation with Malik Betts shortly before his death. The video is clear and compelling evidence of the officer's willingness to use deadly force. Coupled with the officer's prior violence against Mr. Betts, this is a viable defense theory that we must be allowed to present to the jury."

Casey paused, consulted her notes, and looked up at the judge. "Your Honor, the defense concedes that the video's release has prompted shocking scenes here in Portland. But in the controlled environment of a court of law, along with appropriate jury instructions, it can be presented in a way where its prejudicial effect is minimized. In our response to the prosecution's motion, we have identified several cases where a court allowed potentially prejudicial evidence without a negative effect. The video has direct bearing on who killed Malik Betts, and it must be admitted if my client is to receive a fair trial."

Casey sat down. I nodded at her, impressed by how she had presented her case. She gave an uncertain shrug in response.

Judge Obrecht wrote something on his notepad, then put his pen down.

"Thank you, both," he said. "Ms. Raife, I have reviewed the cases you provided, and frankly I'm not persuaded. There's nothing in them that can remotely compare to the incendiary nature of the footage in question. Given the destruction and chaos we have seen in the city over the past week and a half, I fail to see how a simple instruction could address its effect on the jury. I'm afraid I have no choice but to exclude the video from evidence at trial. The prosecution's motion is granted. Do counsel have any other matters before we adjourn?"

"No, Your Honor," Astert said, unable to hide her smile.

Casey put her head in her hands. "No, Your Honor," she muttered.

Judge Obrecht stood up, nodded at us, and left. As soon as he disappeared into his chambers, Astert and her assistant gathered their things and walked out.

Casey slumped back in her chair and let out a deep sigh. "Well, we tried."

I shook my head. "Not letting the jury see the video drops us in a deep hole."

"Yeah, it does. But we have one last throw of the dice. We put Kavanagh on the stand and catch him in a lie. Maybe then we can crawl our way over the line to reasonable doubt."

FORTY-FOUR
STRIKE THREE

I arrived at the office early the next morning. With the trial a few short weeks away, we had a mountain of work ahead of us. Casey arrived an hour after me and we sat down at the conference table to work on Sam Kavanagh's testimony.

"So how are you going to play it?" I asked.

"We open with the obvious. Put his partner Wright on the stand first, use his statement to the investigation to get him to repeat his claim that he couldn't see anything, then hit him with the transcript where he says Elliott had his hands on his head and he didn't see a gun."

"Okay. And what about Kavanagh?"

Casey sighed. "Good question. We can use the same line, show that he lied about seeing a gun. And he also said Elliott tried to flee, but the arrest was only three blocks from the NNC office. So, there's another obvious lie."

I could see from Casey's face that she didn't think it was enough, and I agreed with her. "We've got to get him to testify about his fight with Betts," I said. "And we should bring up his off-duty security work, too. Paint him as a thug for hire. Plus, there's his disciplinary record—you can ask him why he got away with so much crap that other cops would have been fired for."

"I agree with you about the fight and the security work," Casey replied, "but I'm not sure about the disciplinary stuff. That's headed off into conspiracy land and I'm not sure the judge will let us go there."

I paused. How I phrased the next bit was important. "We don't have to go far. It's not about convincing the jury of some big conspiracy. It's about making Kavanagh sweat. You ask him about the disciplinary stuff and he'll be all smug because he got away with so much. Then you ask him why he's locked up. Ask him why those friends who took good care of him in the past aren't there for him now."

"What's the point? Nicole will object and the judge will strike the question."

"Maybe not. And either way, Kavanagh will have heard it," I said. He'd become nervous and defensive when I brought that up on our call.

Casey must have seen the look on my face. "Is there something you're not telling me?"

"No, of course not," I said quickly. "It's just a way to rattle him. If someone did put him up to killing Betts, maybe he'll make a mistake. Give us something we can capitalize on."

She didn't look convinced. "Okay, I'll think about it."

I tried to think of a way to change the subject to avoid any more awkward questions. The last thing I needed was Casey knowing I'd violated ethical rules. And if it got back to the judge, he'd hit us with all kinds of sanctions.

Fortunately for me, Casey's desk phone rang. She got up from the conference table and answered it.

"Hello, Ms. Astert, what can I do for you?" As Casey listened to the response, her face went white. "Are you serious?" she said. "When?"

Casey listened some more, then hung up and stared at me.

"What is it?" I said.

"That was Nicole Astert. Officer Sam Kavanagh was attacked and stabbed by another inmate early this morning. He's dead."

I stared back at her. "You've got to be fucking kidding me."

"I wish I was."

I felt like someone had kicked my legs out from under me. With Kavanagh dead and the video excluded, we had no case. The look on Casey's face told me she was thinking the same thing.

"That was no accident," I said, eventually.

"Of course it wasn't. Not that it matters. We're fucked either way."

"Maybe not. Let's see if we can dig something out of what happened to Kavanagh. And we can still use Elliott's shooting to show the jury something weird is going on."

"We can't put a dead man on the stand, Mick."

"So, what do we do, then? We can't just give up."

"There's something else. The prosecution has offered a plea deal. They'll take the death penalty off the table if Elliott pleads guilty and does twenty-five years without parole."

"That's ridiculous!"

"I know. We have to come up with something in whatever time we have left."

Casey tried to look defiant, but her shoulders were slumped. I felt it too. Ever since he'd been arrested, Elliott's case had been hanging from a cliff by a frayed rope, and now the last thread had just snapped.

"Look, there's no point sitting around moping," Casey said. "Let's go see Elliott, talk to him about the plea offer."

"Okay." I stood up, still feeling numb. Clearly, Kavanagh had been killed to silence him. Sinclair had to be behind it. But what could we do about it? The police weren't likely to dig too deep into what happened. Cops don't do well in jail. No doubt whoever killed Kavanagh would use that as an excuse. Probably some guy already doing life without parole, more than happy to shank a cop in return for a few bucks for them or a family member.

We drove out to Inverness to see Elliott, neither of us saying much. Kavanagh's murder had left me feeling like my insides had been ripped out. I had nothing to say, nothing to do, nothing left.

We parked, went inside, passed through the metal detectors and reported to the duty guard. He logged our entry and another guard led us through to the waiting room. After half an hour, the guard came back and told us that Elliott was ready.

Casey sat opposite Elliott. Normally I liked to stand, but today I sat beside her, not sure my legs would hold me through what was coming.

"What is it?" Elliott said.

"I'm afraid we've got some bad news," Casey said.

"What do you mean?"

Casey looked at me, a plea in her eyes.

"Bad news, buddy," I said. "Sam Kavanagh got shanked this morning. He's dead."

Elliott threw his arms up. "Oh, that's just fucking perfect. First the video gets excluded, now this. Unbelievable. So, what happens now?"

"Trial starts in three weeks. Which means we've got that long to come up with something."

"Come up with what? We still don't have the video or a witness."

I shrugged. "Right now, I don't know. But we'll find something." I tried to sound convincing, but the look on Elliott's face told me it wasn't working.

"There's something else," Casey said. "The State has offered you a plea deal. They'll agree not to seek the death penalty if you plead guilty and accept a twenty-five-year minimum sentence."

"Fuck that," Elliott snapped. "I ain't taking no plea deal."

Casey held up a hand. "I agree you shouldn't take that deal. But what if I could get the sentence reduced further, like to fifteen years? I can't promise anything, but I might be able to make that happen. You'd be out before you're fifty."

"I don't think you heard me, Counselor," Elliott said, his voice low and hard. "I am not taking a plea deal. I don't care if I rot in this shithole for the rest of my life. I ain't never saying I killed Malik Betts when I know damn well I didn't."

"Please, take some time to think about it. With Kavanagh dead, your chances at trial aren't good. A plea might be your best option."

"Think about it? Ain't nothing else to do in here but think about it. Twenty-five fucking years," Elliott muttered. "Locked up in this shithole for being a Black man with an attitude. Same old shit. They think that's going to shut me up. No, fuck them. No deals, Counselor. Not now, not ever."

"Please, Elliott, think about it," Casey said, her voice breaking. "It's better than the death penalty."

"Maybe for you," he said. "Not for me."

"Okay. I understand." Casey wiped her eyes and stood up. "I need to go."

She banged on the door and the guard let her out.

Elliott looked at me. "Be real with me, Mick. What chance have I got?"

"I think you know," I said. "Sorry, buddy."

"Yeah, one more uppity nigger shot down. I ain't surprised. I always wondered how they'd do it.

"People been telling me for years to keep my head down. Warning me that the high and mighty don't like a Black man getting in their way. When the first round of riots started I knew they'd come for me; I just didn't know how or when. Now I guess I do." He pushed himself away from the table and nodded at the door. "You better go see how she's doing."

Casey was already in the car when I got there, staring straight ahead with her hands on the steering wheel.

"Are you okay?" I said.

"I will be." She took a deep breath. "How does he do it? How does he stay so calm?"

"Beats me. But he's one strong dude, I can tell you that."

"Yeah, he is. I don't know about you, but I can't go back to the office right now. Do you want to get a drink?"

FORTY-FIVE

LAST CHANCE SALOON

We ended up at Paddy's. It was Casey's suggestion. As one of Portland's more expensive and classy bars, it wouldn't have been my choice, but I didn't object. Besides, given how today had gone, I didn't care.

I grabbed a Scotch on the rocks for me and a glass of Chardonnay for Casey while she settled in to one of the back booths. When I put the drinks down, she grabbed hers and downed two thirds of it in a single go.

I took a drink and rattled the ice in my glass. "So we've got less than a month to perform miracles."

"Pretty much." Casey sighed. "What do you think happened with Kavanagh?"

"Isn't it obvious? Whoever's behind this whole thing didn't want him spilling his guts on the witness stand."

"But why kill him? If you've been trusting him to do your dirty work for this long, why not just pay him off?"

"My guess is they're worried about his attempted murder charge for shooting Elliott. They don't want him giving them up in return for a good plea deal. Better not to take that chance."

"You're probably right," Casey said. She drained her wine and gestured at me with the empty glass. "Want another?"

"Sure."

I sat back and looked around while Casey went to get the drinks. The after work crowd was already trickling in. More suits and ties than your average drinking crowd. Unlike most bars in Portland, a beard and a plaid shirt put you in the minority at Paddy's. The place liked to present an image, with its carefully maintained Victorian interior and expansive array of liquor bottles lining the mirrored wall behind the bar. There was even a rolling library ladder for staff to reach the upper shelves. But behind the façade, it was just like the dive bars I usually frequented. A place where people came when they needed to push life away for a while.

I watched the crowd. Sam Kavanagh was probably already lying on a cold mortuary slab. Did he tell someone about our call? Did I put him there? Maybe, maybe not. It didn't matter now.

Casey put our drinks on the table and sat down with a heavy sigh.

"I feel like I've been kicked in the stomach," she said.

"I'm not surprised."

"Is this what it felt like for you? At the end?"

I knew what she meant. "Every time I lost a case, I felt like this. Now I'm not even a lawyer and it still feels like shit."

"I get that." Casey took a drink. "You know, part of me is glad Elliott won't take a deal. Even though it means we have to fight for a lost cause in court. That's your specialty, right?" She forced a smile.

"Yeah, there's a reason they used to call me that."

"Speaking of which, you should get a lawyer too. Buchanan's been threatening you with accessory liability all along. With Elliott likely to be convicted, he's going to come back at you."

"Let him try. I've got a good story. We found a body and called the cops. They should be thanking me, not arresting me."

"But what about the gun you tossed in the river?"

I laughed. "He won't go there. He'd have to admit he knew about the gun. And since it was planted by whoever framed Elliott, I'd love to hear him explain that."

"I hope you're right." Casey took another drink. "You know, this isn't even my first murder case. But it is the first one where my client is innocent. It sucks."

"Are you okay?" I said.

"I keep thinking about Elliott spending the rest of his life locked up because I lost his case." She wiped her eyes with the back of her hand. "It's just so unfair."

Casey put her head in her hands and sobbed, her chest heaving with each breath. A few heads turned our way. I moved around to her side of the table, then put my arm around her shoulders and pulled her close. She buried her face in my chest and wept. I held her, making quiet soothing noises to the back of her head.

Eventually, she recovered enough to lift her head. I handed her a napkin and she blew her nose.

"Thanks, Mick. Sorry, I wasn't expecting that."

"Don't worry about it," I replied, my arm still around her.

Casey looked me in the eye, then rested her head on my shoulder, her breath still coming in jerky half-sobs. I stroked her hair and we sat there for a while. Gradually, her breathing became more normal. She sat up slowly, a half-smile on her face.

"Thanks. That was nice."

I didn't know what to say to that, so I moved back to my seat and took a drink. Casey must have sensed my discomfort, because she stood up and straightened her hair.

"I should go home," she said. "See you in the office tomorrow?"

"Of course. Bright and early."

Casey left, her unfinished glass of wine still on the table.

I sat back and sipped my Scotch. I could still smell Casey, and the feeling of her body pressed against mine had stirred something I'd buried for too long. What kind of fucked up day was this? I forced myself to remember Elliott, locked up at Inverness, dealing with the fact that his last hope had gone. I had to keep working for him. Nothing else mattered.

One question kept running through my head: *now what?* We had three weeks to prepare a defense for Elliott, but we had nothing to work with. We couldn't use the video of the cops shooting Elliott. Our star witness was dead. All we held was a busted flush.

No matter how I tried to twist it, I kept coming to the same conclusion. Working this case through the legal system could only end one way—with Elliott convicted of a murder he didn't commit. If I was going to prevent that from happening, I had to find a different way to do it. And I'd had enough of wallowing in my past and feeling sorry for myself. My buddy's life was on the line. It was time to step up.

I was convinced Kavanagh killed Betts, and pretty damn sure Sinclair paid him to do it. But why? Why kill the goose that laid the golden egg? In my experience, there was only one motive stronger than money. Fear.

What was Sinclair afraid of? Find that, and maybe, just maybe, I could crack the case. And I had an idea of where to look.

I finished my drink and called Tony. He answered immediately.

"Hey, Tony, you busy?"

"No. What's up?"

"It's a long story." I told him about Kavanagh being killed, what it meant for our case, and what I wanted to do about it.

"It's worth a try," he said. "When do you want to hit it?"

"No time like the present. Meet me at my place?"

"I'll be there in twenty minutes." He hung up.

Tony was waiting outside my apartment when I got home, a laptop bag slung over his shoulder. I unlocked the door and led us both inside.

"Tell me more about what happened to Kavanagh," he said, as he sat at my kitchen table and took out his computer.

I grabbed my laptop and a couple of beers, then sat down opposite him. "You know as much as I do. He got shanked in jail this morning."

"Shit, man. And you think Sinclair had it done to shut him up?"

"I'm sure of it. Not that it matters."

"Yeah, 'jailed cop killed by convict' is an easy story to sell. So now what?"

I opened the beers and handed him one. "Like I told you on the phone, there's only one way to save Elliott now. We have to find out why Sinclair had Betts killed. You said it yourself—the answer is probably in the information your hacker dude pulled for us. He told us those layers of shell companies meant there's some kind of financial bad action in play. So, we're going to sit here and go through the data until we figure out what it was."

"How do you want to split it up?"

"You take the property sales. I've been over those a bunch of times already and didn't see much beyond Betts paying over market value for condos and selling them at a loss. Maybe another pair of eyes will catch something I missed. I'll work on the construction supply business."

We put our heads down and got to work. I opened the file of transactions for Starlight Supply, the construction supply company Betts had owned—or the company that was owned by a shell company, which was owned by another shell company, which was owned by Betts. Unfortunately, there were thousands of rows. I took a deep breath and started at the top.

The transactions didn't look strange, at first glance. They were mostly bulk orders for various construction materials: drywall, lumber, cement, rebar and so on. Sinclair's company CDS Construction was by far the biggest customer, accounting for over ninety percent of the transactions. I tried different sort and filter combinations to change the way I was viewing the data, but still nothing stood out.

After an hour of finding nothing, I stood up and stretched.

"Found anything?" Tony said.

"No. You?"

"No. Betts was definitely selling the condos for below market value, but not by a lot. Just enough to make sure his units sold faster than the rest."

I had a thought. "Did he buy the condos for cash or finance the purchases?"

Tony poked away at his computer. "Looks like mostly cash purchases. Money's coming from an account at a bank in the Cayman Islands."

"That's unusual." Something else occurred to me. I leaned over and looked at my screen again. Maybe there was something strange in the numbers after all.

"Hold on a second." I went into my bedroom and came out with two bankers boxes.

"What have you got there?" Tony asked.

"It's the discovery materials for that construction defect civil case we worked on for Kristen Campione. There's a pile of supply orders in here too. I want to check something."

I rummaged through the first box, but it wasn't the one I was looking for. I opened the second and dug through the papers until I found what I needed. There were sheaves of supply orders for building materials. That case had been about strip malls and business premises, but the properties were similar in size to some of CDS's condo developments. I took a few of the paper orders and compared them to the Starlight transactions. The difference was obvious. I checked some more and the same pattern came up each time.

"Okay, I need to check one more thing." I pulled up the County Recorder's property transfer records. "Help me out here, Tony. In the 21 North development, how many condos did Betts buy from Sinclair?"

Tony ran his finger down his screen. "Looks like eleven."

"Interesting. How about in Tabor Commons?"

Another pause while Tony checked the numbers. "I count twelve in that one."

I shook my head. "Fuck me, you were right. The answer was right in front of my face."

"You found something?"

"More than that," I said. "I know what Betts and Sinclair were up to, and I know why Sinclair had Betts killed."

FORTY-SIX

BOLD STRATEGY

I showed Tony what I'd found, then explained what it meant in terms of Sinclair's business and his relationship with Betts. We spent ten minutes going back and forth between different documents and transactions, comparing figures and dates, creating a trail that tied the whole thing together. When we were done, Tony shook his head and ran a hand through his hair.

"Damn, that's crazy," he said. "What now? We have to take this to the cops, right?"

"No. Sinclair is untouchable in this city. He's tight with the mayor and Buchanan just about lost his job the last time he tried to investigate him."

"But we've got the proof! It's right here in black and white."

"Doesn't matter. I guarantee they'd fake up some business records to explain it all away."

Tony frowned at me. "What, then?"

"Good question. I have no idea." I paused, then checked the time. Just after 5 pm. "Wait a minute. Maybe there is something we can do."

I looked up Gerald Whitehead, Sinclair's lawyer from his deposition, and called his office. A female voice answered.

"Gerald Whitehead's office. How can I help you?"

"I need to speak to Mr. Whitehead. Please tell him it's urgent, regarding his client Charles Sinclair."

"I'll see if he's available. Who should I say is calling?"

"It's Mick Ward. I was at Mr. Sinclair's recent deposition."

"Thank you. One moment, please."

I was treated to some truly awful hold music, then Whitehead came on the line.

"What is it, Mr. Ward?"

"I need to speak to your client."

Whitehead sighed. "Mr. Ward, you've already deposed my client in this matter, which was a complete waste of everybody's time. He is a very busy man and he has no obligation to speak to you again. In fact, if you want him to do so, you'll need a court order."

"I'll do better than that. Tell your client I know everything about his business arrangements with Malik Betts. I mean *everything*. And if I don't hear back from him in the next hour, the whole sordid mess will be on the front page of tomorrow's *The Oregonian*."

I hung up.

"I don't get it," Tony said. "What are you trying to achieve?"

I explained my plan, such as it was.

"Mick, this is a bad idea."

"You're probably right, but I don't have a better one."

"You could get killed! Come on, sleep on it. Show this stuff to Casey. She'll come up with something."

"No. It's got to be this way. I'm done standing on the sidelines."

My phone buzzed with a text from a number I didn't recognize.

Tomorrow night. 8 pm. Come alone.

My phone buzzed again and a second message gave an address. I showed it to Tony.

"I'm telling you, this is a bad idea," he said.

"Maybe." I shrugged and made a call. "Hey, Sonny. I need another favor. And this time it's a big one."

FORTY-SEVEN

PINCH HIT

Not surprisingly, the address Sinclair had given for our meeting was a construction site. It was only a ten-minute walk from my apartment, so I set off Thursday afternoon to get the lay of the land and make sure I was ready for the meeting with Sinclair. It was another cold, gray day in Portland, a thick wet drizzle hanging in the air. That gave me an excuse to wear a bulky jacket with the hood up and a ball cap pulled down low, to reduce the risk of being recognized.

The development was yet another condo complex, this one on Southeast Ankeny, close to 20th Avenue. Just east of downtown, Burnside's bars and restaurants were a block away. These places were going to cost a fortune, and Nike drones and tech bros would snap them all up in a heartbeat. The development was called Heart of Portland, which was ironic given that it was another nail in the coffin of whatever heart Portland had left.

The site buzzed with activity, despite the dreadful weather. Two tower cranes unloaded bundles of steel framing studs from a semi-trailer, stacking them at the front of the site. A crew with a smaller mobile crane picked up individual studs and held them up while workers bolted them into place. Another crew worked on pouring the cement base for the second floor. An electrical crew flitted between the activity, running mains wiring from spools of cable. There were two construction office trailers at the back of the site, with a steady stream of men going in and out. The overall impression was of a finely choreographed dance.

I walked a few blocks past the site and turned around for another look, then went home to get warm and dry for a while. I was taking a big chance, agreeing to meet Sinclair there alone at night. But I'd spent the last twenty-four hours running through alternatives in my head and I hadn't come up with a better idea.

I set out again at 7:40pm, wearing the same bulky jacket and hat. A heavy darkness had fallen, made thicker by the wet winter air. Streetlights cast sickly yellow pyramids of light in the drizzle. The occasional car hissed by, but the smart people stayed tucked up at home.

There was a bus stop two blocks east of the future Heart of Portland, so I used it to position myself where I could see the site without being seen myself. It was quiet and dark now, all the machinery shut down and the workers gone home. A sharp wind cut the air and I huddled in the corner of the shelter.

At five to eight, a black Lincoln Town Car eased to a halt outside the construction site. The driver got out and opened the back door, and a tall, thin man in a long trench coat emerged. The driver held an umbrella over the man's head as he unlocked a padlock on the site gate, and the two of them hurried to one of the office trailers. They stepped inside and a light went on in the window.

I waited a few minutes, then took a deep breath and walked to the site. This was it—my last throw of the dice. If my plan worked, Elliott would soon be a free man. If it went badly, I'd be joining Betts and Kavanagh in the great beyond.

I pushed the gate open, deliberately making a lot of noise, and walked toward the trailers at the back of the site, my boots squelching on the muddy ground. Sinclair let me get most of the way before he emerged. The other guy came out behind him and I recognized Officer Wright, Sam Kavanagh's old partner.

"Hey, Dwayne," I said, and waved. "Sorry about your buddy Kavanagh."

Wright bristled, but Sinclair held up a hand.

"That's far enough, Mr. Ward." He lowered his hand. "Search him."

Wright marched over and patted me down from head to toe, deliberately ramming his clenched fist into my balls as he checked my legs. I winced, but forced myself to stand tall. No way was he going to get the satisfaction of seeing me hurt.

He took my phone and handed it to Sinclair. "He's clean."

Sinclair nodded. "So, tell me what's so important that we have to go through this charade."

"I'm here to offer you a deal. You help me get Elliott Russell out of jail, and your secret stays buried forever."

"And what secret would that be?"

"Money laundering. You and Betts. I know how the whole scheme worked, beginning to end. And I know why you had him killed."

"My, that's quite a story." Sinclair tried to sound causal, but I could hear the tension in his voice. "Ridiculous, but quite a story all the same."

"It's a story all right. Let me see if I got it right. Each time you built a new development, Betts would order a bunch of condos. Let's say a dozen. He'd pay you for all twelve, but you'd only transfer title to nine of them, leaving you holding about a million dollars of his money. Then, you'd order construction supplies from his company, Starlight Supply. But you'd order and pay for ten times more than you needed. Betts only delivered what you needed, so he and his Mexican cartel partners got their cash back, minus a fat cut for you. And the cash, which of course came from drug sales, is now nice and clean, with a chain of business records to back it up. Money laundering 101.

"You and Betts had a good thing going. But he got flashy, didn't he? The Bentley was just the start. Showing up loaded at your fundraiser, raising hell at Blazer games. You knew it was only a matter of time before he did something stupid and got caught, so you had Kavanagh kill him and dump the body in Elliott's yard. Nice bit of improvisation, by the way. Frame the guy whose activism cost you ten million dollars."

Sinclair's face grew darker as I continued. He jammed his hands into the pockets of his trench coat. "All right. No more games. What's this deal you mentioned?"

"Simple. We work together to pin Betts's murder on Sam Kavanagh. He did it anyway, and he's already dead, so no great loss there. I reveal what I found out about Kavanagh and Betts fighting at your fundraiser. You tell the cops Kavanagh threatened to kill Betts, and you saw him with a gun, or something like that. We can stitch it together easily. In return, no one ever finds out about the money laundering or any other connection to you."

"And if I say no?"

I shrugged. "Like I told you yesterday. The whole thing's on the front page of The Oregonian. Chapter and verse."

"Interesting, Mr. Ward," Sinclair said. "I must admit I'm tempted. But there's one small problem with your clever little plan. What's to stop you from leaking all the details anyway, once your friend is out of jail? No, I don't think I'll take that chance. Get him, Wright."

Wright pulled a gun from his pocket and stomped toward me.

"You sure you want to do that?" I said to him. I jabbed a thumb at Sinclair. "This guy leaked the video of your old partner shooting Elliott Russell. You could be next. It was a lot easier to have Kavanagh whacked once he was inside, wasn't it, Sinclair?"

Wright ignored me. He stopped a yard away from me and pointed the gun at my chest. "Turn around. Hands behind your back."

I did what I was told. Wright snapped handcuffs on my wrists, then cracked me across the back of the head with the butt of his pistol. I collapsed face-first in the mud, a screaming pain racking my skull.

"That was for Sam," Wright muttered, and spat on the back of my head.

"Enough of that!" Sinclair snapped. "Get him up."

Wright grabbed the collar of my jacket and hauled me up, then rammed the barrel of his pistol into the base of my skull and shoved me forward. I spat mud and tried not to stumble.

Sinclair followed us. "We're going to go for a drive Mr. Ward, while you tell me everything you've figured out. And then we'll find a quiet place in the forest to put a stop to all this nonsense. Play nice and it will be quick and painless. One bullet, just like poor Malik. If not, well..."

I couldn't see him, but I could hear the shrug in his voice. Wright's gun ground into my neck, cold and hard. I flashed back to an earlier memory, my chilling vision of Betts's last moments as he stared up past the barrel of Sam Kavanagh's gun. Was it my turn next? It took all my strength to keep my knees from buckling.

"You can't keep covering up murders!" I yelled.

"Oh, I don't know. I'm doing quite well so far."

My breath fogged in the night air. Somehow, I managed to put one foot in front of the other.

A blur of shadow moved in from my right, then I heard a meaty smack. I spun around to see Wright groan and collapse in the mud. The giant frame of Junior Gradzinski loomed over him, holding an aluminum baseball bat.

Sinclair reached for the inside pocket of his trench coat.

"I wouldn't do that if I were you," Sonny Gradzinski said. He stepped out of the darkness, a Smith and Wesson revolver the size of a small cannon pointed at Sinclair's head. Sinclair raised his hands. Sonny reached into his coat pocket, pulled out Sinclair's gun and tossed it aside.

"You okay, Mick?"

"I will be when I get these cuffs off."

Junior planted his knee in Wright's back, driving him deeper into the mud. Sonny tossed Junior a roll of duct tape, which he used to bind Wright's arms and legs, then fished a set of keys from the cop's pocket and uncuffed me.

I rubbed my wrists, then ran a hand over my head where Wright had clocked me, wincing as I felt warm blood oozing from the bump forming there.

"Did you get it all?"

Sonny patted his pocket. "Audio and video."

Junior taped Sinclair's wrists, then kicked his legs out from under him. Sinclair landed on his side in the mud and Junior bound his legs.

"Easy, Junior," Sonny said. "You'll ruin the nice man's coat."

I knelt down and rummaged around in Sinclair's pockets until I found my phone, then made a call.

"Detective Buchanan, it's Mick Ward. Remember when you said you wouldn't look at Sinclair again? You might want to reconsider that."

FORTY-EIGHT
ALL GOOD THINGS

The DA withdrew all charges against Elliott first thing the next morning, and Judge Obrecht ordered that he be released immediately. I had rented a wheelchair-accessible van in anticipation of the ruling, and I drove out to Inverness as soon as we heard from the judge.

Elliott had already been processed by the time I got there. He was waiting outside the public entrance, dressed in jeans and a sweater, when I pulled up.

"Taxi for Mr. Russell?" I said.

He smiled and wheeled himself over to me. I leaned down and hugged him, tears in my eyes.

"Oof, take it easy, man," he said.

"Sorry." I let him go and stood up. "Damn, it's good to see you, buddy."

"You too." Elliott looked up at the cloudy sky. "I still can't believe this is real. What the hell did you do?"

"Let's get away from this shithole and I'll tell you about it."

I pushed Elliott up the ramp into the van. I locked him in place, then we drove away. I glanced up at the rearview mirror, happy to see those barbed wire fences disappearing for the last time, then moved the mirror so I could see Elliott's face.

"Okay," Elliott said, "they told me Sinclair has been arrested, but that's about all I know. What's the deal?"

"Yeah, turns out he was behind it all along. He'd been helping Betts launder Mexican drug money. Betts got out of control, so Sinclair paid Kavanagh to execute him before he blew the whole scheme. Dumping the body at your place was an attempt to kill two birds with one stone." I didn't say anything about the stunt I pulled last night. He'd hear about that soon enough.

"How did you figure that out?"

"Well, we'd known for a while that there was something weird about the business dealings between Betts and Sinclair. Tony and I took another look at the data. What tipped us off was that Betts was paying cash for the condos. Normally those kinds of deals are mortgaged out the wazoo. So we looked at the purchases some more. We found several transactions where Betts would order and pay for a dozen condos, using an offshore bank account. But Sinclair would only transfer title to eight or nine. Each time, it left Sinclair holding about a million bucks in cash for condos he never delivered. Right after that deal, Sinclair would deliberately over-order construction supplies from Betts's company. For example, if he needed two tons of concrete, he'd order and pay for two hundred. Betts delivered two tons and the rest of the cash went back to a different offshore account. Hey presto, a million bucks in drug money looks like legitimate business proceeds. Betts and Sinclair both took a cut, of course, but there was plenty to go around."

"Shit. How did you figure it out?"

"Like I said, paying cash for the condos was the first clue. As for the over ordering, I did some contract legal work on a civil construction defect case a while back. I still had copies of supply orders in the discovery documents. I compared them to Sinclair's orders from Betts. The difference was obvious and I worked backward from there."

"That's pretty damn smart."

"Thanks. Now that you're out, what are you going to do?"

"First thing I'm gonna do is see about getting into a physical therapy program, get my ass out of this damn chair." He nodded. "Then I'm gonna get my City Council election campaign back on track. The election is six weeks from now. I'm gonna milk this Sinclair bullshit for every damn vote I can get."

"If you want any help, I'm all in," I said.

"Thanks, Mick." Elliott gazed out the window and took a deep breath. "Right now, though, I wish Casey hadn't scheduled this press conference. I'm tired. I just want to go home."

"Hang in there. You'll be home soon enough."

We drove the rest of the way downtown in silence. I parked on the street, a block up from the Justice Center, and helped Elliott out of the van. He looked around. The sandwich store we'd parked outside was boarded up and the wood was scorched where someone had tried to set it alight. All of the other storefronts on the block bore similar damage.

Elliott shook his head. "Man, we got work to do."

A crowd of about a hundred people was gathered outside the Justice Center. They turned our way as we approached. A line of uniformed police held them back from the entrance. There were reporters from each of the major networks amongst the crowd, waving microphones at us and backed up by cameramen, along with several print reporters holding recorders outstretched.

"Mister Russell! Mister Russell!"

"Come on, guys, make room," I shouted. I moved ahead of Elliott and cleared a path through the crowd to where Casey and Tony stood at the bottom of the steps by the main entrance.

The crowd let us through, then closed behind us and shouted questions at Elliott again.

Casey held up her hands and waited for the noise to subside.

"Ladies and gentlemen," she began, "thank you for being here. I know you have a lot of questions, but before we start, I'd like to make a short statement. Back in June, I stood in this same place and told you that my client Elliott Russell was innocent. Today, all charges against him have been dismissed. As a result, a terrible miscarriage of justice has been avoided. Unfortunately, that won't heal Mr. Russell, but perhaps it will be a small step toward healing the divisions that have done so much harm to our city and our society."

Casey paused and the shouted questions started up again immediately. She waved her arms for silence, but the noise kept coming.

"I'd like to say something."

Elliott had spoken. The crowd instantly fell silent.

"I'd like to say something," he repeated, his head held high. "I know a lot of people are angry about what happened to me. Hell, I'm angry. But violence is not the answer. It breaks my heart to see our city torn up in my name. Please, no more riots. No more violence. Take your anger, turn it into energy, and put it to good use. We need to rebuild our community, physically and spiritually. Come together, help each other, work for positive change."

Elliott stopped and the crowd stayed silent for a while. People nodded their heads and spoke to each other softly.

A reporter from Fox News held out his microphone and shouted, "Mister Russell, will you be suing the City of Portland?"

"My client is considering his options," Casey said.

The questions kept coming and Casey batted most of them

away with softball answers. Elliott sat there calmly, looking straight ahead. In front of a crowd, he was transformed. He may have been in a wheelchair, but he seemed to be ten feet tall.

"Okay, that's enough," Casey said. "Thank you all for your time."

One of the uniformed cops stepped forward. "Okay, you heard the lady. Show's over. Move along."

At first, no one moved. Several other cops stepped forward and the crowd slowly began to disperse. Casey set off in the direction we'd come from. I pushed Elliott up the hill after her, with Tony by my side. We had just about reached the van when I heard footsteps hurrying up behind us. I spun around and put my body between Elliott and whoever was approaching, then relaxed when I saw it was Detective Buchanan.

"What is it, Detective?"

Buchanan was breathing hard.

"Damn, I'm out of shape," he said. "Sorry to come after you folks, but I need to get something off my chest. Mr. Russell, I know this is too late, but I'm sorry for what happened to you. If there's anything I can do to help you, give me a call."

Elliott looked him up and down. "Do you mean that, Detective?"

"Yes, I do."

"Good." Elliott waved his arm at the burned and boarded-up buildings. "Because this mess needs fixing and the police gotta play their part. So I'm going to take you up on that."

"I hope you do," Buchanan said, and walked away.

Casey was waiting by the van. "Let's get Elliott home," she said.

"Sounds like a damn good idea to me," he replied.

"Tony, can you drive Elliott?" Casey said. "I need to talk to Mick about something."

307

"Sure," he said. I tossed him the keys and helped him get Elliott situated, then stood back as they drove off.

"What is it?"

She put her hands on her hips. "You know you could have been killed last night, right?"

I fingered the bruise on the back of my head. "Yeah, I noticed."

"Why didn't you just go to the cops once you'd figured it out?"

"I couldn't take a chance. After all the crazy shit that's gone down in this case, I didn't know how deep Sinclair had his hooks into the department. Hell, after Kavanagh got whacked, who knows what could have happened to Elliott? Or me, for that matter, given the way Sinclair deals with problems."

"Still, what you did was crazy."

"Maybe, but it worked. Anyway, I'm guessing you didn't just want to tell me off. What's up?"

Casey looked down. "This could probably wait, but I wanted to strike while the iron's hot. I've been so busy working for Elliott that a lot of my other cases got backed up. Plus, this case has attracted a lot of attention. I've had half a dozen new client calls this morning alone. Tough cases, too. The sort of cases that would be perfect for the patron saint of lost causes. If I promise to pay you a real salary, will you join my firm full time?"

"You're serious, aren't you?"

"Of course I am."

I didn't know what to say. I thought about everything I'd been through these past few months, being back in the defense law world. How at first, I'd just wanted to hand Elliott off to Casey and walk away. How incensed I'd been when Elliott was shot. All the sleepless nights. The sheer devastation when it had looked like all hope was lost. But I'd stuck it out, and stood up when it mattered. I still had the fire. The fire that drove me to put my life on the line for my friend. Before this case, I'd been running away from myself for too long. Now, I realized I was exactly where I needed to be. Back in the ring, fighting for people who needed me. *Maybe the lost cause I'd needed to save was my own.*

I took a deep breath. "Sure. Let's give it a shot."

We shook hands, then Casey grabbed me and hugged me tightly. I hugged her back, not sure I ever wanted to let go. Judging by the way she buried her face in my chest, she felt the same way.

Eventually, we stepped back, both avoiding each other's gaze.

"I'm not a lawyer anymore, you know," I said.

Casey laughed. "Yeah, someone told me that already."

THE END

ACKNOWLEDGEMENTS

Writing a book requires a lot of help – at least it does for me. First of all, thank you to the awesome crew at Bloodhound Books, especially Betsy Reavely, Tara Lyons, and Abbie Rutherford, for taking me on the journey from rough manuscript to the book you're holding now.

Thank you to Daniel Pearse and Rankin Johnson, whose feedback made Black Mark a much better book, and whose encouragement kept me writing when it seemed like I'd never make it to the end. Rankin also helped with the criminal law details, as did Kasia Rutledge, Josh Pond, and Jake Kamins. Of course, any errors are all mine.

Amanda Bourne from Polly's International Bookshop deserves a big thank you for editing the first draft, and starting me on the road to publication. Thanks also to Emily Chenowith, Melissa Rush, Zack Schomburg, Lisa Metcalf, Emily Redimbo, Phillip Pearson, and everyone else at the Portland Literary Arts novel writing group. I can't begin to describe how much I learned from you. And I took your advice, so I'm going to send the negative reviewers your way.

ABOUT THE AUTHOR

Paul Spencer was born in London, grew up in Australia, and has traveled extensively ever since. He lived in the United States for many years, where he became a lawyer. His experience in criminal and anti-discrimination law inspired him to write *Black Mark*, his first novel. *Black Mark* won the Daphne du Maurier Award for Excellence in Mystery/Suspense. In addition, Paul's short fiction has been published in several journals, and longlisted for the Crime Writers' Association Short Mystery prize and the Uncharted Magazine Short Story Prize.

Besides writing, Paul enjoys reading Tartan Noir, making sausages, and messing around with cars. He lives in Spain with his wife, a lazy old Labrador, and an obnoxious cat.

A NOTE FROM THE PUBLISHER

Thank you for reading this book. If you enjoyed it please do consider leaving a review on Amazon to help others find it too.

We hate typos. All of our books have been rigorously edited and proofread, but sometimes mistakes do slip through. If you have spotted a typo, please do let us know and we can get it amended within hours.

info@bloodhoundbooks.com

www.ingramcontent.com/pod-product-compliance
Ingram Content Group UK Ltd.
Pitfield, Milton Keynes, MK11 3LW, UK
UKHW040636030125
453013UK00004B/35